COLLIDE

COLLIDE SERIES
BOOK ONE

J.C. HANNIGAN

Cover Design by Yosbe Design

Edited by Nikki Colligan

Formatted by J.C. Hannigan

ISBN 978-0-9951911-7-4 (paperback)

ISBN 978-0-9951911-1-2 (ebook)

www.jchannigan.com

ACKNOWLEDGMENTS

So many people have helped me along this journey of publishing my first novel. I'd like to thank Sarah Fader, for pushing me to "sit down and actually write it", Elizabeth Barone, for her sage wisdom on the publishing world, my husband Matt for dealing with my temperamental frenzied writing spells (and handling our wild children so I could focus), my father, for being the first person to ever tell me that I could do this, that my dream of becoming a writer wasn't silly or foolish, and my incredible team. Allie Burke, one of the most intelligent woman I know, for her incredible ability to keep me on track. Cassy Roop, for her remarkable cover designs and way of understanding exactly what I want my books to "look like", and Nikki Colligan, for proofreading (and loving) Collide.

I'd also like to thank all of you who have supported me and eagerly awaited the release of Collide. Thank you all so much!

DEDICATION

DEDICATION

...to every strong willed woman I know that would give the shirt off their back for someone else and still kick some serious ass.

CHAPTER ONE

I stood in front of the bathroom mirror, critically studying myself.

I don't know why I was so concerned with my appearance when I had never overly cared about it before.

Maybe I was fretting because it was the first day of school. My long black hair had a natural slight curl to it. I rarely had to do anything to it short of brush, run some product through, and blow dry. My eyes were a striking dark, deep green—or so many guys had told me. They were usually the creepy old men I encountered at every place I worked. They were also quick to compliment me on my breasts. For a 17-year-old girl, I had quite the voluptuous curves that gained me a lot of attention with the opposite sex, which was probably the cause of my unpopularity among the other females for the duration of my high school career thus far.

Somewhat begrudgingly, I finished critiquing myself and expertly applied my signature look· liquid eyeliner, mascara, and bold red lipstick. Whenever I had the chance, I wore black, although my new school required I wear the typical Catholic schoolgirl uniform. I had done my best to add my own personal flair, but it was pretty much hopeless. I looked like a slutty Catholic schoolgirl, which could have been fun, but not when everyone else was going to look like slutty Catholic schoolgirls.

"Lord save me," I said sarcastically, rolling my eyes. If I made it to graduation, I would need to reward myself with a new tattoo.

Mom told me that I would be attending a Catholic school with a scared look on her face. We had never been religious before Mom's new husband, Larry. I wasn't surprised in the least that Mom jumped aboard the Catholic train and embraced her "newfound faith" with an insane schedule of church, fundraising meetings, and volunteering in the Sunday school classroom, but I was pissed that she wanted me to jump aboard too. I didn't understand what she saw in Larry—the sex couldn't be *that* good. Larry was an overweight 57-year-old man who ran the Catholic School Board in the region, which was probably how Mom weaseled a spot for me.

"It's the best education you can get," Mom countered when I forcefully said no. "They choose students that graduate from this high school over others in college and university applications."

That got my attention. Despite my outward appearance and rebellious behavior, school was very important to me. I had always effortlessly excelled in school. I wanted to graduate top of my class and get into a top university. I would be an English major. I had a passion for writing, a love for the written word, and saw the beauty of poetry.

Still, I found the whole thing with Larry and my mom somewhat creepy. He wasn't the kind of guy I would have picked out for her in a thousand years. My mom was a stunning woman. She ate healthy and exercised regularly so that her body stayed toned and thin. She had great skin and looked much younger than her 38 years. She could do so much better than lumpy Larry.

Mom and Larry hadn't known each other all that long before Larry proposed and Mom said yes. Suddenly we were leaving Southern Ontario for the great North. I think Larry had some kind of twisted desire to save us both or something. He was forever trying to play the overly concerned father card. It was annoying. I had been on my own with Mom for so long; we'd gotten along just fine without him. I had been able to come and go without her interference. She'd let it go, convincing herself that I was the good responsible daughter who couldn't possibly be up to no good.

When she met Larry all that changed. I guess I was partly to blame. I started getting into more and more trouble, and with Larry there noticing everything, it got harder and harder for Mom to pretend that there wasn't a problem. There wasn't *really* a problem. I didn't do hard drugs; I just got myself into a couple bad situations when I fell in with the wrong crowd.

My mom's desire to move us up North with Larry increased after last winter. I was in a car accident that killed my best friend, Lauren. My boyfriend, Rhys, was driving us home from a party, completely coked out of his mind. Lauren and I hadn't had the slightest clue that he was high. We were young and stupid and had no idea what the signs were. Granted, both of us were drunk, but I hadn't seen Rhys do a single thing. He'd been in and out of the bathroom a few times, but how was I to know? It wasn't until after the accident that I learned of his cocaine habit.

Lauren's death was a traumatic experience for me, and I missed her more than I could even begin to express.

The attention I received after the funeral was too much for me, especially with Lauren gone forever. When Mom put her foot down about moving up North with Larry, it surprised us all, but I went willingly. There was nothing tying me to Toronto, and a new start sounded alluring. I wouldn't be "that girl whose boyfriend killed her best friend and almost killed her" or worse, what I was known as before Lauren's death: the school whore. That reputation was harder to stomach without my best friend by my side.

So far, I hadn't made any friends. A week after we moved in with Larry, I got a waitressing job at a local diner down the road from my new high school. I was a little young to pull off the gig, but the diner owner didn't care too much, since I was only four months away from being 18. The clusters of high school girls that came in didn't enjoy my company, nor did I enjoy theirs.

"Honey! Are you just about finished?" Mom asked timidly, tapping against the bathroom door. "I can give you a lift to school."

I threw open the door, my jaw clenched and my eyes hard. I was still punishing her for, well, everything. I avoided looking into her pale hazel eyes—one of only a few differences between the two of us, and a slight one at that. I'd also inherited my father's plump lips while Mom's were thin. Despite those two things, I looked exactly like she had at 17, which I didn't mind. She had been gorgeous, and still was, if not worn and exhausted looking...probably thanks to me.

Unluckily for her, luckily for me (depending on how you looked at it), I had also inherited my dad's rough personality opposed to her needy clingy one. I knew she was concerned about me and always had been, and I knew that my attitude did little to diffuse that concern.

"I'll take the bus," I said, brushing past her and down the hallway. Luckily, Larry was already gone for the day. So far, he hadn't done anything to merit my feelings of discomfort, but still. I didn't trust anybody. Not even my mom. She knew it, and she was forever going to ridiculous lengths to prove to me otherwise.

She was constantly hovering over me, asking me if I was all right. She always had this concerned look on her face, and it would immediately put me into a foul mood. Mom treated me like fine china, which I hated. I was far from weak. However, there were a few perks. She typically allowed me to get my way with most things if it meant that I was happy.

Part of me felt guilty for making her jump through hoops, but I couldn't stop myself. I couldn't stop punishing her for things that couldn't be changed now, and I couldn't stop feeling as if she'd failed me. There was guilt that rode along with those feelings, which made me typically act out in anger toward her.

I slipped into my black leather jacket (the last thing I had that belonged to my dad) and put in my headphones, walking out the front door and down the suburban street to the bus stop. I took my time and smoked a joint, enjoying the sense of calm that took over. Lauren had been the one to introduce me to the benefits of marijuana. I found it was one of the only things that calmed my frazzled nerves.

A small group of other high school students was already waiting for the bus. They looked younger than I was. Regardless, I had no plans on talking to anybody right then and there. I ignored their stares and finished my joint, tossing the roach onto the road as if it were a simple cigarette. A couple kids dared to look at me, but I met their gazes with a challenging one of my own. No one knew what to say, so they didn't say anything at all.

The bus was overcrowded, and I had to sit with some ninth grade kid with greasy hair and terrible skin. If I wasn't on a mission to avoid making small talk, I would have told him about the wonders of deodorant and how it could potentially save his social status, but who was I to talk about social status? Instead, I breathed through my mouth and focused on the vinyl seat in front of me, thinking about how I really needed to buy a car. This was one of those times where I physically had to restrain myself from sending a text to Lauren. She would have found the whole thing hilarious. I felt a sharp pain in my chest at the thought that I couldn't talk to her anymore, but I brushed it aside and stared at the seat in front of me.

Stepping off the bus was a relief, although the ninth grade kid's scent lingered for a few moments longer than I would have liked. I adjusted the strap of my book bag and followed everyone up the stairs into the school. It was loud, as high school hallways are. Nobody stared at me as if I were out of place as I walked down the hall; I guess they were used to seeing unfamiliar faces the first day. A few of the male students did a couple double takes, whispering, trying to discover who I was. I smiled my flirtatious, seductive smile at a group of guys hanging out by the cafeteria doors. They looked like my type, the stoner group. It was the glassy eyes and overuse of Axe body spray that tipped me off.

"Hey, what's your name?" one of them asked when I had almost passed them. He was tall, scrawny, and very cute with shaggy brown hair that was almost a little too long and soft brown eyes. A band T-shirt peaked out from under his uniform: Metallica, from the looks of it.

"Harlow, yours?" I replied, not stopping. If he wanted to talk to me, he was going to have to keep up, although I had no idea where I was planning on going. I had to find all my classes, and considering I'd never to the school before, I knew that was likely going to be a challenge. The last thing I was going to do was appear helpless, despite the anxiety I was feeling. I pushed up the sleeves of my jacket, feeling overheated. The guy followed me.

"Jake Patterson," he answered, giving me a large grin. His teeth were slightly crooked, but there was something endearing about him. He was like an adorable little puppy. "You're new here?"

"It would appear so." I smiled, entertained by his eagerness and all the while searching for the principal's office. I needed to check in before I headed to class.

"How come you look so familiar?" he asked, peering at me as if he was trying to remember where he had seen my face before.

"I'm in a couple of porn movies," I replied airily. I didn't even laugh at his bewildered expression. People rarely knew how to take me, since I always looked serious and spoke seriously. "Kidding. I work at that diner down the road."

"Oh right! You're a waitress there!" Jake laughed. I gave him a steady look, slightly amused but more or less just waiting to see where this was going. Now that he'd mentioned my looking familiar, I realized that he—and his friends—also looked familiar. They were the group of guys that frequently came in smelling of my favorite scent: marijuana.

"And you're the group that comes in every once in a while and tips really crappy," I said, giving him another smile before I spotted the sign for the main office and breezed away from him.

It was significantly quieter in the principal's office. A receptionist with huge brown 80s hair was answering phone calls. She held her chubby finger up at me, silencing me although I had yet to speak.

"Yes, I'll put you through to Mr. Osborne," she was saying into the phone. "Have a great day! Can I help you?" I was staring at the boring speckled tile, thinking about how wonderful it would be to skip class indefinitely. Lots of kids were getting their high school diploma online, so why couldn't I?

"Excuse me. I said *can I help you?*" she repeated slowly, as if I were deaf.

"Oh, sorry." I stepped forward. "I'm new here. Harlow Jones."

"Hello, Miss Jones. I have your schedule here," the chubby receptionist said, handing me a timetable and a map. "Enjoy your first day! If you have any questions, please feel free to ask!" I reached out with my right hand, following her gaze down to the tattoo on my inner forearm that was only half covered by the sleeve of my jacket. I'd forgotten I pushed them up. It was my most recent tattoo: a quill and an inkpot. It symbolized my love of writing. The detail in the feather was breathtaking. My other tattoo was a cherry blossom tree that crept up my right rib cage and cupped under my breast. Across my left collarbone, there were six minimalist black birds in flight. Cliché, I know, but I loved them. Lauren had had the same tattoo across her right collarbone. It was our "friendship tattoo," an idea she had one rainy day last year when we skipped school. We'd gone to Rhys' shop. That was actually the first day that I met him. Rhys and the other tattoo artist, Alex, did the tattoos without questioning us on our age because Lauren and Alex were dating. I drew in a breath, ignoring the pang that my jog down memory lane had brought on.

The receptionist pursed her lips and her tone iced over. "You'll need to cover those up, dear. Dress code, you see. Have a great day," she said, dismissing me coolly. I was used to the pursed lips and dismissal that my appearance brought on in most communities, particularly religious ones. It didn't bother me. It amused me that I, of all people, was supposed to attend a Catholic school, but that's irony for you. I nodded but didn't make a move to cover my arms.

I glanced at my timetable and map before I headed out of the office. English, room 302. Upstairs. I made my way through the crowds and up the stairs. Everyone was still taking their time, as the warning bell hadn't rung yet. Still, I tried the door-knob anyway. I didn't want to hang out in the hall by myself. It was unlocked, so I slowly pushed it open.

You know in movies, how things move in slow motion when something significant happens? That's what happened when I opened that door. I was somehow able to take in my surroundings quickly. The classroom was your typical high school classroom, the walls were an off-white, maybe cream color, and there were rows upon rows of empty desks, but that wasn't the significant part.

My eyes were immediately drawn to the man sitting casu-ally behind the desk. His feet were up and he was leaning back comfortably in his chair, drinking a coffee and looking at some papers on his lap. He was quite the specimen: dirty blond hair trimmed closer to his head at the sides, longer at the top, a little bit of stubble dusting across his jaw line like he hadn't shaved in a few days. He was muscular for an English teacher, and young. If I had to guess, I'd place his age around 28 or so. He was dressed in the typical teacher uniform, but dress pants hugged quite snugly to his muscular legs. He looked up when I walked in, and his eyes were very piercing—the color of the bluest Caribbean sea. My heart skipped a beat and my stomach clenched, the body's natural response to attraction. A response I hadn't felt in a long time.

"Hello," he said, smiling easily. Play it cool, I warned myself. I ran a hand through my hair and smiled sensually back as I walked toward him. That threw him off a little, and his easy smile turned into one of caution as he looked me up and down.

"Hi, I'm new here....Harlow Jones," I said, extending my hand.

"I'm Mr. Bentley." His grasp was strong. His hands were callused but somehow soft. The clenching in my stomach didn't release, but intensified. I'd never been attracted to a teacher before. Of course, I'd never had a super hot young one before either. He tried not to look, but my chest was at perfect level with his eyes and I naturally hadn't buttoned up the first two buttons of my uniform shirt, despite the receptionist's warning about the dress code. It wasn't intentional; things around my neck, like tight collars, legitimately made me panicky. I watched his eyes take in the tattoo across my collar-bone before I broke his gaze with my voice.

"Is there a seating arrangement?" I asked. He still had a hold of my hand. Dazed, he dropped it and smiled again. I took that opportunity to assess his hands, and he didn't appear to have a ring on. It amused me that I was concerned about that, of all things.

"Nope, sit wherever you'd like." Mr. Bentley motioned around the room. Just then the warning bell rang, the sound ringing through my body. I stepped back, still smiling sensually. "Where are you from, Miss Jones?" he asked after a moment of charged (on my part, anyway) silence.

"Toronto. I used to attend Trafalgar's All-Girl School," I said rather suggestively, just to gauge his response. In reality, I had only attended the school for a couple of months. He swallowed hard—the typical reaction guys gave when an all-girl school was mentioned. I watched his Adams apple bob up and down and smiled a little wider. He smiled back.

I was pretty good at gauging men. I had a lot of experience reading people, and I was naturally talented at it. I knew he found me attractive, but that didn't mean anything would ever come of it.

When I saw something I wanted, I went for it. It didn't matter who or what it was. I was typically assertive and self-aware. This personality trait didn't just apply to men—and hadn't, really, as I was distrustful of most. This personality trait did create friction amongst my female peers, who all typically assumed the worse out of me, like I was a harlot or something. But that's the thing with girls, if another girl is fairly decent in the looks department, she's branded a whore whether or not she enjoys casual sex. That bit didn't matter. If she was pretty with a nice body and guys were interested in her, other girls got catty.

Although I had a reputation, I didn't typically go out of my way to get affection from guys, at least not intentionally. I hadn't met anyone that made me want to actively pursue them. I didn't typically do "random hookups" and I stayed clear of the guys from my past high schools after ninth grade.

Rhys was different from other guys. For one, he had not gone to my high school. For two, he'd been just as disconnected from me as I'd been from him. We only ended up together because Lauren had been in love with his best friend, Alex, and they had spent nearly every available moment together. Rhys was cute and a stereotypically punk guy, but what I was feeling now, that impossible to ignore attraction for my English teacher, I'd never felt with Rhys. In fact, I wasn't sure I had felt it with anyone before. At least not to this extent.

Iain Bentley was different. I felt as if I was awakening, finally, after months of being in a daze.

I couldn't just go for a teacher...and I didn't want to anyway. Or at least not just in the way that women imagine being with their favorite Hollywood actor. Innocent, because it'd never happen, but if the opportunity arose, then there wouldn't be a moment's hesitation.

I couldn't help but wonder what the chances of an opportunity were. I knew exactly what Lauren would say: *Make an opportunity for yourself! Go for it!* I could almost hear her singsong voice in my head, daring me to make a move.

Before either of us could say anything else, students started to file into the classroom.

"Later, Mr. Bentley," I said softly before snagging a desk toward the back of the room. I would have the perfect view of the front of the class, which would be a bonus. My heart was pounding as I sunk down into my seat.

It didn't take long for Mr. Bentley to recover from our encounter, or for the classroom to fill up. He kept glancing over in my direction, which made me smile. The last to arrive were three girls, chattering away mindlessly about some party that happened the weekend before at some kid named Riley's house. They came in as the final bell rang. Mr. Bentley waited until everyone was seated before he stood up.

"Welcome back," Mr. Bentley said. His voice was smooth yet rugged, and I think pretty much every single girl—and a few guys—in the room swooned when they saw him. Mr. Bentley turned to the blackboard and wrote his name in blocky letters. "I'm Mr. Bentley. It's my first year teaching so go easy on me."

Not at all, I thought. My eyes were drawn to his tight ass as he turned away from us to write on the blackboard. I wondered if he looked just as muscular with his clothes off as he did with them on. An entertaining thought, one that most of the girls (and those few guys) were probably sharing. I noticed the three girls near me staring at him with appreciation and giggling in whispered tones.

Mr. Bentley decided that instead of doing actual work on

the first day, that we'd play a "get to know one another" game. We each had to say our names and one word about ourselves. Then he wanted us to write a short essay on ourselves so that he could both get to know us and ballpark what kind of students we'd be. The essay was due on Thursday.

I could have a lot of fun with this activity. I thought about all the possibilities while I watched each of the students say something about themselves.

"My name's Jenna and one word to describe me would be fun!" one of the girls, who was one of the last three to arrive, declared flirtatiously. She had shoulder-length blonde hair cut in layers, with all-American baby blue eyes. I got the impression that she was one of the self-declared popular girls. Every high school has them: the group of well-groomed, somewhat pretty girls that think they own the school. She was sitting with two other girls, and they all giggled along with her.

"I'm Callie and one word to describe me is playful!" the platinum blonde girl in front of Jenna said.

"I'm Tara and I'm happy!" the dark haired girl in their trio said with a high-pitched laugh that made me wince. I rolled my eyes, frowning. Soon it was my turn.

"My name's Harlow, and one word to describe me is *single*." I said, pointedly looking at Mr. Bentley with wide, innocent eyes. I might as well go in with a bang, since I was likely to go out with one.

Several of the guys turned in their seats to check me out, and I smiled. I was almost in my element. It still stung, knowing I was missing my comrade in arms, but still. I knew she'd be proud.

Being flirtatious and sensational was...fun. I'd always been a flirt, especially when Lauren was around. She had been just as bad, if not worse, than me.

Aside from Lauren, I had always gotten along better with

guys because they were easier to read than girls and they typically had less bullshit attached. Sure, the occasional guy didn't fit that description, but even with my past, I'd encountered more crappy girls than guys, which was saying something.

Jenna, Callie, and Tara sent me a dirty glance. I could feel the waves of dislike coming off them already. Whoa. I'd never moved that quickly onto the popular group's radar before. Impressive, even for me.

"Well then." Mr. Bentley cleared his throat, trying not to laugh. "I'm sure a lot of the guys here are glad to hear that, Harlow." His eyes brushed over me again, flickering with interest before moving on to the student behind me.

"My name's Riley and I'm horny," the guy behind me declared, trying to go along with what I said. Everybody but Mr. Bentley and I laughed. I looked over my shoulder. Riley was pretty hot, although he paled in comparison to Mr. Bentley. I was now likely to compare every guy I met with Mr. Bentley. He'd set a high bar, one that I doubted anyone would come close to. Riley had fair hair cut close to his head and styled expertly, light eyes, and a smile that suggested he was popular and accustomed to getting what he wanted. He must be the same Riley that the girls had been talking about before class. "What are you doing tonight?" he asked me in a lower tone, raising his eyebrow.

"Sorry, working," I replied before turning back to the front of the class. I had a smile on my face again. I enjoyed getting hit on and asked out; what girl didn't? Although dating a guy who spent more time doing his hair than I did definitely wasn't on my list.

"Alright, that's enough." Mr. Bentley looked visibly aggravated. "None of that in my classroom, please, Mr. Douglas. Can you think of another word?"

"Disappointed," Riley shrugged. "But determined."

"Alright then," Mr. Bentley said, clenching his jaw slightly. I couldn't read if he was jealous or simply irritated by the exchange happening in his classroom. I hoped it was the first one. "Moving on. Next?"

The rest of the replies were safe and boring, and toward the end of class Mr. Bentley again reminded us about our essays. The bell rang, singling the end of class, and people started to pack up their books.

"Homework already," Riley groaned loudly.

"Oh, don't sweat it, Riley. You'll have no trouble writing about yourself. It's your favorite topic," Jenna said, tossing a curious look over her shoulder at me. Callie and Tara were both staring with open hostility.

"True," Riley replied, laughing. I finished shoving the rest of my books into my bag and stood up. I breezed past the group of girls and a few other stragglers, who were clearly waiting around to get a few more minutes of Mr. Bentley. He was standing at his desk, organizing some papers. He looked up at me, and again it felt like time slowed down a bit—to me, anyway. I raised my eyebrows suggestively at him as I passed, and he quickly looked down. I was making him uncomfortable, but I couldn't tell why just yet.

The rest of my morning wasn't nearly as interesting as my English class had been. Math was next, and Jake was in that class. He eagerly sat beside me and stared at me for practically the entire time.

"Look, I'm sorry about the crappy tips," he said at the end of class. "Let me make it up to you."

"How?"

"A little sesh, perhaps?" Jake offered, cocking his eyebrow and smiling.

"Alright." I sighed, smiling and shaking my head slightly. I grabbed my book bag and we walked toward the cafeteria to meet up with his two friends.

They did a double take when I walked up to them with Jake. They were typical stoners, wearing their hair a bit on the long side. They were nice guys, I learned as I smoked up with them inside Jake's Jeep. Kind of dull, though. I had to friend zone them; they just didn't spark my interest. Jake too, although I could tell he wanted to not be in that zone by the way he was looking at me.

I was pretty high by the time we were done. I pulled out my trusty Visine and squirted some into my eyes. I didn't like evidence, so when we got out of the Jeep, I also sprayed some Chanel perfume on myself. It was the only "designer" thing I had, and I only had it because my mother gave it to me for every single occasion.

"We're headed to the caf. You wanna come?" Jake offered.

"No thanks, I'm good," I answered. I had seen something I wanted to investigate.

"Okay." Jake shrugged, heading back toward the school. I adjusted my skirt and walked toward the figure staring at me a couple parking spots down.

"Were you smoking pot?" Mr. Bentley asked, studying me suspiciously. He was coming back from his car with a paper bag from Mr. Sub.

"No, I was just involved in a four-way," I replied sweetly, laughing at his expression. "Kidding! I wouldn't do anything like that. And smoking pot is illegal, Mr. Bentley."

"So there must have been another reason for the inside of that kid's car to be hotboxed full of smoke," Mr. Bentley said, smiling back and shaking his head. I could tell he wasn't about to get us into trouble.

"Maybe I was telling the truth about the foursome," I said slowly. "Maybe it was steam." I don't think it was any secret that I was trying to seduce him, and he knew it. He glanced around the parking lot nervously. My heart thudded quickly in my chest like a hummingbird. I couldn't believe I'd actually said it. I had never done anything quite like this before. The only time I'd ever said overly sexual things was back when Lauren and I would try to get as many guys as we could to ask for our numbers. It was a silly game, one that I hadn't played in months and had never played with an authority figure before. They were usually just classmates or guys we met at parties. I could almost feel Lauren cheering me on, as stupid as that was. It made me feel all that much closer to her.

"I hope that isn't true," Mr. Bentley said, frowning and looking away, a faint blush on his cheeks.

"You think so little of me already," I said, sounding hurt. "I prefer to focus all of my attention on one person at a time." I looked at him suggestively, and although his jaw had dropped slightly from shock, his eyes betrayed his true feelings. I hadn't expected that at all. My heartbeat increased even more as he looked at me. His mouth opened and closed as he tried to think of an appropriate response. I didn't give him the chance, and there wasn't one. Instead I started walking toward the school, looking over my shoulder briefly.

"See you later, Teach." He was still standing there with his jaw open. He looked the way I felt inside. Totally shocked and intrigued.

That was ballsy, even for me. Despite the rumors, I hadn't really had a lot of boyfriend experience. I'd only really dated two guys before, and both relationships had ended terribly. But I couldn't seem to help myself from saying those things around Mr. Bentley. I knew it wasn't a good idea, but it was almost like I could only watch from the outside. I was on a mission and even I couldn't stop myself. That feeling of awakening, it had been a taste of something I really needed. I'd felt so dead inside for months, and I was finally starting to come alive again. How could I not crave that feeling? Nevertheless, I scolded myself. I had to tone it down a bit. I didn't want to cause trouble. I still had my ambitions and dreams of going to university at the front of my mind.

Despite that, I couldn't stop the show. I didn't know what I hoped to achieve. It wasn't like I actually thought I'd be able to seduce my English teacher.

I put a lot of effort into my essay. At first I just wanted to sound alluring to Mr. Bentley, and I think I succeeded, but then I fell into my writing. I escaped.

I wrote about how my parents met, about my dad playing in a semi-popular band in the 80s and about him overdosing when I was three. I wrote about how I'd been with him, alone, when he died, and about how my mother came home from work to find me clenching his body and crying for him to wake up.

I wrote about the trouble I got into from 12 on. I wrote about my tattoos— the feather pen and ink pot, the six black birds in flight, the cherry blossom vine tattoo, and the very significant meaning they each held for me. I wrote about my ex-boyfriend Rhys and how we'd dated for six months. I wrote about Lauren, our adventures together, and about nearly dying in the very car accident that killed her. I wrote about closing off from everyone after that. Once I started writing, I couldn't stop. The words flowed out of me without my control and I let it happen. The release was euphoric. I sat at my desk after-wards, proofreading and smiling. It was personal, it was raw, and it was the way I loved to write. Despite how open I'd been, I still left out a lot about my life.

I didn't write about my mom's second husband, Rodney, or about how she walked in on him masturbating over me when I was 8. I didn't write about my first ex-boyfriend, star of the basketball team, and how he drugged me on my 15th birthday and let his friends take turns sexually assaulting me. I didn't write about the bullying that happened afterwards, the reason why I switched to the all-girls school, or my general distrust of men. At first, I wanted to write about that stuff...just to tell someone. Lauren had been the only one who knew every horrible detail, and she was gone now. But I didn't want Mr. Bentley to look at me with concern and pity. I wanted to build myself up. Telling him about Lauren's death had been difficult enough.

I was satisfied with the end result when I handed it in Thursday. "Happy reading," I said, giving him a sarcastic smile.

I carried on with my day. At lunch, I went out with Jake and his friends to his Jeep for another "sesh." All day long, I ignored the not-so-warm reception I was getting from my female peers. Females were petty and jealous, and very distrustful of one another. I knew they saw me as a threat and I didn't try to win them over. Instead, I focused on hanging out with the guys. Even after all that I'd been through with my ex and his friends and with Rodney, the step-monster from hell, I was more comfortable hanging out with guys. I had learned from that mistake with the basketball team, and that was to never let someone else mix my drinks and to never give up the control. As for Rodney...well, I had only been 8 and asleep.

Girls were harder because they were stabby, and you could never tell which way they were going to stab you either. They act all trustworthy and understanding, all the while learning information about you so they can turn on you the moment the opportunity presents itself. So I avoided them, or most of them, anyway. Lauren had been different. We had been kindred spirits. We met at the beginning of tenth grade, and had been inseparable until the day she died. She was the first person I really connected with in a long time, possibly ever. She was my rock when I went through rough times. We were often mistaken for siblings, too. She had wide hazel eyes and naturally blond hair, but when she dyed darker we could pass as sisters.

I suppose I kept my distance from the other girls because I knew they'd be nothing like Lauren, and I didn't want to feel like I was replacing her.

After school I had to work, so I started walking toward the diner. I had my earbuds in and listened to Lacuna Coil during the 15-minute commute. I pushed open the door and stepped inside. I hated themes, but somehow this 50's diner was charming and the atmosphere was great. You couldn't help but want to be cheerful. I felt like I could almost be someone else... almost. All my co-workers were pretty nice. I knew a few of them liked to gab behind other employees' backs, but at least they didn't outright make you feel like crap to your face.

Tonight, like most nights, I was working with Danielle, the most tolerable of all my co-workers. She was 22, very pretty with auburn hair and soft brown eyes. She was one of the rare ones who was warm and kind to everyone and didn't talk trash behind anyone's back. She was wholesome through and through, and not in a superior way. She was sweet. I liked her, and I enjoyed working with her.

"Hi, Danielle, just need to get dressed," I greeted her, holding up my uniform. I went into the back, past the kitchen guys who whistled at my school uniform, and toward the staff bathroom where I quickly changed into my work clothes: a black knee-length skirt and a turquoise uniform shirt with the name of the diner on the left breast. I pulled my hair up into a high ponytail and applied some fresh lipstick. Then I put my apron on and made my way back out to the front.

The diner wasn't packed yet; it wouldn't be until about 5 p.m. I spent the next hour topping off the table toppers and making sure we were fully stocked. Danielle had the bigger section, since she had been there longer, and I had the smaller, more reclusive section. A couple regulars that enjoyed the privacy even more than my sunny disposition would frequent back there. I served each table with a small smile on my face, allowed witty comments when merited, and did pretty good with tips. I could be nice when it was needed.

"How was your first few days of school?" Danielle asked, making conversation as we rolled up cutlery for the morning shift when all of our customers were tended to. It was nearly 8 p.m., and the dinner rush was finally over. I enjoyed the quiet moments at night, watching the patrons enjoying their meals, doing side work, and chatting with Danielle to keep myself entertained.

"Good." I shrugged.

"I wish I could go back," Danielle said, sighing wistfully. I looked at her curiously. "Oh, I had to drop out...I'm doing correspondence now so I can stay home with my son."

"Oh, right," I said, feeling awkward. I had almost forgotten Danielle had a kid. She certainly didn't look like it, but she'd told me the first time we worked together. Plus, the other girls gossiped enough about her that I really should have remembered. "Well, if it's any consolation, I wish I could do correspondence."

"Really?" Danielle laughed, delicately tossing her head back slightly. "Why is that?"

"I hate people," I said with a shrug. "Mainly people our age. Not you," I added quickly, seeing her hurt expression. "But the majority of the other ones. They're all two-faced."

"Yeah, I know what you mean." Danielle sighed. "I guess I don't miss that! I just miss the days of little to no responsibility...when my biggest concerns were what I should wear or if so-and-so liked me."

Before I could reply, the door chimed as another customer walked in. I looked up and saw Mr. Bentley heading straight toward my section. He was carrying the laptop bag that I always saw beside his desk. I don't even think he noticed me at first, since I was behind the cashier counter talking to Danielle. He picked a corner booth and sat down. Danielle was watching him too and nudged me with a wide grin on her face.

"Go get him," she whispered, winking. I rolled my eyes at her, grabbed a menu, and walking up to him with a flirtatious smile.

"Fancy seeing you here, Mr. Bentley," I said, bending over slightly to give him the menu. "How did you know I worked here?"

"I didn't," he said a little uneasily, straightening up and looking surprised to see me.

"Is it just you, or will someone else be joining you? Your girlfriend perhaps?" I asked.

"Just me," Mr. Bentley answered, smiling sheepishly. "No girlfriend." He ran a hand through his tousled hair and avoided making eye contact with me. I resisted the urge to lean forward and run my own hands through his hair.

"Can I get you anything to start?" I asked instead, smiling. This was going to be fun.

"Coffee would be good," he answered, keeping his eyes focused on the menu.

"Coming right up, Mr. Bentley." I went to turn around. He gently grabbed my arm.

"You can call me Iain," he said, still holding my arm and looking at me intently. He realized what he was doing and dropped his hand. "Here, anyway. I'm not at work...and Mr. Bentley makes me feel old." He looked surprised by his words and the personal contact.

"Okay, Iain." I couldn't ignore the thrill just saying his name gave me. I brought him a cup of steaming coffee.

"Thank you," he said, distractedly. He was reading a couple of the essays. I noticed mine was on top of the pile.

"Are you reading mine?" I asked, curious.

"Not yet..." he said. "Right now I'm reading the menu." he smiled at me. I blushed a little, noticing the menu to the left of the papers.

"Well then, have you decided what you want?" I asked, trying to regain composure. A guy hadn't made me blush in so long. It was almost weird.

"Oh, no, actually," Iain said. His eyes left my face and focused back on the menu.

"Might I suggest tonight's special? Spaghetti and meatballs with garlic bread?" I said.

"That sounds good," he said, nodding. I wrote his order down on his bill and took it to the kitchen window. I pinned it up and grabbed a couple plates for one of my other tables.

Since rush hour was done, I was getting kind of bored. I actually loved the diner best when it was busy, especially at night. Side work only lasted so long, and the regular customers made me laugh, and they were easy to get along with. Especially the ones that tipped well.

Tips paid for my indulgences, my clothes, my tattoos, and my marijuana, although I could now officially score that for dirt cheap, thanks to Jake. After my cell phone bill, I saved the rest of my paychecks. I was very good at saving my money. I was intent on getting the hell away from my mother and Larry and out on my own as soon as possible, so every penny counted and the busier the better. With only an hour until close, I knew I'd be hard pressed to find things to do to keep myself preoccupied and not stare at my high school English teacher.

I checked up on Mr. Bentley when I noticed he was pretty much finished with his dinner. He had a few bites left but was focused on reading the papers in front of him.

"Mr. Bentley, I mean Iain...can I offer you some dessert? Maybe cherry pie?" I asked, half a smile playing on my lips. His eyes shot up and he looked shocked for a moment. "The cherry pie is our best pie..." I trailed off awkwardly, surprised that I even felt awkward in the first place. Usually, I made sexual innuendos with ease, but I hadn't really intended for that to be sexual. "Or there's apple, or Boston cream pie..."

"No, thank you, another coffee would be good," he replied. He loosened the collar of his shirt, his eyes lingering on my face for a moment before he went back to reading papers. I didn't bother trying to peek at what he was reading. I knew he'd get to mine eventually and I'd hear about it, likely at school. Besides, I didn't really want to remind him that I was a student of his, and I didn't want him to read it with me standing nearby.

I topped off his coffee and asked if he was finished with his dinner. When he nodded, I cleared his table and left a bill. Then I breezed toward the counter, where a couple was waiting with their bill. I rung them out and started on tomorrow's morning prep, filling the cutlery tray and listening to Danielle chat. At five until nine, we started prepping for close. Mr. Bentley was still reading at his table.

Danielle bit her lip and looked at the clock.

"Seriously, Danielle, head out. I'll lock up," I offered. I knew she wanted to get home to her 5-month-old. From what I'd gathered from the other girls at work and what she'd told me, Danielle was a single mom who lived with her parents after her boyfriend ditched her and their unborn child.

"Are you sure?" Danielle asked.

"Yeah, whatever. I'll just wait until this guy goes, then I'll vacuum and close up shop." I had done it a couple times before. The manager liked to make sure that all the evening waitresses were trained on how to lock up. One of us had to stick around for sure, and one of the kitchen guys too. Ryan was still closing the kitchen, and I really didn't mind sending Danielle home. Especially not tonight, when Mr. Bentley was still sitting in the diner.

"Thank you so much, Harlow." Danielle hugged me, and her boobs felt like rocks. I knew she was breastfeeding—that's why she had to take off for twenty minutes to pump every four hours.

"Don't mention it. See you later!" I watched Danielle grab her purse and keys and dart out. When she was gone, it was just Mr. Bentley and I—and Ryan, but he was in the kitchen. Out of sight, out of mind.

I took a deep breath, tossed back my hair, and approached him. His eyes darted up off the page as I walked up to his table.

"Oh, sorry. I lost track of time," he said, taking in the fact that we were alone. I raised one eyebrow suspiciously. Did he really not see everyone leave and us prepping for close?

"Do you mind if I ring you in now so I can shut my till down?" I asked.

"Oh, sure." He fished his wallet out of his pants and pulled out a twenty. "Keep the change," he told me, shoving his papers into his laptop bag. He was suddenly in a great hurry.

"Thanks! See you Monday, Iain," I said coyly. He flinched slightly and was out of the diner before I had even finished ringing his bill through. I bet he was regretting telling me to call him that. I was a little disappointed; part of me hoped that he was in the parking lot, waiting to offer me a ride home, but that would have been weird.

By that point, Ryan had sauntered out of the kitchen. Ryan was a really nice guy. He was a little on the chubby side, but he had a lot of muscle behind him too. I was pretty sure he was in college to be an electrician. He wasn't anything remarkable to look at, but he was very sweet and hilarious. He was madly in love with Danielle, but perpetually shy. He sat down and waited for me to count out the till and deposit the money in the office and grab my stuff. I typed in the security code while Ryan waited outside, then I made sure the door was locked.

Ryan and I parted ways, both of us living in opposite directions from the diner.

When I got home, Mom was in bed but Larry was sitting in the darkened living room. Instantly, the hairs on the back of my neck went up.

"Hi, Harlow," Larry said cheerfully, taking off his reading glasses and putting them on the table beside his reclining chair. He was still dressed in his typical attire of a button up shirt and dress pants. "I've missed you the past few days. I haven't gotten a chance to ask you how your first day of school went."

I relaxed, but only slightly. There was something about this situation that made me feel extremely uncomfortable.

"Fine," I answered, taking my coat off and hanging it up in the closet. I kicked my shoes off and put them away too, feeling Larry's gaze on my back. My guard went up again.

Larry and I hadn't really spent any time together alone. I was very careful to avoid it, and he had never waited up for me before. It made me uneasy that he had.

I held my breath as I heard Larry get up and cross over to the front hall.

"Your mother is very worried about you," he said softly, almost kindly. "She just wants you to be happy, you know?"

"I know," I replied stiffly, backing away. My flight response had kicked on and I just wanted to get away. He was standing too close to me.

"Just go easy on her," Larry told me. "I know you're mad at her for making you move up here, and that you think all of this is too sudden. But she's really trying to find her own slice of happiness too."

He lifted his hand and gently squeezed my upper shoulder. I stood, frozen. Half a second later, he dropped his arm.

I didn't know what else to do, so I nodded. "Well...I have school tomorrow. So, bye." I turned around and quickly walked down the hall to my bedroom.

One of the first things I'd done the moment we moved up north was have a lock installed on my bedroom door. My mother hadn't questioned me on it; she knew exactly why I'd want it: for the comfort. I quickly locked my door and leaned against it, trying to steady my breathing.

While Larry had done literally nothing aside from a harmless touch that I'm sure he meant as comforting, I couldn't help but fight off the panic attack of having him near me. *Larry isn't Rodney*, I told myself firmly, squeezing my eyes shut.

Typically, I was okay around him if my mom was around. But usually, it wasn't that bad; it wasn't panic attack inducing.

CHAPTER TWO

The next day was Friday. After a night of restless sleep, I overslept and missed the bus. Begrudgingly, I allowed my mom to drive me.

"I don't understand why I can't just drive the car," I grumbled. I had my G2 for almost a year. I knew how to drive.

"I need the car during the day, Harlow. You know that," Mom said, keeping a cheerful smile on her face. I could tell it was forced, though.

Mom tried to make small talk on the drive to school about all her recent and upcoming church volunteer projects, but I just didn't have it in me to listen. I was exhausted and my nerves were still frazzled from my panic attack the night before. I didn't tell her about it, although I probably should have. She had to know that being around Larry made me uncomfortable, since she had been the one to find out what Rodney was doing, but it wouldn't surprise me if she acted oblivious to my discomfort. Not that it really mattered. Larry was right, she did deserve happiness. I didn't want to inadvertently ruin that by crying wolf when nothing had happened aside from my own paranoia.

When we pulled up to the school, Mom parked the car and looked at me. "Harlow...I need to ask. Are you okay?"

"What do you mean?"

"It hasn't been that long...since Lauren." Mom was looking at me with concern. She definitely knew how close Lauren and I had been.

"I'm fine, Mom," I said, trying to keep my voice even and my expression neutral. The truth was, I wasn't fine. But it didn't help to tell her that. Telling her that I felt empty and blank would only make her want to send me to a grief counselor, a route that Larry had already tried to push.

Mom nodded, accepting this answer, and attempted to kiss me goodbye on the forehead. I dodged it and got out of the car quickly. "Bye!" I said, slamming the door and cutting her off. She looked at me sadly for a moment before pulling away.

The one upside to Mom driving me meant that I had arrived earlier at school than I would have had I taken the bus. I quickly headed over to the smoking section for a joint. I felt my muscles release the tension they'd been holding, and I started to relax. I rolled my shoulders and took in a deep breath.

"Okay, now I know that's not a cigarette," a familiar, sexy smooth voice from behind me said, jolting me from my moment of peace. I smiled an actual smile, not a forced one. I didn't even need to turn around to know who it was. His voice was already very familiar to me. It even accompanied my dreams...well, the better ones, anyway.

"Mr. Bentley," I said, knowing better than to call him Iain on or near school grounds, especially after he'd flinched the night before. I casually flicked the joint to the ground and squished it with the toe of my shoe, burying it in the dirt.

"What are you doing, Harlow?" Mr. Bentley asked, frowning slightly. "You're a smart girl. You don't need to do drugs."

I turned to face him. He was standing with a hot coffee in his hand, apparently walking over from the nearby Tim Hortons.

"Marijuana is hardly a drug," I replied, trying not to show how nervous I was. I technically got caught red-handed smoking an illegal drug by a teacher. "There are a lot of health benefits to it. It helps with depression, anxiety, and a crap ton of other illnesses. Besides, I get the sense that you hit the bong every now and then yourself."

He laughed, but before he could reply more students came over to the smoking session. "I'll see you...later," he said.

I drew in my lip, watching him walk away. What did that even mean? *Nothing, Harlow,* I thought, almost amused with myself, *It means he'll see you in class.*

The following Monday in English, I tried my hardest to not stare at Iain Bentley. It was difficult, but I managed to avoid his eyes almost the entire class, until the very end when he started handing back our essays.

"Most of you need to work on your paragraph structure, grammar, and spelling. But I was pleasantly surprised by a few of you. A few of you have a great talent for writing, and I'm eager to see what else you present to me throughout the year." Mr. Bentley said this last bit as he handed back my essay. I glanced down at the paper. He'd given me a solid A, but also a Post-It note that said, "*See me after class.*" Normally I'd be disappointed, but since Mr. Bentley was asking, I was curious and looking forward to it, even if I was in trouble. Which I likely was. Horror rose in the pit of my stomach as I worried if Mr. Bentley also wanted me to see a grief counselor. I was regretting being as open as I had been.

"Next Monday, I'll be assigning another essay topic. But the majority of you need to read over how to structure a proper paragraph." The class laughed awkwardly. "If you don't, I'll know by the end of next week. This will count for 5 percent of your final mark," Iain added, ignoring the groans from the majority of the class.

The bell rang, and I kept my head down as I slowly packed up my things. Students spilled out of the classroom quickly; however, someone lingered behind me.

"Harlow! What are you doing this Saturday night?" Riley asked, leaning forward from his desk so that his head was just behind my left shoulder.

"That depends. It's forever away. What's going on?"

"Party at my place. Tell Jake. He knows where it is. Starts at 9." Riley grinned.

"Is this party going to be a 'my parents are home and in the basement' party, or is it going to be a *party*?" I asked skeptically.

"Do you even need to ask?" Riley grinned, standing up. "Hope to see you there," he added before walking off.

I watched him leave the classroom and glanced over to Mr. Bentley's desk. He was leaning back slightly, arms crossed and looking straight at me, his brows slightly furrowed.

I grabbed my bag and stood up, walking over to him. He kept his eyes on me the whole time, and I felt my heart racing, only in a good way. Not like last night.

"Well, you couldn't have hated it that much. You gave me an A," I drawled, giving him a half smile and raising one eyebrow. He smiled.

"That's not why I asked to see you," he said, leaning

forward slightly. I kept my expression even and tried to tell myself that he wasn't saying what I thought he was saying—what I wanted him to say.

"Why did you ask to see me?"

"I wanted to tell you that you write beautifully and articulately. You have a real talent and I'm looking forward to reading more of your work," Mr. Bentley said sincerely, his eyes meeting my gaze and holding it. There was meaning behind his words that I couldn't decipher, and he was wearing a secretive, sincere smile. Normally, I was very good at reading guys, but Iain Bentley was different. "Have you thought about a career in writing?"

His words had humbled me. "Thank you..." I didn't know what to say for once. I hadn't expected him to enjoy my essay that much. I hadn't expected him to have me stay after class just so he could tell me I had talent. It was the first time that someone had actually said that to me and meant it. Then again, it was the first time I had been really open like that. "Yes, I've thought about becoming a writer...maybe someday."

"No problem. You'd be very good at it," Mr. Bentley said. I smiled and looked away. "I also wanted to tell you that I'm sorry about the passing of your friend. That couldn't have been easy for you. If you need anything at all, please don't hesitate. Unfortunately, I know a thing or two about losing a friend."

I glanced back at his face and he looked open and honest. "It sucked, but that's life. You live and you die. The ones you leave behind get to feel...left behind." I shrugged, feeling like my statement was more stupid than wise.

Mr. Bentley nodded thoughtfully. "That's true, but...like I said, I'm here."

"I'm fine." I smiled, and I found I was fine with him around. "If that's all?"

"One more thing," he said, giving me a sheepish half-grin.

"Those tattoos, they sound...very interesting." His topic choice shocked me, although I didn't show it.

"You'll have to see them sometime," I replied coyly, raising an eyebrow and quickly making my sweeping exit. I tried to ignore the fluttering of my heart in my chest. I thought I heard a sharp intake of breath before I closed the door behind me, but it was impossible to tell if it was his or mine.

What are you doing, Harlow Jones? I demanded, instantly putting my hand on my forehead to massage my temples. The word FORBIDDEN danced across my mind in big bold letters. But suddenly, he didn't seem so forbidden, so unattainable. That both scared and thrilled me.

It was almost as if I couldn't control myself around him. I didn't let myself lose control, and if I found I was going to, I backed out. Or at least I had learned to do that in recent years. Only what could I back out from? It wasn't as if Mr. Bentley and I were...involved. I just had a massive, irresistible attraction to him. He just set me on fire every time he looked at me. He was so close yet so far. I thought my crush was an impracticable dream, but now I wasn't so sure. Iain seemed to want me. After all, dreams can and do come true...for some people. Not necessarily me.

On weekends, I usually worked the morning shift on Saturday and the evening shift on Sunday so that I could have Saturday night to cause mayhem. Since moving, my social life wasn't as booming as it had been, and the only mayhem I got into was reading books or writing in my room. I knew my staying at home every weekend actually concerned my mom. When Lauren was alive, we were out all the time.

I hadn't really wanted to go to Riley's party at all, but I was so bored and tired of not doing anything. As much as I hated people, I hated constantly being alone too. I hadn't been to a party since Lauren died and it was surreal getting ready without her by my side, competing for more bathroom counter space to lay her makeup out on.

I dressed in a pair of my favorite ripped faded dark denim jeans and the corset style top that Lauren had picked out for me during one of our shopping trips. My mother hated it, especially now that she was married to such a religious nut.

"Are you going out dressed like that?" she asked when I came into the front hall, the shock evident on her delicate features. I grabbed my coat and high heeled shit kickers.

"Yup," I answered simply, pulling my long dark hair out from under my jacket.

"That sends the wrong message. The wrong kind of guy—"

"It's a little late for you to be protecting me from 'the wrong kind of guy' isn't it, Mom?" I snapped, my words harsh. Mom flinched at my voice, almost shrinking. She opened her mouth to reply, but a horn sounding from the driveway cut her off.

"I've got to go," I said, feeling guilty. "See you later."

I don't know why I couldn't apologize. I don't know why I blamed her for all the things that she hadn't been able to shelter and protect me from, but I did. It was impossible to ignore those feelings too, not when they were constantly just below the surface. A small part of me feared that she blamed me for what happened with Rodney, although she'd never even given the slightest hint toward that.

I thought about all that as I walked toward the old, beat up Jeep Jake was driving. He'd forced Cory and Troy into the back seat so I could ride shotgun.

"Before I get in," I said, extremely seriously, standing in the driveway and holding the passenger door open. "If you're going to drink tonight or get stoned beyond belief, you have to tell me."

"Don't worry about it," Jake assured me. "I don't drink, and I won't be getting stoned. I'm going to make a profit tonight."

"Okay," I could believe that...maybe. And even if he did get drunk or stoned, I was resourceful. Since the accident a year prior, I definitely knew better than to get in the car with someone who'd been drinking or doing drugs ever again, even if it was just pot.

I jumped inside and buckled up, and Jake drove to the rich end of town. Huge houses were tucked away into the massive hill that the rest of the town had affectionately named "Snob Hill." The house where Riley lived was fairly huge and very new and was jam packed full of people already.

"He always says invite only, but everyone always comes from our school and the surrounding schools," Jake explained, motioning toward the house with his head. He found parking and we piled out of the Jeep. I took a steadying breath, hoping my nervousness wasn't showing on my face. I had a reputation to uphold.

I tucked my hands into my leather jacket and followed the guys up the perfectly manicured lawn and down an impeccable walkway. Music was booming from the doorway, and people kept streaming inside.

"Harlow! You're here! Ayyy Jake! You're here too!" Riley's voice was even louder than the music, and it was the first thing that greeted us when we walked into his massive foyer. He threw a heavy arm around my shoulder in a drunkenly friendly manner. "And then you two...whatever your names are!" Riley was clearly wasted already, and it wasn't even 10 p.m. yet. Classy.

"Hey Riley." Jake inclined his head slightly in greeting.

"Harlow, do you want a drink?" Riley shouted over the

music, shaking me with almost every word. I shook my head, lifting his arm off my shoulders. I didn't drink, at least not with already drunk high school students in an atmosphere like this. Not since the accident. *Why did I come again?* I thought, trying to hide my uneasiness.

"Nah, but I will have a joint," I said out loud instead, looking at Jake. He nodded and we made our way to the back patio with Cory and Troy following behind.

"Suit yourselves! Have fun!" Riley shouted after us, his red cup sloshing liquid out all over his hand. He didn't even seem to notice and was already approaching another group of girls.

It was slightly quieter outside, but not by much. Loud, drunk kids were everywhere. I stayed out back with the stoners, laughing it up. I wasn't comfortable, but I wasn't about to let them know it. But being uncomfortable meant that I was aware of my surroundings. I barely smoked anything, and I only drank from a water bottle that I'd brought.

About two hours after we got there, I went inside to try to find the bathroom. Riley cornered me in the hallway, holding a red cup.

"Take this!" he slurred, shoving it at me. I smiled sweetly and took the red cup. He then proceeded to yap at me for 10 minutes while I tried to edge around him.

"Thanks, Riley. But I need to use the washroom. Is it upstairs?" I asked. He nodded.

"It's on the right, with the toilet. Want me to walk you up?"

"I'm sure I can find it. I'll see you in a bit." I waved him away, still holding the red cup.

As I headed toward the bathroom, I heard male laughter and crying coming from one of the bedrooms across the hall. My attention snapped to the door, and I went to take a step toward it. I could hear a female begging and a guy's voice gruffly telling her to shut up.

"No!" she said, more forcefully this time. I heard the sound of skin hitting skin, and her whimper.

A bad feeling in my stomach welled. The hairs raised on the nape of my neck, and I was instantly transported back to the night my ex-boyfriend and his friends had drugged me. The girl whimpered again, then her whimper became muffled, as if someone was covering her mouth.

"Shut up, bitch! If you make another sound, you'll regret it. You know what I can do to you, easily," the guy's voice said harshly. I stepped toward the door, my hand hovering over the knob. My heart was racing. I knew exactly what was going on behind the door, and although I wanted to burst into the room and stop it from happening, I hesitated. My fear kept me in place a moment too long. I heard the guy moan in pleasure, which prompted me to finally break free of the fear. My hand shook as I opened the door. I forcefully flung it wide, and it clattered with a bang against the door stopper.

I didn't really know what to do, so I instinctively started acting drunk. "Oops, sorry, this isn't the bathroom." My giggle was a little too high, a little too fake, but it did the trick. I put a hand over my mouth and staggered a bit to buy myself some time as I assessed my surroundings and searched for some kind of weapon in case things got ugly. I quickly spotted a bat leaning against the wall.

The big, stocky guy on the bed whipped around to stare at me. He looked at the red cup in my hand, and a sly smile pasted across his Hollywood features. He would have been semi-attractive, but all I could see was the girl underneath him. It was Jenna, from my English class. Tears were streaming down her face, mixing in with the snot from her nose. She was panicked, and looking at me with wide, fear-filled eyes. Her cheek was red, as if she'd been struck. Her underwear was around her ankles and her skirt was lifted up. The big stocky guy was rolling off the bed, tucking himself back into his jeans, still looking at me with that sly sneer. A wave of nausea and rage hit me.

"A little lost, are we?" The guy smirked, standing up and walking slowly toward me. He was tall, much taller than I was. And a lot stronger.

Instantly I threw the cup down, spilling its entire contents all over the pristine white carpet, and grabbed the bat, lifting it with both my hands. "What the fuck are you doing?"

"Whoa...easy there." The guy mockingly raised his hands. I glared hard at him. He had muscles that no teen guy should have; he definitely didn't look like a high school student. His black hair was a little longer, tight curls close to his head. I stole a look at Jenna. She was trying to dress herself with trembling arms.

"Get the fuck out of here!" I raised my voice, the rage I was feeling keeping it steady although inwardly, I was shaking.

"Nah, I don't think we will. See, you intruded on us; we were just having a good time," he said, taking a step toward me. "I think you should leave."

"I'm not leaving, and she doesn't look like she's having a good time with you," I said, looking at Jenna again. Fresh tears were pouring down her cheeks. Her right cheekbone was beginning to bruise. I looked back at the guy, my hands clammy as he kept walking toward me. "Take one more step, and I'll hit you."

"You wouldn't dare." The guy laughed, throwing his head back. He kept walking, and I swung the bat. It connected with his knee. He buckled, shock crossing his features as he fell. The shock was quickly replaced with rage.

"You stupid bitch!" he roared, somehow managing to get back to his feet and lunge at me.

I tried to swing the bat at the last minute to hit him again, but he was too quick; his body smashed into mine and I fell back against the wall. The impact made me bite my tongue and my vision wavered as I hit my head against the wall. The bat dropped from my hands. Frantically, I scratched at his face. He punched me in the stomach, knocking the wind out of me. I kicked my knee up and it collided with his precious family jewels.

"What the fuck is going on in here?" boomed a voice from behind me. I tried to turn my head, but it spun unpleasantly. "You need to get the hell out of here before I call the cops." Jake stood in the doorway, eyes blazing with anger.

"I'll find you," the stocky guy hissed in my ear, leaning forward to lick my face. "And I'll fucking finish this, bitch." I spit at him as he shoved me back.

"Get out now!" Jake roared angrily. He'd managed to pick up the bat. I wavered against the wall, disoriented.

The guy took another look at me, then shrugged. "Whatever, man," he said, leaving the room as if he hadn't just raped a girl and nearly beaten the crap out of me.

Jake was at my side, offering his arm out to steady me. "Are you okay?" he demanded. "Riley said you came upstairs. I came to find you...we were gonna bail..."

"I'm fine," I muttered, my head still spinning slightly. I ignored the unpleasant sensation and forced myself to stand up straight with a little assistance from Jake. I don't think he even realized that someone else was in the room. I quickly went over to the bed where Jenna was sitting, her legs drawn up and her arms tightly around them. Her inner thighs were covered in dried blood.

"Oh my god," Jake managed, quickly averting his eyes to offer Jenna what privacy he could. She didn't even seem to notice him though; she was sobbing hysterically and shaking.

"Can you go and get me a cold wash cloth and some

water?" I asked, not thinking about myself. I leaned toward Jenna, gently brushing back her hair from her sweaty forehead.

"I didn't want to..." Jenna hiccupped. "I wanted to save myself."

I couldn't think of anything to say, so I gently rubbed her back as she cried, my heart breaking for her. By the time Jake returned with a cloth and a glass of water, Jenna was more aware. She'd stopped talking, although she was still shaking as silent tears streaked down her face.

"We need to call an ambulance or take her to the hospital," I said.

"No!" she weakly cried. "D-don't." She looked at me, fearful, then she looked at Jake. Her face was red from embarrassment and shame.

"I know you're scared, but you should go," I told her, gently brushing her hair from her face again. "You did nothing wrong."

"No," she said, firmer this time. "I'll get into trouble. I'm not supposed to be out."

I bit my lip, glancing back at Jake. He shrugged; he didn't know what to do either.

"Jenna, we need to report this," I told her, keeping my tone gentle but persuasive. She looked at me as if I was insanely stupid.

"Do you even know who that was?" she demanded, fresh tears pouring down her face.

"No..."

"Andrew Cooper," Jenna said, her voice shaking. Jake made a sound of recognition. I looked toward him for an explanation, as it was clear Jenna wasn't going to elaborate.

"His dad is the Chief of Police," Jake answered my unasked question.

"I just want to go home," Jenna said, fresh tears streaming

down her face. My heart ached, the situation dredging up an all too familiar past.

"Okay, we'll take you home. Can you walk?" I asked. Jenna was unstable on her feet, but between Jake and I, we were able to get her out the door and to Jake's Jeep with minimal people noticing. The only people who did notice were Callie and Tara, who both just glared and rolled their eyes, and Riley, who quickly started walking toward us to cut us off.

"Leaving so soon?" he practically whined. The three of us ignored him and walked around him.

Jenna lived in a nice area of town in a cute little bungalow a few blocks away from downtown. By the time we got to her house, she was steadier on her feet.

"I've got it from here," I told Jake.

"I'll wait. Give you a lift home," Jake answered. I nodded, helping Jenna up the pathway to her house.

"Are your parents home?" I whispered when we got to the door. She shook her head and struggled with her house key. Her hands were trembling still. I helped her open the door, and inside.

Jenna pushed away from me once we were inside her foyer. She stumbled down the hall to the bathroom and sat on the toilet, her eyes blank.

"Jenna, I really think you should go to the hospital," I told her, kneeling in front of her.

"I'm fine," she insisted, but her voice shook.

"Look...I know it's hard but the best time to go is right now, before you wash any of the evidence away."

"I can't report it," Jenna said, looking horrified at the suggestion.

"I know that his dad is Chief of Police, Jenna," I tried. "But surely—"

"Surely not." She was crying again. Her cheek was starting

to bruise where she'd been hit. "Who will they believe? Andrew has his father to back him."

"Fuck." I frowned, exhaling the breath that I hadn't been aware I was holding. I had no idea how to pursue her to change her mind, or if a thing like that was even possible.

"Please, please don't tell anyone. Your boyfriend either." She looked at me desperately. "I...I don't want anyone to know."

I nodded, unable to think of anything else to say or do. I made sure Jenna was tucked into bed before I left. Jake was waiting for me in the driveway to give me a ride home, just as he promised.

I woke up at about 2 p.m. I was scheduled to work at 5. My body felt as if it'd been hit by a truck, but I bore no bruises from the encounter. I took a long, hot shower to try and ease my aching muscles, but I barely felt a difference.

My shift was uneventful. Surprisingly, I didn't run into anyone who'd been at Riley's party.

"You go home early," Danielle insisted an hour before close, looking around the dead diner. "I'll close up tonight. I owe you one anyway."

"Thanks," I told her, grateful. My body was still sore, and I stiffly went to the back to grab my purse and jacket.

It was getting dark out, but not overly so. I felt wary about walking home after last night, but I didn't want to call my mom. Her fussing over me about my emotional state was getting on my last nerve. I didn't need another thing for her to freak out about. Besides, I knew Larry would be with her too. I peered outside and looked around, not seeing anything or anyone suspicious. I adjusted my bag and started walking, knowing it would take me only fifteen minutes at a brisk pace. Almost halfway into my walk, I heard catcalls from behind me —three of them. I didn't want to turn around, so I started walking faster. Their voices grew louder, and I recognized the one. I tossed a quick glance over my shoulder to see for sure. Andrew was standing between two other guys. They were holding beers, drinking in a nearly empty parking lot beside a couple of parked vehicles. He looked right at me, anger and recognition crossing his face.

"Hey! You're that girl from last night!" he said, throwing his beer can down on the ground as he started walking toward me. "Hang on, I think we need to finish our...conversation!"

I started to run, ignoring the ache in my legs, real panic setting in. Panic that hadn't had time last night during my adrenaline rush, at least not as strong. Panic that was always there. I heard three sets of feet pounding the pavement after me.

I was running when a house I'd walked by a thousand times caught my eye. It was an old brick one, and it had caught my attention because there was a figure heading up the walkway with groceries. The first person I'd seen in a while, and I knew the three guys behind me were catching up. I didn't think I could outrun them.

"Slow down! We just wanna....talk," Andrew was saying.

"Come on, sweet cheeks—there's no reason to be afraid!" the second guy added while the third guy laughed. The person, hearing the commotion, turned around. I was too panicked to register that it was Mr. Bentley until I had already run up the walkway and collided into his arms, his groceries falling from his hands to land on the ground.

"Please," I said breathlessly, my side a painful stitch. Iain quickly assessed me, concern apparent on his face, and then glared toward the three figures quickly retreating the way they'd came.

"Harlow? What happened?" Mr. Bentley asked, brushing back a strand of my hair. My shaky legs gave out, and he caught me in his arms.

Moments later, I found myself carried into Iain Bentley's house and placed on the couch. I was trying my hardest to fight off a panic attack on my own, but there was no stopping it.

"Can you hand me my bag please," I managed between breaths. He quickly handed it to me and, shaken, I searched for my bottle of Clorazepate. I popped one, but knew it wouldn't help immediately.

"I'm going to make you tea," Iain said, standing up. I couldn't focus on anything but my hands and my breathing. He went outside for a moment, likely to retrieve his groceries from the walkway.

A few minutes later, he returned, glancing at me with concern as he walked toward the back of his house with his groceries. Five minutes later I heard the kettle coming to a boil, and the sound of water pouring and spoons tinkling against the mugs as he stirred.

I was finally steadier with my breathing by the time he came back. Iain's face was full of concern and anger. I shrunk back into the couch. Maybe he was angry that I had involved him, that I was there. He saw my expression and his face softened.

"I'm not angry at you," he said, sitting on the coffee table in front of me and holding out a mug of steaming tea that I gratefully took in my hands. "I'm angry that I didn't get a good look at those guys. They were following you, right?"

I willed myself to become the sensual and confident Harlow, the face that I tried to wear whenever anyone else was around. It was difficult, what with my face chalk white and clammy and my heart pounding extremely fast in my chest. I held my head higher and steeled my jaw, trying to appear unaffected and strong.

"Yeah. A party I went to last night. I walked in on the one guy...taking advantage of a girl. He raped her," I replied, leaving out that the girl had been Jenna.

"Jesus." Iain ran a hand through his hair, his eyes hard with anger. "If I had known, I would have..." he trailed off, glaring out toward the street.

"Would have what? You would have chased them down?" I scoffed. Iain gave me a look.

"I should call the police so you can report this to them," he said after a moment of looking at me.

I chewed on my lip and looked out the window, thinking about the promise I'd made and about how the culprit was the Police Chief's son. "I'd rather not. They can't really do anything."

Mr. Bentley sighed. "Harlow, that girl at the party...it'd help her case, especially because you witnessed what happened and that guy attacked you that night and followed you tonight."

"Won't I get in trouble for being here?" I asked, curious. I was suddenly very aware that I was completely alone with my English teacher, and that he was inches away from me. I heard his breath intake, but I didn't dare look at him. Although I'd been fighting to get my confidence back, it just wasn't coming. I felt vulnerable and worse, insecure. Why couldn't I have run into some old gentlemen who would make sure those guys had gone before sending me on my way? Why did it have to be Mr. Bentley's house that I randomly ran to? I hadn't even known he lived nearby. I thought about all this as I stared into the mug of tea.

"Why would you be in trouble?"

"Because, you're my English teacher and I ended up on your doorstep. It's going to look...suspicious. Even if it was totally random. I swear I had no idea this was your house. Had I known, I would have kept running." I couldn't help but think about how openly I had hit on him. What if he thought I was stalking him?

"That would have been stupid." It was Iain's turn to scoff at me. He gently reached over with one hand and tipped my chin up so I was looking at him. "Had you kept running, they would have caught up to you, and you could have been seriously hurt." He said this softly, his voice filled with...something. I frowned, dropping my gaze. The look in his eyes and the feel of his hand on my chin was making my heart rate increase again. Normally, that kind of contact would make me uncomfortable —very uncomfortable. But with him, I welcomed it. I *enjoyed* it. He dropped his hand, sighing again.

I took a sip of the tea I was holding, just to give myself something to do. My hands shook, and I couldn't tell if it was from the near-miss or from him. I could still feel his eyes on me.

"I promised the girl," I said, shrugging. "I can't give away anything without involving her...and she doesn't want to report it. As much as I don't agree with her, it is her decision."

Iain quietly observed me for another minute, then sighed. The silence we fell into was charged—by me, anyway. I didn't dare look at him again.

"Okay, well. Let me drive you home then," Iain said suddenly, standing up directly in front of me. He held out his hand and I took it. He gently pulled me up, and I was closer to him than I'd ever been before. He smelled intoxicating, the combination of books and the woods. He still had a hold of my hand. He was about a head taller than me, so that when I tipped my head up to look at his face, he was still peering down.

His smoldering blue eyes were full of longing. He wanted me. I leaned into him, almost without meaning to. He inhaled sharply and backed away, releasing my hand.

"Where do you live?" he asked, looking away from me and clenching his jaw.

"Prince Edward Street," I whispered, suddenly overcome with embarrassment. Maybe I'd read him wrong. *What were you thinking, Harlow?* I scolded myself. My cheeks felt hot, and I stared down at my feet.

He grabbed his keys from a ledge near the door and slipped into his coat. I was still wearing mine. I picked up my bag and followed him out the door.

CHAPTER THREE

On Monday, the party was all anybody could talk about. How awesome it had been, how drunk so-and-so had gotten—the usual.

English class was a challenge. I looked for Jenna beforehand, but it was obvious that she wasn't coming by the comfortable way Callie and Tara were gossiping about her.

"I can't believe she'd get that drunk," Callie was saying, tossing her hair over her shoulder and rolling her eyes judgmentally.

"I know, I also can't believe she'd hook up with Andrew," Tara was saying, her voice full of disgust.
    "She knew you guys were going to get back together! What a slut!"

I gritted my teeth, resisting the urge to slap both of them so hard that their heads spun.

In addition to them, Iain was also a challenge. I felt his eyes on me, but every time I looked up, he'd pointedly be looking in another direction.

"This week's essay is going to be about struggles. Write about a time when you struggled and overcame it," he told us at the end of class. "It's due next class. Remember, proper paragraph structure, grammar and spelling are crucial," he added as the bell rang, signaling the end of class.

Great, I thought, stuffing my notebook into my bag. I could write an entire book on struggles, but the last thing I wanted was for Iain to read any of mine. I was still feeling the sting of rejection from our not-so-near kiss. I didn't want him to think I was some obsessed student.

"Hey, Harlow...did you have fun Saturday?" Riley asked, looking at me with an almost wounded expression on his face. "You left early."

"Oh yeah, it was great," I said dryly. "Gotta go. Late." I took off without saying another thing to him, but I did spare a peek at Mr. Bentley. He was watching me with a guarded, vulnerable look on his face. Maybe he thought I was going to tell on him. For what, I wasn't clear. It wasn't like anything had actually happened.

The rest of the week passed by in an uneventful manner. By Friday, Jenna had finally returned to school, but she was not her usual bubbly ditzy self; she looked pale and sullen. I saw her head into the bathroom alone during morning break, so I followed her.

"Hey, are you okay?" I asked, seeing her leaning over one of the bathroom sinks.

"I'm fine," she whispered.

"Look." I took a step toward her. "Let me know if you need anything, if you need to talk...or anything."

She looked up at me with dull eyes. "Thanks. For everything," she said, her voice void of emotion. "I really appreciate it."

I nodded, resisting the urge to hug her. The last thing I wanted after the incident with my ex and his friends was to be touched by anybody. I sighed, fishing in my bag for a piece of paper and a pen. I scribbled my cell phone number on it and handed it to her.

"Seriously, if you need to talk or anything, don't hesitate," I told her as she took the paper from me and stared blankly at it. She nodded, and figuring I had nothing more to say, I left.

I had a low-key weekend, picking up a couple extra shifts at the diner, and at the end of the Saturday night shift that I had picked up. I decided to do something impulsive and probably stupid.

"Catch you later," I told Ryan as we parted ways. I looked behind me, watching his retreating figure for a couple minutes.

I started walking. My heart was pounding, I didn't know what I'd hoped to accomplish, but the questions were driving me crazy. I needed answers.

In no time at all, I was walking up the steps to the red brick house and tapping firmly on the door.

The door opened, and Iain Bentley filled the doorway, staring at me. He didn't look the least bit surprised or put out to see me. The chilly October wind was tossing his hair pleasantly. It had grown since the first day of school; he still had a 5 o'clock shadow too.

"What are you doing here? Is everything alright?" he demanded, sticking his head outside to look around for anyone pursuing me. I didn't respond. My heart was pounding in my ears. I pushed him back inside and followed him in, closing the door behind me.

"I'm getting a vibe from you," I said, my heart racing.

He looked at me, startled. "A vibe?" he almost stuttered, drinking me in hungrily. He shook his head, trying to clear his thoughts. He ended up staring at the wall beside me. "I don't—"

"It's alright. I'm not an idiot." I rolled my eyes, feeling very much like an idiot and desperately hoping that my intuition was right. "I know you want me." My voice was steady, although I felt anything but.

"I—" his mouth opened and closed as he struggled to find something appropriate to say. His eyes shot back to mine and he held my gaze. I could feel the heat in his eyes. "I feel like I owe you an explanation," he finally said, his rugged voice low and intense as he continued to look at me. He had taken three big steps away from me, but I could feel the heat radiating off him, warming me on the crisp autumn night.

"For what?" I challenged. "Almost kissing me?" Even if I wasn't sure that had been his intent, even if I'd sort of initiated it.

"For wanting to," Iain amended, seriously. "For...still wanting to. You were vulnerable, and you came to me for help, and I nearly took advantage of that. I'm not that kind of person."

"No, you didn't." It felt odd that we were finally having this conversation, but it had to happen. I took a step toward him. I was trembling. "Trust me, I've been taken advantage of before, and that wasn't even close. I wanted you to—"

"Was that supposed to make me feel better? Because it doesn't." Iain frowned. He shook his head again, seeming to clear his thoughts. "I shouldn't feel this way about you. About a *student*. It's wrong." He seemed to be talking to himself.

"Feel what?" I whispered.

"Attraction, longing, desire, vulnerability..." Iain trailed off, looking torn. He frowned as if he was angry at himself for telling me. I took another step toward him and he watched me.

"I feel that way too," I told him. "For the first time in a long time, I feel...alive. Awake."

It was another one of those "time stood still" moments. I walked toward him and he gently grabbed my jacket, pulling me close to him yet holding me at a distance. He was a good head taller than me, so I had to look up at him. He slowly lowered his face to mine. He didn't kiss me. He just put his forehead against mine and inhaled deeply. I felt his breath cascade across my nose and lips. It smelt minty and fresh, and it warmed me from the inside out. I felt myself thawing out, not realizing how frozen I'd been before.

I looked up at him, filled with a need I couldn't fully comprehend. It took seconds before I felt his lips against mine, softly, gently, and yet setting me on fire. I kissed back, just as gentle and vulnerable as he kissed me. He moaned, then kissed me softly again and pulled away, returning his forehead to mine.

"Harlow..." his whisper was almost a plea. "I should take you home. This is wrong." Iain massaged his temple with his left hand; his right hand was still grasping my jacket.

"How is it wrong if it feels right?" I asked, standing as still as I could. He smiled, almost pained. "You're what, maybe seven years older than me? That's not so bad."

He laughed softly. "More like ten" he corrected, sighing. He frowned as if that number was truly overwhelming. His hand released my jacket.

"Age is but a number," I said, bringing my face closer to his. He closed his eyes, inhaling me.

"I'm your teacher. You're my student," he said, reminding us both. He ran his hands up my arm. That detail seemed so insignificant.

"I think we've already crossed that boundary," I whispered. His hands gently squeezed my arms through my thick jacket.

"I won't lie. I've been attracted to you from when I first saw you," he confessed again. "But...this can't happen. I'll lose my job if anybody finds out. Or worse."

"What if nobody finds out?" I whispered, promise behind my words. I didn't want him to lose his job, but I couldn't stop thinking about him. I couldn't resist this urge. And I didn't want to. It had been easy to do when I thought he hadn't wanted me—when I thought I'd misread him—but now that I knew differently, resisting that would be even harder.

"You're seventeen." He sighed, releasing his grasp on my arms.

"I'll be eighteen in January," I answered, raising an eyebrow. I didn't wait for him to reply. I ran my right hand against his jaw and behind his neck then I pulled him toward me, joining my other hand on the back of his neck. He came willingly, and his lips crashed against mine with fevered intensity. I had never been kissed like that before; he set me on fire as he trailed kisses along my neck and ears. He was breathing almost as heavily as I was.

After what seemed like ages, he slowly pulled away. "But you're still my student." I could hear his resolve weakening.

"And I won't tell," I replied. "You'll be Mr. Bentley at school, and in public, and Iain here." I didn't know why I was trying to convince him. It was a bad idea; I knew that. He could get into trouble, and lots of it. But I wasn't planning on telling anyone and I didn't want to go back to feeling that emptiness I'd felt before. I was addicted to...whatever this feeling was.

I could literally see the battle between desire and reason that he was having, so I took a step back.

"Let me know what you decide," I said, turning around and heading for the door. His hand grabbed mine, and I looked back at him. His brows were furrowed with frustration and confusion. He looked torn. He still held my hand.

"I can't seem to let you walk away, so I guess it's decided." Iain exhaled, running his free hand through his hair. "I can't get you out of my head, and I want to be with you. And not just... like that," he added, seeing my expression.

"Then how?"

"You know, be with you. Be yours." It was amusing watching my English teacher struggling to find words, but it was more amusing because it was harder for me to look at him as my teacher. It had always been hard, but now it was even more challenging.

He didn't really give me an opportunity to reply; he pulled me toward him for another earth-shattering kiss.

"Oh," I mumbled, almost dazed. He grinned at me and I laughed.

Suddenly, the mood got heavy. He gently helped me out of my coat and tossed it on the ground. My heart was pounding in my ears. I was no virgin—far from it—but I felt just as nervous as one. I kicked off my boots and he picked me up and carried me to the couch. The same couch I'd sat on a few short weeks ago, having a panic attack. We fell onto it, him onto me and me onto the couch, never breaking the kiss. My hands roamed his body through his clothes, and I was pleased to see that my prediction of his body wasn't that far off. He was in shape, each muscle defined and hard, and he was packing. I could feel him pressing into my pelvis through both our jeans. I moaned into his mouth, and he gently nibbled my bottom lip in response.

"I wanted to wait," he said heatedly. "But if you keep kissing me like that, I won't be able to."

"Me?" I laughed, trying to duck away from his lips. "You're the one kissing like that."

"Fair enough," he amended. "But you're irresistible."

I laughed. He was still poised over top of me, his blue eyes full with longing and amusement, a delectable half-smile playing on his lips. I drew in my lower lip and bit it gently, my stomach tingling with desire.

Iain Bentley was amazing. He was gentle and he was passionate. He was impressive on all levels, and extremely skilled. I hadn't been with many people willingly, only Rhys, and he had been completely all about him. With Iain, I'd never been more pleasured in my life, and likely never would know pleasure of that intensity after him.

Afterwards, he wrapped us both up in a warm afghan from the back of his couch, and we lay there tangled up in each other's arms, breathing peacefully. I rested my head on his chest while he rubbed my lower back and played with my hair.

"I should go soon..." I trailed off, figuring it was nearing midnight.

"Mmhmm." Iain yawned, pulling me tight. "You could stay, if you wanted to."

"I sort of have a curfew." I hated to remind him of my age now, especially considering what we'd just done, but it was true.

He laughed, showing no traces of regret. "I didn't take you for the type to obey curfew," he joked.

I feigned offense. "What kind of type do you take me for?"

"The independent, strong willed, assertive kind that doesn't follow any rules but her own," Iain replied, suppressing a yawn.

"That's accurate, and although I hate obeying curfew, I also have my own rules for hook ups. One of them is no sleepovers," I informed him, making it up as I went along.

"You think this was just a hook up?" Iain actually did look offended. "Weren't you listening to a word I said prior?"

"Well, I've learned from a very early age that guys will say anything to get in your pants...so, I did hear you, I just didn't believe you," I answered honestly.

Iain looked thoughtful as he pondered my words. "Okay, fair enough. Well, I meant it. This is more than a hook up to me. I'm saying it now and I've already been in your pants," Iain added, smiling. "What about you? What are you looking for?" He looked at me, almost vulnerable.

"I don't know," I answered. "I don't want it to be just a hook up, but I told you, I'm not expecting anything."

"Well, let's just take this slow..." Iain trailed off, seeing my expression. "Slower, I mean. But know that I believe in monogamy. Even if we can't be open about our...relationship with anyone else."

"Good to know." I smiled. "And don't worry, your secret is safe with me."

"*Our* secret," Iain whispered, pressing his lips against mine for another kiss.

———

That Monday morning, I was a little late for class after accidentally sleeping in. The weekend had caught up with me. I hadn't gotten home until nearly 3 a.m. on Sunday morning, then I worked from 8 until 2 and crashed hard.

"Nice of you to join us, Miss Jones," Iain said sternly when I finally walked into the classroom, nearly an hour late.

"Sorry, teach. Busy weekend," I replied, tossing my hair over my shoulder as I walked past. I caught a hint of a smile at the corner of his lips, but I didn't dare look directly at him. I went to my seat and sat down, ignoring Riley's obvious chest stare.

"What did you do this weekend?" Riley whispered as Iain continued the lesson, trying to be oblivious to me. I knew he was watching out of the corner of his eye by the slight set of his jaw.

"Worked. Hung out. The usual," I replied, not really wanting to encourage conversation with Riley. I wanted to be left alone to discreetly stare at Iain's body and bask in the sweet memories of what it looked like unwrapped from all those layers and what it was capable of doing to me. But instead, knowing that Riley was staring at me, I opened up my notebook and started doodling.

In the last ten minutes before class ended, Mr. Bentley gave the writing topic. He sat on the edge of his desk and observed us all.

"This week's topic is chance. Write about what chance means, or about what happened when you gave something—or someone—a chance," he said. "And pick out a novel from the reading list to read and do a book report on. The book report will be due two Mondays from now."

The class groaned in unison, except for me. I loved reading, and I enjoyed doing Iain's writing topics. I enjoyed pouring bits of my soul into them, especially when he chose topics that were extremely relevant to what I was going through. Not that I openly wrote about him—he always knew by the metaphors, just as I knew by the topic.

The bell rang, signaling the end of class. I packed up my things and stood up. Riley reached out and grabbed my arm, smiling cockily at me.

"You up for dinner tonight?" he asked.

"No," I replied, pulling my arm from his grasp. "I'll pass... indefinitely." I ignored the disappointed look on Riley's face and stole a look at Iain, who was discreetly watching from his desk. He suppressed a smile as I walked by with a smile of my own on my lips.

As I joined the overwhelming amount of students in the hallway, I caught sight of Jenna, Callie, and Tara. She'd gone back to hanging out with them, although their friendship seemed to have changed. Jenna was looking a little better these days though, and she had yet to text to me. I figured she'd moved what had happened to her into the filing cabinet of denial. I didn't want to force her to talk about it or deal with it.

"Harlow! Wait up!" I turned my head toward the sound of my name, seeing Jake trying to push his way through the clusters of students clogging up the hallway. He reached my side and kept up with my pace. "Hey, I meant to ask...how's that girl? Callie?"

"Jenna," I corrected. "I think she's okay." I shrugged, frowning. "I don't want to force her to talk about it so..."

"Yeah," Jake said awkwardly. "That's probably...a good idea." He looked completely out of his element. "You haven't seen him around again, have you?"

Jake knew about how Andrew had chased me after work one day, although I'd left out the part about running into Iain completely.

"No, I haven't. Thank God." I sighed.

"Good." Jake nodded in agreement, pursing his lips angrily. "God, I want to teach that guy a lesson."

"Why hasn't anybody?" I asked. "He's an arrogant prick. Oh, and a rapist."

"Because..." Jake raised one eyebrow. "His dad."

"Oh right." I rolled my eyes. "Let's just let Junior get away with everything." I stomped off, not waiting for Jake to catch up.

CHAPTER FOUR

My secret relationship with Iain was effortless. I didn't have anyone to tell, and I didn't want to. I wanted to keep every delicious detail to myself. Iain and I maintained our teacher/student relationship while at school, and we didn't often see each other during the week. We hung out every Saturday, except for the occasional quickie during the week after work. Every time with Iain was incredible, and I couldn't help but feel as if I was free falling into something wonderful. It wasn't just about the sex either, although that was definitely amazing. Iain and I were just great together. We couldn't do anything in public, obviously, but we'd spend hours curled up on his couch just talking and laughing.

Iain was always very open and honest with me. It wasn't long into our relationship that he had told me a lot about his life—that he'd been the middle child of three boys and one girl, and that all his siblings had been heavily into sports and he'd been very into books. He told me about taking the advance track programs in university so he could become a teacher sooner because he'd always known that was what he wanted to do. He told me about the six months he backpacked around Europe with friends straight out of high school, about all the crazy adventures they'd gone on. He told me about the book he wanted to write, then joked about it—what English teacher didn't want to write a book? Then he told me about the girl he nearly proposed to two years prior, who had broken his heart.

Iain's openness made me want to be honest, but...I couldn't. The only person who had known every gruesome detail had been Lauren; I hadn't even attempted to tell anyone else. Lauren only knew because she just *knew*. She was incredibly skilled at reading people—better than even me—and it was almost like the scars of my past had been written on my forehead. I wasn't ready to share that much of myself with anybody else, and I didn't know if I ever would.

One Saturday night in mid-October, as we curled up together on his couch, Iain started kissing me, exploring my mouth with his like he never had before. It was almost disorienting.

"Why me?" I suddenly asked, unable to stop myself. "I mean...you don't have flings with all the students, do you?"

"Yes, every last one of them. Even the guys." Iain pulled away slightly and rolled his eyes. Then he realized that I was asking him a serious question. "No, I've never had a fling, or even a desire to have a fling with a student before. Although I suppose that's not saying much, considering this is only my first year of teaching."

"Comforting," I joked.

"There's just something about you..." he continued. "I felt it the moment I saw you. This impossible pull. I know it's too early for declarations of adoration, but just know that this isn't a random need I want to fill."

"Okay," I said, unable to think of a more brilliant response to that. My heart was pounding from his kissing expertise, his closeness and his words. He leaned toward me to continue kissing me, and paused when I frowned.

"What is it?" he asked, concerned.

I shook my head, unable to voice it. Never before had I felt so strongly for someone, and it felt like it was all happening impossibly fast. Like a train going at warp speed, it left me dizzy and disoriented, but pleasantly so. I didn't want to get off. I wanted to stay for the ride and see where we ended up. Even if we crashed. Even if there was a lot at stake. I wondered how it was possible to feel so much for someone so quickly, and to give every bit of yourself without really giving it. That's what I was doing. I was open and vulnerable, only not with my words. At the same time, it was easy to forget everything else when I was with him.

"Just kiss me," I said huskily, trying to push down the overwhelming amount of feelings. I'd deal with them later.

The next few weeks passed by in pretty much the same manner. I went to school, I worked, and I hung out with Iain late at night. I told nobody about our relationship.

One day at school, I was in the bathroom washing my hands when I heard someone burst in. It was Jenna. She was wearing a larger cardigan than usual, and she looked ashen and clammy. She barely spared me a glance as she raced toward a stall and slammed the door behind her. It pounced off the lock and remained half opened. She vomited loudly into the toilet, her shoulders heaving.

"Jenna? Are you okay?" I asked, drying my hands on a paper towel and watching her carefully.

"No." Jenna clamped a hand over her mouth and returned to the stall to vomit some more.

Dread settled in my gut. "Jenna, are you...could you be...?" I trailed off, not wanting to voice my concerns. She looked back at me, tears welling up in her eyes, and nodded once. "Jesus."

She laughed bitterly. "I know, right? I was saving myself for marriage," she said, sounding embarrassed at her confession. "My first time and I didn't even want to, and now..." The tears finally rolled down her cheeks. "I don't know what to do. I haven't told anyone. My parents are extremely religious. They're going to kill me."

"Are you..." I didn't know how to ask her, so I closed my mouth. She lifted her head up to stare at the ceiling.

"I don't know. I don't know if I can keep it," Jenna sobbed. "But I can't...kill it."

I grabbed another paper towel and ran it under the cold water, ringing it out before I stepped up to her stall door and offered it to her. I wracked my brain for something to say and could find absolutely nothing of comfort. "I'm sorry," I finally said. She nodded, fresh tears spilling out of her eyes. "Are you going to tell your parents?"

"I'm going to have to, I think." Jenna sighed. "I've thought long and hard about getting an abortion, but I...I can't do that. I can't kill an innocent child."

"It's not a child yet; it's an embryo, a cluster of cells," I replied. "It's your body, your decision. If that's how you feel, that's how you feel, but you can't look at it like a child when it's still a cluster of cells." I tried to be diplomatic and scientific about it to give her a little hope.

She smiled weakly. "I know, but that cluster of cells will be a person, if it's given the chance. What if it grows up to find the cure to cancer?"

I shrugged, unsure of the correct response. That was a heavier track of thought than I had expected of her.

"Or what if it grows up to be like...its father?" Jenna whispered, fresh tears pouring out of her eyes. She covered her face, sobbing heavily into her knees. The bell rang, signaling the beginning of another class before I could think of anything to say to this poor, broken girl.

"Just go," Jenna sighed, leaning her head against the wall. "I'll be here a while."

I hesitated for a half a second, then pulled myself up onto the bathroom counter.

"What are you doing?" Jenna asked, looking over at me.

"When you're done tossing your cookies, we're gonna blow this joint." I shrugged, looking at my nails. I felt a pang in my chest. I hadn't really been a friend to anyone in...well, a long time. I was rusty and it felt awkward.

"I can't. My parents will know," Jenna tried, but stopped at the look on my face. I had one eyebrow raised.

"Jenna. You're gonna have to face them sooner rather than later, especially if you don't go with plan B."

Jenna's face paled.

"Sorry, I'm very blunt." I inwardly kicked myself.

"No, it's okay." She sighed, pulling herself up. "You're right." She leaned against the bathroom stall, picking an imaginary thread on her cardigan.

"You done?" I asked. She nodded, brushing back a strand of her blond hair. "Let's go."

We ended up going to the mall to grab coffee and shop. Lauren had always believed that retail therapy was a wonderful distraction, and luckily Jenna was in agreement. I wasn't a big shopper, but I wanted to distract Jenna.

"So, what about your friends? Dumb and Dumber?" I asked, examining a cute low-neck top while glancing at Jenna curiously.

Jenna snorted. "Dumb and Dumber. That's accurate." She exhaled sharply. "I just...I don't trust them. Not anymore. They've never been really good friends, if you know what I mean. And Callie, she used to date Andrew. She's still obsessed with him." Jenna looked out the window. "She definitely wouldn't understand and Tara goes with whatever Callie says."

"Ahhh," I said, nodding as if I suddenly understood when I had all along. "So my early prediction of them being super bitches wasn't that far off."

Jenna laughed, then her head snapped up as she looked at me. "Wait, you thought they were super bitches? What'd you think about me?"

"Same." I shrugged without apology. "There's nothing wrong with being a super bitch; I'm a super bitch."

Jenna shook her head, chewing on her lip as she pondered whether or not to be offended by my honesty. "Well, I wasn't always a bitch. Their personalities kind of wear off on you."

"Why don't you ditch them?"

"'Cause we've kind of been hanging out for years. But who knows...I doubt they'll have my back for this," Jenna answered softly. I kept my mouth shut. I already knew they wouldn't.

Jenna and I hung out at the mall until school was over, then we both went our separate ways. I had a very rare evening off, so I decided to walk to Iain's house.

It was about a half hour trek from the mall, but I didn't mind. I pulled my sweater hood up, put on my headphones and started playing Lorde's new album. The walk was peaceful, despite battling clusters of high school students headed to the mall. I made sure nobody was watching me when I turned down Iain's street. Nobody was paying me a lick of attention, but I still shuffled nervously on my feet while I waited for Iain to answer the door. Usually, my visits happened after dark.

"You skipped class," he remarked when he opened the door to find me standing impatiently at the door.

"How do you know? I didn't even have you this afternoon."

"I'm aware of all that happens at the school," Iain joked.

"Well, I had good reason to."

"There's never good reason to skip out on class," Iain lectured, crossing his arms over his chest. He looked ridiculously handsome, somehow still demanding authority despite the fact that he was standing barefoot in the doorway. I smiled.

"I came here for sex, not the third degree," I teased, leaning up to kiss him as I slid out of my coat. He distractedly ran his hand up my waist, pulling me against him. I moaned into his mouth, pressing harder to him.

"I really want to know why you skipped though. I went an entire class without staring at you discreetly," Iain said, after breaking the kiss and taking my hand. He led me into the kitchen where he put on the kettle for tea, somewhat of a ritual whenever I came to visit.

"Wait, what?" I asked, confused. Normally, I only had Iain Monday mornings.

"I covered for Mr. Parsons," Iain explained, referring to my

Science teacher. "He ended up leaving halfway through the day with the flu, so I took over his class."

"Well, that's too bad," I said, exhaling. I chewed on my bottom lip in consideration. "Do you remember that girl at the party?" Iain nodded. "I ran into her...and...well." I absently grabbed a strand of my hair, twisting it around my fingers. "She's...pregnant. From that...encounter."

Iain leaned back against the counter, his eyes full of sympathy. "That's terrible. What does she plan on doing?"

"She has no idea. She doesn't believe in abortion, but she definitely doesn't want..." I trailed off awkwardly. I felt like I was betraying Jenna, but she hadn't asked me to not tell our English teacher. *That's kind of an assumed thing though*, I thought.

Iain was still frowning. "This wouldn't happen to be someone in our English class? Someone who has missed a lot of time lately?"

"You weren't supposed to make guesses, Iain," I replied, frowning.

"Don't worry, I'm not going to tell her that I know," Iain said quickly. "I'm just trying to piece everything together."

"Why?"

"I have a need to know every detail of things." Iain shrugged shamelessly. I nodded in understanding. That made sense. I was the same way.

"Well, okay. It was Jenna. Is. And she still doesn't want to go to the police or anything," I added before Iain could suggest the legal route. "That won't work."

"Why not? Now she's got physical proof," Iain pressed. The kettle started to whistle, and he absently took it off the burner and poured water into two already prepared mugs.

I was definitely a little uncomfortable with this conversation.

"Do you trust me, Harlow?" Iain asked, tipping his head as he looked at me inquisitively.

I paused, thinking about it for a moment. "I do, actually," I said, surprising myself.

His smile was radiant. "I won't tell anyone anything you say to me, or anything we do. I would never jeopardize you. I guess I just want to know so I can help you help her."

"Okay." I sighed, sitting down at the tiny table in Iain's little kitchen. He finished making the tea and handed me mine before sitting down across from me. "Jenna can't report this because the rapist is the Police Chief's son. Apparently, he would just have it swept it under the rug."

"Jesus." Iain's brows furrowed again. "That's a tougher situation than I expected."

"Tell me about it," I said in agreement. "I literally have no idea what to tell this poor girl. I suggested abortion, but she was against it."

"Are you? Against abortion?" Iain asked, interested in my answer.

I froze. I wasn't. Had I gotten pregnant from one of my rapists, I would have...but I didn't want to tell Iain that, because I'd have to talk about my reasons.

"I'm pro-choice. A woman's body is her body. If she doesn't want a pregnancy, especially one that resulted from a rape, I think she should have the right to make that choice," I said instead, looking into my tea.

"I agree, actually," Iain said. "I know I teach at a Catholic school, and was raised Catholic, but I'm very modern with my beliefs."

"Well, she's against abortion...as I said. So I really don't know how to help her...aside from suggesting she skip school for some retail therapy, I mean."

"What about adoption?" Iain asked.

"I could suggest that," I offered. "But I think she's terrified of her parents' reaction."

"I'm sure their reaction wouldn't be nearly as terrifying if they knew the circumstances."

"I don't think she wants to share with them," I pointed out. "In any case, that's what's going on."

"Well, thanks for telling me," Iain said soberly. "If adoption is something she'd consider, I have some contacts I could get to you to give her."

"Contacts?" I asked.

Iain scratched the top of his head and smiled gently at me. "Yeah, adoption agencies and what not."

"Why do you have that?" I pressed, instantly envisioning him visiting adoption agencies with the blank faced woman he'd been engaged too.

"My sister is infertile. She and her husband have been dealing with many adoption agencies over the years."

"I'm sorry," I said, feeling a little embarrassed at having pried into his family's personal life.

"Don't be." Iain's hand reached across the table and took mine. I felt the sparks of lust firing up in my belly, as they always did when I was around him.

CHAPTER FIVE

The next morning, Jake hunted me down in the hallway. "Have you been avoiding me?"

"No, sorry." I yawned, exhausted from my late night with Iain. "I've just been...busy."

"With who?"

I gave him a level look, wondering what his deal was. I knew Jake had a thing for me, and that he would probably continue on having a thing for me unless I did something to put me off limits.

"With my boyfriend," I answered.

"You have a boyfriend? Since when?" The disappointment was evident in Jake's face.

"A few weeks. Why?" I tried to play dumb.

Jake shook his head, forcing a look of indifference on his face. "No reason." He shrugged. "Wanna meet in the parking lot for a mid-day sesh, or would your new boyfriend object to you hanging out with me?" He said the last bit with a little more bitterness than he intended, and tried to ease his question with a smile.

"He'll be fine with it." I rolled my eyes. "I'm always up for a mid-day sesh. See you then," I said, heading into the stairwell before he could follow me.

I was getting my notebooks out of my locker for my morning class—anthropology—when Riley sauntered up to me with an invitation to his Halloween party that Saturday. I had to physically refrain from rolling my eyes at him.

"I don't know, Riley; I'm probably working," I told him, barely looking at the invitation. I knew that wasn't true. I still kept my Saturday evenings and Sunday mornings free so I could hang out with Iain at his place.

"Come on," Riley drawled. "It's gonna be amazing. Best costume wins a 40."

"I'll think about it," I told him. But there wasn't anything to think about. I wasn't going to go.

For one, I didn't want to risk the chance of running into the Police Chief's son. I didn't let fear overtake my every thought, but I was smart enough to know that going somewhere he was likely to be was definitely not a bright move. Second, it was the one-year anniversary of Lauren's death. It was a Halloween party we'd been driving home from when we got into the accident. Lauren and I had gone as a sexy cop and a sexy prisoner. Third, Iain and I had already made plans. We were going to have a scary movie marathon. The idea of cuddling up on Iain's couch, wrapped up in his arms while I tried hard to not relive the accident and Lauren's death was much more appealing than going to a party at Riley's, where I'd undoubtedly be reliving it. By myself, because Iain wouldn't be able to go, obviously.

"Suit yourself." Riley shrugged and started down the hall toward his cluster of friends.

The school day dragged on and on, and finally, I ran into Jenna after last bell. She was walking away from Callie and

Tara with an irritated look on her face. I quickly approached her.

"Do you have a moment?" I asked, wanting to relay Iain's suggestion to her. She looked surprised to see me walking beside her.

"Oh, yeah," she said, slowing down a little. We both glanced behind us at Callie and Tara, who were scowling in our direction. "Did you want a ride home? I've got my car here. It'd probably be better to talk there." She added the last part in a hushed voice, barely above a whisper.

"Well, I work, but a ride to work would be cool." I enjoyed walking, but I wasn't about to turn down a free ride when it was offered.

"Okay, where do you work?"

"The diner," I answered as we walked out the doors that led to the parking lot. Jenna led me to a gunmetal gray Hyundai. It looked a couple years old, and the interior was perfect. "Whoa, nice car."

"Thanks, my dad bought it for me," Jenna answered, looking a little embarrassed. She hit the unlock button on her key remote. I opened the door, sliding quickly into the passenger seat.

"So...what was up with Tara and Callie?" I asked, unsure whether I should just dive in or talk a bit first. My friendship skills were still a little rusty.

"Oh." Jenna frowned. "They're pissed at me because I don't want to go to Riley's stupid Halloween party. It's all anyone's talking about, and I just don't want to go."

"Understandably so," I said. "I won't be going either."

"Really?" Jenna looked at me, surprised.

"Yeah...really. Last time wasn't exactly fun." I regretted saying it. Obviously it hadn't been fun. "I'm sorry. Didn't mean to remind you."

"No, it's okay." Jenna sighed. She put her car in reverse and carefully backed out. "It's not like I don't have a daily reminder already."

"Have you told your parents yet?" I asked gently.

Her eyes widened in horror. "No! I can't tell them. They'll definitely disown me. I guess one of Dad's co-workers daughters is pregnant. She's in high school too, and you should have seen how they were carrying on about it." Jenna drew in a shaky breath.

"You're going to have to tell them," I said. "They're going to start to notice."

"I know." Jenna took another breath. "I just feel like I need a plan."

"Have you thought about—" I started to say, but she cut me off.

"I can't have an abortion!" she almost yelled.

"Jesus Jenna, chill out." I clenched my teeth in aggravation at her outburst. I was only trying to help, and I didn't enjoy being yelled at, it made me feel defensive. But I knew she was going through a very traumatic experience. It couldn't be easy. I softened my expression when I looked at her. "I was going to ask if you'd thought about adoption yet."

"Oh, sorry." Jenna blushed, looking thoughtful. "No. I haven't really thought about that. Stupid, huh?"

"No, you've got a lot on your mind," I told her. She frowned, looking dejected. "What is it?"

"Who would want to adopt a...rape baby?" she whispered, looking horrified. "I mean, if I don't want it, who else would?" She looked extremely crestfallen and guilty to even be suggesting such a thing. I was rendered speechless.

"I'm sure that doesn't matter," I tried, inwardly cursing myself when I realized how that sounded. "I mean, I'm sure there are some couples out there who have all the love in the world to offer a baby. It's not the baby's fault...Ugh, I'm making this worse, aren't I?"

Jenna had tears streaming down her cheek that she wiped away furiously. We were waiting for our chance to leave the school parking lot—it was always congested at 3:05 p.m.

"No, it's not you, it's my stupid emotions." Jenna laughed bitterly. "Anyway, I'll give it some thought."

"I could get you some pamphlets," I offered.

"That'd be good." She nodded. "Um...there was something I wanted to ask you."

"What is it?" I asked.

"Would you come with me to my first ultrasound appointment? I don't want to go alone. I have to drive to Sudbury—I don't want to run into anyone that knows me." We exited the school parking lot and drove toward the diner. It would only take three minutes.

"Yeah, of course!" I answered immediately. "When is it?"

"November fifteenth..." Jenna trailed off, pulling into the diner parking lot. "Sorry to ask. I was going to just suck it up, but..."

"No, it's alright. I'll be there, promise," I assured her. "I've gotta go in now, but if you wanted to grab something to eat—"

"No thanks, I can't handle greasy food right now," Jenna said, looking a little green at my suggestion. "No offence or anything."

I laughed. "I don't cook the food, so none taken. Thanks for the ride!"

"Thanks...for everything." Jenna smiled weakly.

I got out of her car and went to close the door.

"Wait!" Jenna said, hesitating slightly and looking even more embarrassed. "If you don't have anything to do that night of the party, I'll be free if you want to hang out."

"Yeah, that sounds...good," I said sincerely, smiling at her.

She waved again and I closed the door. I stood in the parking lot for a couple of minutes and watched as she sped off.

I was working with Danielle again. She waved at me warmly when I walked inside. The entire diner was decorated for Halloween; I had to duck under a curtain of spider webs upon my arrival.

"Isn't it great?" Danielle squealed, excited. "I did most of it. Ryan helped! Halloween's my favorite time of year. Especially this year! Liam's first Halloween. He's going to be a penguin!"

"Cute!" I genuinely smiled at Danielle's enthusiasm, and the mental image of cute little Liam in a penguin costume. I tried to ignore the dull, hollow ache in my chest. Halloween used to be one of my favorite holidays too, but this year, it would be a difficult. Hard to believe it would be one whole year since Lauren had died.

"Okay, what's up, Princess of Darkness?" Danielle asked seriously, one hand on her hip.

"Nothing!" I quickly said, schooling my features. There was no way I was going to talk to Danielle about anything going on in my head.

She looked at me skeptically. "I don't believe that. If you change your mind and need to talk, you know where to find me."

"Thanks, " I said, a little awkwardly. I made my way into the back room to change into my uniform, completely thrown. Where had my ability to appear like a stone statue gone? Suddenly, people were reading me easily. Or maybe the difference was that people were starting to care about my moods.

It made me incredibly uncomfortable. What if they could read what was happening between Iain and I? So far, nobody had made any comments or given any looks. Then again, I was careful to avoid looking at Iain in class, or talking directly to him.

I went about my shift in a little bit of a distracted daze as I pondered this slight predicament. When I was halfway through restocking the condiments, Danielle nudged me from behind.

"Oooh, Harlow," she whispered. "Check it out! That hottie from before is sitting in your section again. Oh my God! I think he likes you!"

I glanced over, seeing Iain seated at the same table I had served him the first time he came to the diner. He smiled warmly at me, winking, when Danielle turned her focus to me.

"Oh..."

"Oh what? Go serve him before I do," Danielle joked, tossing a menu at me. I rolled my eyes and approached Iain's table.

"What can I get for you tonight?" I asked, trying to hide my nervousness with an easy smile. I was ecstatic that he was there, but he hadn't been back to the diner since that one time —since before our relationship started. Aside from our classes together, we weren't seen out in public. I couldn't help but worry that Danielle was reading our body language, that'd she'd tell someone and someone would know that Iain taught at the Catholic high school and then our relationship would be out in the open. I pictured Iain behind bars and frowned deeply. That was the last thing I wanted.

"The special, and maybe some of that famous cherry pie for dessert," Iain replied, not even bothering to look at the menu. He was looking at me like I was the dessert, which I'm sure was the intention. Then he leaned forward so that only I could hear. "This is for dropping your pencil in class today," he whispered, winking.

I blushed, thinking about how I had purposely dropped my pencil and reached forward to grab it, knowing that Iain would be able to have a full frontal view.

"Alright then. I'll get you the special and once you've finished with that, I'll bring you some cherry pie," I said, smirking. "Would you like a coffee while you wait?"

Iain nodded, pleased with himself for successfully bringing me out of my foul mood. I shook my head as I walked away from him, quickly grabbing a hot cup of coffee. I returned to his table, leaning forward a little more than necessary to put his hot beverage down in front of him.

"Enjoy," I said, smiling coyly. I bit my lip a little, knowing that he was staring at me and knowing exactly what I was doing to him. Then I stood up quickly and went to check on a couple other customers in my section and do my side work. I made sure to lean forward a few times while scrubbing the table in front of him vigorously, occasionally making eye contact with him and licking my lips. Two could play at this game, and I was so enthralled in it that I forgot where we were.

"Wow, he's so into you," Danielle whispered, shocking me. I hadn't known she'd been paying attention to our display. I cursed myself; we hadn't been very discreet at all.

Despite the nervousness I was feeling at having Danielle pick up on our game, I gave a mischievous, uncaring smirk. "Poor soul."

"What do you mean?" Danielle asked, playfully shoving me. "He's hot. Are you nuts, lady?"

"I already have a boyfriend," I said, shrugging. I scowled in Iain's direction and he suppressed a grin.

I ignored Iain for the rest of the time he was there. He frowned slightly as I handed him his receipt, sensing my mood was no longer playful. He looked down at the single word of "*after*" written on it and nodded as he read. He slipped into his jacket and left the diner without looking at me again.

I wonder if I had offended him by my sudden mood

change. Oh well. I sighed inwardly. I still had another hour left of my shift before I could explain myself.

It was Danielle's night to lock up, so I left a little earlier. Daylight savings time meant that it was darker than dark out, and instead of feeling like 9, it actually felt more like 11 p.m. I shivered against the cold, late October chill, pulling my sweater hood up over my hair. I put my ear buds in, turning up my iPhone music to fairly loud. Despite not being able to hear anything but Five Finger Death Punch, I kept full attention on my surroundings, making sure that I was constantly aware of who was around me. My heart was pounding, it was so dark and of course my thoughts instantly imagined Andrew lurking in the corner, waiting to pounce out and attack. I inwardly laughed at myself. *Don't live in fear*, I scolded. I knew better than that. But still, it was hard to calm my nerves, especially because I had the sensation that someone was watching me.

I started thinking about Jenna again, and how she must have been feeling. I mulled over the entire situation for what seemed like the thousandth time that week.

By the time I got to Iain's house, I still wasn't any more enlightened on Jenna's predicament, and I just wanted to forget about it all for a bit. Luckily, I was in the right place. Iain certainly was a great distraction.

"Hey," he greeted, stepping back to let me into the warmth of his foyer.

"Hey yourself," I said, frowning slightly as I remembered Danielle's intense line of questioning after he'd left.

"What's wrong?"

"Nothing's wrong." I sighed, slipping out of my coat and

hanging it on the hook. I dropped my bag by the door. "Danielle just...Danielle thought you were into me."

"I *am* into you," Iain growled sensually, stepping forward and embracing me. My heart felt as if it was jump starting.

"Well, isn't it dangerous for people to know that?" I asked, despite the betraying fluttering of my eyes as he kissed my neck. I hated swooning, but Iain constantly made me swoon. I pushed on his chest, trying to get him to take this conversation seriously.

Iain paused. I could feel his lips frowning against my neck. Then he sighed.

"You're right." He stepped back, running a hand through his tousled hair. It was getting even longer. He still hadn't gotten it cut. I rather liked it that way.

"I don't want to get you in trouble," I almost whispered. I tentatively reached out a hand, touching the side of his face.

Iain nodded, his jaw clenching under my fingers. I assumed he was angry at me, so I took an unconscious step back.

"I'm not mad at you," Iain said, sighing. "I just...I'd love to make it known that you're mine. I'd love to take you out, show you off..."

"But we can't do that," I finished.

"Nope." Iain sighed again, deeper this time. He smiled as he grabbed my hand, his blue eyes alight with an idea. "At least...not in this town..."

"What do you mean, not in this town?" I asked, arching an eyebrow. He gently led me to the living room sofa. We sat down, his hand still clasping mine and his eyes still lit up with excitement.

"I want to take you to Niagara Falls," he said sincerely, looking right into my eyes. "The weekend of November 15. We'll leave on the Friday and be back on Sunday."

"Why Niagara Falls?" I asked, a little surprised that he already had a place in mind.

"It's far enough away from here that we can go out in public and don't run the risk of people recognizing us. And it's...I don't know, touristy."

I nibbled my lip, thoughtful. It did sound extremely appealing. I'd never been to Niagara Falls, and I was a little tired of feeling like a mistress, although I wouldn't trade any time I got to spend with Iain. Even if we were holed up inside his house, eating Chinese take-out and watching terrible B-movies.

"Okay," I said, hesitating a bit as I thought about the entire weekend in shifts I would miss out on. Iain would more than make up for it.

"Great." Iain grinned, kissing me slowly and softly.

"Oh!" I said suddenly, breaking away from Iain slightly. "I told Jenna about your suggestion—adoption." Although I'd interrupted our make-out session to tell him this, Iain didn't look the least bit frustrated. He pulled away slightly, looking intrigued and concerned.

"What did she think about that?" he asked.

"Well...she's not sold on the idea yet. She doesn't under-stand why someone would want a...'rape baby,' as she called it."

"Ahh." Iain flinched; the same reaction I had.

"It's still early," I reminded him. "She's still processing the actual rape...so. I can understand her thought process. But I think she'll eventually warm up to the idea."

"That's good." Iain nodded. "Adoption agencies have coun-selors that can help process all that for perspective birth parents."

"Oh, that's good to know," I said, making a mental note to tell Jenna. "And...I know we said we'd hang out on Halloween, and we will, but Jenna asked if I'd go over there first." I said this as I twisted my hair around in my fingers nervously. I wasn't really sure why I felt nervous. I guess I was worried about disappointing him.

Iain's fingers gently touched my chin, directing my face so that I was looking at his face. "That's totally fine. Sounds like Jenna could use a good friend like you."

"I wouldn't call myself a good friend," I countered. Iain rolled his eyes, kissing me gently on the nose.

"You're too harsh on yourself," he told me. I nodded, not really believing him. I personally didn't think I was harsh *enough* on myself. I still had a lot of self blame. My boyfriend had been the one to kill Lauren, and I hadn't even noticed he was high. I should have noticed, and I should have stopped it. What kind of friend doesn't notice something like that?

"Whatever you're thinking, you're wrong," Iain whispered, frowning at the look on my face. My eyes started to water, and I willed myself not to cry in front of him.

"Okay, change of subject," I demanded, leaning toward him and pressing my lips to his. I focused on the lust welling in my lower belly and ignored everything else. I teased his lips with my tongue, smiling at his increased breathing as my hand roamed the outside of his jeans. Smilingly seductively—all traces of my formal depressive mood gone—I crawled up on his lap and straddled him, kissing him deeply and intently. Iain's hand gripped the hair at the back of my neck as he kissed me back with the skilled expertise that always made me moan.

"One more thing," I muttered, almost out of breath. He looked at me, his eyes saying he'd give me anything. "Try to avoid my work if you can. I can only control myself so much."

Iain laughed in my mouth, nodding as he unbuttoned my shirt and I allowed myself to lose control.

CHAPTER SIX

The next week, I endured the relentless chatter about Riley's upcoming Halloween party, and about how anybody who was anybody would be there. On Friday, people were even louder about it. Jenna hadn't even bothered to show up; I figured she was tired of hearing about it too. I was feeling almost nauseated by it all, and I hadn't even gone through what Jenna had.

At the end of the day, I made a final trip to my locker to get all the books I'd need over the weekend. I had a math test on Monday that I needed to study for, and yet another English paper due. I smiled thinking about Iain's homework assignment. *Write about change. A time you changed, or something you want to change.* His topic choice made me smile because there were so many options for me to write about, and I was rather excited about it. I loved writing for Iain now, mainly because he sang the highest phrase but also because I was always able to pour a little bit more of myself in my assignments. He got to learn about me a little more. My thoughts were interrupted when someone walked into me from behind.

"Oops, sorry," Callie sneered, not sounding sorry at all. She stopped at her locker, which just so happened to be five down from mine. Tara leaned against the locker beside Callie's, blocking Callie nearly completely from my view. Not that I minded. I quickly grabbed my math textbook and shoved it into my book bag; I was suddenly in a hurry to get out of there.

"I can't believe how bitchy Jenna's being lately!" Tara was ranting. "After you forgave her for hooking up with Andrew!"

"I know," Callie said, shaking her head sadly. "She really can't see what good friends we've been."

"Who are you kidding? You guys are horrible friends," I spat, unable to contain myself. I slammed my locker, glaring at them both. "You're both bitchy, two-faced, conceited assholes who back a rapist. But yeah, you're *such good friends* to Jenna."

Callie and Tara stared at me in open-mouthed shock, but I didn't bother giving them a chance to reply. I spun around on my heel and stomped off, eager to get the hell out of the school.

"I really need to get a car," I muttered, zipping up my coat and pulling my sweater over my head as the chilly air nipped at my exposed skin. I was supposed to be at work at 3, and I had less than ten minutes to get there. Thankfully, the walk from school was a short ten minutes. The cold, fresh air also worked to calm my nerves. I regretted saying anything to Callie and Tara. For all they knew, the hook up was just a rumor that I had now pretty much confirmed, even if it wasn't a consensual thing.

No point in worrying about it now, I told myself ruefully.

My shift was not helping my foul mood at all. For one, I wasn't working with Danielle. She had the evening off, so I was working with one of the middle-aged waitresses named Sally. While I generally enjoyed Danielle's company, Sally was a little harder to be around. She was a curvy woman in her mid-to-late forties who spent way too much time tanning. She also tried to dress and act younger than she was. She was extremely loud and her voice just grated on my nerves. She flirted relentlessly with anything with legs, and she told the grossest stories of her sexual encounters that nearly made me want to vomit. I tried to avoid talking to her at all costs, but sometimes it was unavoidable.

Since it was Friday night, the diner was packed full of families and couples out on dates. I was constantly running around, and my feet were on fire. At fifteen to nine, Sally leaned across the cash register and turned on a ridiculous version of puppy dog eyes. "Mind if I take off early, sugar?"

I glanced around the diner; there were still five tables of customers finishing up their meals. We were supposed to close in fifteen minutes, but I couldn't shut everything down until all the customers had paid and left. Doing it alone would take a lot longer than having Sally there to help tackle some of the closing duties.

"I have a hot date," she explained, as if that immediately meant she didn't have to stay. I sighed in exasperation. I had two choices: stay a little later than I wanted to, or continue hearing all about Sally's hot date and the things she was planning on doing to him.

"Fine," I sighed. "Have a good one."

Sally grinned, bending over to grab her coat and purse. She was out the door before I could even say bye. Thankfully, the remaining customers ate quickly and paid by 9:15. I locked the door behind the last person to leave so that I could close my till.

Ryan waited for me, sprawled out in one of the booths and

playing Angry Birds on his phone. I finished up quickly, giving a final glance around the diner to make sure everything was in place. Satisfied, Ryan waited for me outside the door while I armed the alarm system. I pulled the door shut, making sure that it was locked. I turned to face Ryan to tell him goodnight, when two figures jumped out and grabbed him. They started laying punches into him while I screamed. A large hand clasped over my mouth, cutting off my screaming. Frantically, I brought my hands to my mouth, trying to pull away the huge hand. It was useless; the person was much stronger than I was.

"Got you, bitch," he hissed, his words full of hatred. It was Andrew. Of course it was Andrew.

"Stop it," I tried to say, but his hand silenced my words. I looked at Ryan with wide eyes. He was curled up on the ground, trying to cover his head with his hands as Andrew's two friends delivered kick after kick into his ribs and stomach. There was no way I could turn my body to free myself. Andrew's grip was too strong. Hot tears poured down my cheeks and onto Andrew's hand, and I heard him chuckle.

"Alright, boys, that's enough," Andrew ordered. Both guys immediately stepped back from Ryan. I couldn't tell if he was okay. I tried to go to him but Andrew yanked me back.

"You and me? We're gonna go for a little drive," Andrew said, his lips too close to my ear. I shivered in disgust, desperately trying to think my way out of this situation. He started dragging me toward a truck that I hadn't noticed parked in the diner parking lot before. I tried to dig my heels into the asphalt, but it was useless. Andrew had to change his grasp on me to grab his keys from his pocket. I took that opportunity to shove at him as hard as I possibly could. Miraculously, I was able to loosen his hold on me and knee him hard. Unfortunately, Andrew was taller than me, and my knee collided with his thigh, not the tender spot I'd been aiming for. Still, it threw him off and he released me ever so slightly.

I didn't bother wasting my breath; I took off running as fast as I possibly could. I couldn't go back for Ryan. I wasn't strong enough to take on three males, and they seemed to lose interest in Ryan as they started chasing after me.

Adrenalin pumped through my body, giving me more speed than I ever thought I possessed. I ran to the street, hoping that people would notice the guys chasing me and think it was odd enough to stop and offer help. Cars drove by, but nobody stopped. I didn't have time or breath to waste swearing, so I continued running. I raced down Iain's street, hearing footsteps in close pursuit behind me. Iain's place was still a couple houses down, and I knew I wasn't going to make it. A hand reached out from behind me and grabbed the hood of my jacket, yanking me back with force. I screamed as loud as I possibly could before Andrew's hand clasped over my mouth. This time, I bit down hard. Swearing, his hand dropped from my mouth. I heard the revving of an engine, and realized with a panic that not all three guys had chased me. One of them had gone for the truck.

"What's going on out here?" Iain's voice was like a Godsend. Andrew instantly released my jacket and ran for the truck, too much of a coward. His friend following quickly behind them. By the time Iain reached my side, the truck had sped off down the street.

"Ryan!" I said in a panic as Iain reached for my hand. I couldn't look at him yet. "They jumped Ryan outside the diner and beat him up pretty bad, I need to—"

"Let's get in my car, Harlow," Iain said, his voice full of calm authority.

I nodded, allowing him to lead me to his car. He started it

and quickly pulled out of his driveway, speeding to the diner. I jumped out of the car before we even came to a full stop.

I ran over to Ryan's crumpled body, falling to my knees beside him. I tried to wake him. He groaned, and I let out a sigh of relief.

"We need to get him to a hospital," I told Iain, feeling his presence behind me.

"We'll call an ambulance, Harlow," Iain replied. "I don't know where he's been injured. I don't want to move him."

"That makes sense," I said, grabbing my cell phone from my jacket pocket. I dialed 911 and told them I needed an ambulance. While we waited for them, I looked at Iain with newfound worry.

"You shouldn't be here," I whispered. "What if..." I trailed off, looking at Ryan quickly. He didn't appear to be awake, but I didn't know for sure if he could hear me.

Iain frowned, seeing the direction of my thoughts. He nodded. "You're right." He hesitated. I knew he wanted to stay.

"Just go," I told him. "They won't be long, I'll...text you."

"Keep your phone in your hand. If they come back, call me. I'll be nearby," Iain said, looking at me intently. I nodded. He leaned forward, brushing a strand of my messy hair out of my eyes. He looked as if he wanted to kiss me, but was startled by Ryan's soft groaning. He glanced down, thought better of it and stood up, giving me a wistful look that communicated how badly he wanted to stay. I watched him drive away, then focused my attention back on Ryan. His face was bruised and bloody, swollen in so many places. My heart hurt for him, and rage was boiling in the pit of my stomach.

We didn't have to wait long for the ambulance. Soon, Ryan was being loaded up and I was accompanying him to the hospital since I'd been with him when he got jumped. Two policemen found me in the waiting room while a doctor and nurse assessed Ryan's damage.

"Were you with him when the incident happened?" the first one, a middle-aged, seasoned cop asked, approaching me with a look of authority. His partner was a little younger, his chest puffed out proudly as he studied me with hard green eyes.

"Yes, I was," I said, standing up and brushing back a strand of my hair. "He was jumped by three guys."

"Did you happen to get a good look at them?" the first cop asked, exchanging an almost bored look with his partner.

"Yeah, I did," I replied, my own eyes hardening slightly. "One of them was Andrew Cooper. I'm sure you know who that is."

The older cop didn't look surprised, but the younger guy's eyes sparked with recognition and interest.

"Who were the other guys?" the older cop asked, staring me down. I described them the best way I could, all while making occasional eye contact with the younger cop. He seemed more interested in what I had to say, while the older one seemed to be simply taking my statement out of routine. I glanced at the older cop. He had jotted down most of my statement on the incident, but didn't appear to write down Andrew Cooper's name or the detailed physical description of his accomplices.

"Aren't you going to write down Andrew Cooper's name?" I demanded.

The older cop moved the incident report from my view, and gave me a steady gaze. "I have, ma'am. Thank you for time. That'll be all," he said, giving me a challenging look. When I said nothing, he turned on his heel and left the waiting room, casting one glance at his partner with a raised brow.

"Just a sec, Jim," the younger cop said. He waited until his partner, Jim, had shrugged and left our sight.

"Give me a call if any more...incidents arise," the younger cop said, holding out his card with his name and number on it. I read it over then looked up to give my thanks, but he'd already joined his partner in leaving. I was alone in the waiting room.

CHAPTER SEVEN

I didn't get home until 3 a.m. and accidentally slept in the next morning. I woke up panicked, my heart racing from last night's near miss. I had waited an additional two hours in the hospital waiting room until a nice, elderly nurse came in to tell me that Ryan was awake and well. He had bruised ribs and a fractured cheekbone, but aside from that, he was alright.

I hadn't gone in to personally check on him. His parents had been at his bed side almost immediately after they'd been called by the hospital, and it felt...wrong to intrude on that. Ryan and I weren't really friends and it was almost my fault that he'd been jumped.

If I didn't hurry, I was going to be late for work, although work was the last place I wanted to be. I forced myself to shove the blankets off my body and get out of bed when all I wanted to do was hide there all day. I couldn't do that, not if I had any hopes of talking to Jenna about last night. I was supposed to hang out with her before I went over to Iain's. Talking to Jenna was essential. I couldn't shake the feeling that she'd change her mind if she heard what happened to Ryan, and to me. I hurried to the bathroom, trying to brush my hair and do my makeup in record time. Mom knocked tentatively on my bedroom door, offering a ride to work. I took her up on it, knowing that I would be late if I tried to walk.

I made it through my shift. I had to work with Trixie, another middle-aged woman that I didn't particularly get along with. She harassed me the entire shift, demanding details on what happened to Ryan the night before. I told her the basics: that we'd gotten jumped by Andrew and his friends. She didn't seem to believe me at all.

"That sweet boy? Really? Are you sure it wasn't someone that just *looked* like him?" she asked, demanding more and more information.

"I really don't want to talk about it anymore, okay, Trixie?" I said, glaring at her.

She touched her dyed red hair, offended. "Well, all right then," she sniffed, walking away from me. She left me alone for the rest of my shift.

When I was getting ready to leave, the manager, Bruce pulled me aside to tell me that he was having cameras installed out back for more security. It made me feel a little better, hearing that he was being proactive.

Jenna was waiting for me in the parking lot. She waved at me, smiling until she saw the expression on my face.

"What is it?" she asked, looking at me warily as I climbed into the passenger side of her car.

"I ran into Andrew last night," I started, trying to keep my hands from shaking.

"Ran into him?" Jenna looked fearful and concerned. She didn't make any move to drive out of the diner parking lot. I didn't blame her.

"He showed up at my work with a couple of his friends. They jumped my co-worker, beat him up, and tried to drag me to Andrew's truck. I got away and ran until I saw someone. They took off."

"Oh my God." Jenna looked ill. She opened her door and lurched out of the car toward the snowy ditch and began to vomit. I winced. I kept forgetting she was pregnant, although I honestly hadn't thought my bit of news would upset her like that. I took a steadying breath—listening to someone throw up was never a pleasant experience.

"Are you okay?" I asked when Jenna had finally stopped vomiting and returned to the car.

"I'm fine," she said, turning to face me. "Okay...so I'm not fine. Not at all."

"Neither am I," I confessed. "Honestly? I'm a little scared. I feel like I'm being hunted."

Jenna nodded, understanding. She looked scared too.

"Has he...has he tried to contact you or anything?" I asked after a moment of silence. Jenna shook her head. "Well, that's good at least."

"What do I do?" she whispered. I wasn't sure if she was asking me or asking herself.

"I think that you do need to press charges. About what he did," I told her gently.

She bit down hard on her lower lip. "I...I can't. If I do that, I have to tell my parents and I'm just not ready yet..." she trailed off, looking ashamed. She wouldn't meet my eyes, and I knew it was because she thought I was angry at her for not coming forward with what I was experiencing. The truth was a part of me was angry. I didn't want to look over my shoulder for the rest of my days. I didn't want to dread leaving work. I didn't want to feel scared and anxious, but I could see the toll that everything had taken on Jenna. I sighed heavily.

"It's alright, Jenna. I just thought you should know...and maybe think about pressing charges. I don't think Andrew's going to go away, or stop what he's doing. There will be more girls, too." I didn't voice my fear: that I would end up one of them. Andrew's interest in me was alarming.

"His dad is the Chief of Police," Jenna reminded me, although her argument was weakening and she knew it. Regardless of who his father is Andrew shouldn't be getting away with the kind of things he was doing.

"So what?" I rolled my eyes. "If you come forward, I'll testify with what I saw. I'll also testify with the two occasions that Andrew's tried to hurt me."

"Two?" Jenna interrupted, surprised.

"Yeah. He chased me when I was walking home from work just after the party. But it was daylight, and I...ran into someone," I said. "Anyway, his dad is going to see the evidence piled against Junior and not be able to do a thing."

"He can still make my life hell, and this baby's," Jenna whispered, eyes on her steering wheel.

"That won't happen," I replied. "I've done some research. No matter what happens, leave him off the birth certificate. He will have no rights to anything, considering how the baby was conceived."

"I don't know, okay!" Jenna looked utterly and completely torn.

"I'm not saying any of this to upset you," I told her. "I hope you know that."

Jenna sighed, looking away. "I know that. It's just..."

"Hard," I finished. "I know that. But trust me, that doesn't go away if you try to forget it.."

"How would you know?" Jenna asked accusingly.

It was my turn to look away. "Because it's happened to me. An entire basketball team drugged and raped me. I didn't press charges, and they're still walking free like it hadn't happened."

Jenna opened and closed her mouth, speechless. "Sorry," she said finally. "I hadn't realized."

"It's okay," I quickly said. "That's not the point. The point is I wish I had pressed charges, because guys like that don't deserve to walk free."

Jenna sighed again, wrapping her arms around her body. "I'd...I have to think about it."

"That's all I'm asking."

The remainder of the weekend was both uneventful and intense. Jenna and I hung out at her house until 8 p.m., watching movies and talking about anything but what we'd discussed when I first got into her car. I texted Iain when I was ready to leave, and he met me a few blocks away from Jenna's house so that I wouldn't have to walk. We watched scary movies, just as we had planned. Only I couldn't focus.

I was so tired from the attack on Friday and the heavy conversation with Jenna. Plus, all the anxiety and emotions I was carting around, and I couldn't stop thinking about Lauren. The anniversary of her death had crept up, and I felt exactly how I expected to feel.

Iain tried to get me to talk to him about it, but aside from giving him short answers, I couldn't really spill it all. He understood, not demanding more than I could give.

My exhaustion finally caught up with me, and I slept in, missing my entire first period and half of second period. I rushed to catch the tail end of my second period class. I nearly ran into someone in the hallway, and would have fallen back if two hands hadn't steadied me. I looked up into Jake's face, feeling relieved. For a split second, I had almost feared that it was going to be Andrew or one of his friends. My nerves were still frayed.

"Hey," he said softly.

"Hi." I backed away, looking at him curiously. He dropped his hands to his sides.

"Are you okay?" he demanded. He frowned, studying me carefully, as if checking for bruises.

"I'm fine...why?"

"Ryan," Jake said in a clipped tone, his eyes narrowing slightly. "He's Troy's cousin. I heard what happened. Grapevine is saying that you're saying Andrew did it."

"Andrew and his friends, yes," I replied. "How is Ryan?"

"He's okay. He'll live," Jake told me. He glanced around, making sure that nobody was within earshot of us.

"What is it, Jake? Why are you being so sketchy?" I asked, feeling nervousness bubbling up.

"Andrew," Jake said, glancing around again.

"What about Andrew?" I was beginning to lose my patience.

"There was this one girl a few years back who tried to press charges," Jake answered, giving me a funny look. "She got run out of town."

I frowned. "Jenna hasn't pressed charges yet."

"I'm just saying be careful," Jake said seriously. "The both of you. I want that shit to stop as much as you do, but be careful. There's an old quote: *don't cross the Coopers*."

"Is the entire town afraid of the Coopers?" I griped. "They're just people."

"You think Andrew is bad?" Jake's tone was sharp. "His old man is five times worse. And he's Chief of Police."

"What does that even mean?" I asked, raising my arms in annoyance. I felt confident that surely any jury or judge would see past this trivial nonsense and toss Andrew were he belonged—on the registered sex offender list—and Andrew's dad, Carl, away in jail for abusing his position of power and apparently covering up all these incidents.

"I hope you don't find out." Jake's voice was serious. I opened my mouth to reply, but we were interrupted.

"Shouldn't you two be in class?" Iain's voice startled me. He was a couple feet away, standing in the hallway and frowning deeply.

"Sorry, Mr. B, on our way now." Jake shrugged, giving him a careless grin. Jake gave me another pointed look that said *We'll talk more later*, and continued walking down the hall toward the men's bathroom.

I was suddenly aware that the hallway was now completely empty, and Iain was only a few steps away from me. I think he was aware of it too. He took a deep breath and sighed. I felt him reach out and gently touch my arm as I passed him. I shot him a surprised look, then quickly checked that nobody had caught it.

"See you after?" he mouthed. I nodded and kept walking as the bell rang, signaling the end of second period.

I sat through the rest of the day with an icy feeling in the pit of my stomach that felt heavier than the feeling I'd woken up with.

I had to work after school, but I texted Iain that I would see him after my shift. I walked quickly to work, hugging my arms to my chest—and not just because the early November air bit against my exposed skin. The icy feeling in the pit of my stomach hadn't lessened as the day wore on; it grew even more. I tried to choke back the panic that now came with simply walking to work alone. I kept glancing around, obsessively checking for a blue truck or anyone following me.

I rushed into the diner and quickly changed into my uniform, grateful for the warmth. Danielle was already working, greeting people with a large grin on her face. I wondered if she had heard about Ryan yet. When she turned away from her customer, the look on her face told me that yes, she had. Her pretty, easy smile was replaced with a look of gnawing worry as she approached me. She put a gentle, tiny hand on my arm and examined me with her green eyes.

"Are you okay?" she asked, her voice soft so as to not draw attention to us. I nodded, trying to find my brave face and put it on. All I could find were images from Friday night and the fresh memory of the panic I'd felt, the panic I *still* felt.

"Ryan is—"

"Doing better," Danielle assured me. "Once I heard, I visited him at the hospital. He's supposed to be released today. He'll be off work for a week."

"Oh," I said, surprised. I hadn't expected Danielle would know more than me. I looked at her, curious. "You visited him?"

She blushed, her cheeks glowing pink under her pretty freckles, and laughed uneasily. "Yeah, I did. I needed to see him. Make sure he was okay."

I nodded, accepting her answer as it was, and headed to the back to change into my uniform.

I tried to loosen up, to not let that icy feeling completely turn me into a rigid robot. It was hard to slip into my diner girl role, and it took some time, but I did so about an hour after my shift started.

It was fairly busy for a Monday night, but I still had plenty of time to do some side work alongside Danielle while she chatted animatedly about her Saturday night and taking Liam trick-or-treating for the first time.

As Danielle was finishing up the tale about how Liam had started bawling his eyes out after a scary wolf gave him Halloween candy, the diner door chimed as it was pushed open. A gust of cold wind rustled my hair, and I distractedly turned to see who'd come in.

It was Andrew Cooper and an older man that looked remarkably like him, dressed in his police uniform with his Chief of Police badge proudly displaced. I froze, petrified, as they made their way over to my section. Danielle had fallen silent and stiff beside me as she watched my reaction.

"What's wrong?" Danielle asked, her voice full of concern. She tenderly touched my arm and looked at me with her wide green eyes. I realized that she had no idea that one of the people who had jumped Ryan was Andrew.

"It's...nothing," I muttered, swallowing hard. I wanted to tell her, but I wanted to avoid a scene at the diner, too. Other customers were eating. I grabbed some menus and headed over to their table, forcing myself to appear calm and composed as my stomach rolled with nerves and disgust.

"Good evening," I said, too formally to be friendly. "What can I get you to start?" I gave myself major kudos for my voice not shaking or wavering. I sounded self-assured and polite.

"We'll both get coffees to start," the man—Carl Cooper—said as he eyed me with keen interest.

I nodded, walking off to get the coffee, my head spinning with Jake's warnings. I brought them their coffees with a forced smile on my face, much to Andrew's delight. I met both their stares with one of my own, not breaking eye contact until they did first. I wanted to appear unafraid and determined, not like a scared little mouse that would bend at their will. Because I wouldn't.

"I'll be back soon to take your orders," I told them, heading off to the kitchen window to grab plates for some of my other tables. I forced myself to be professional, even though I wanted more than anything to leap across the table and claw Andrew's eyes out. That would knock the sly smile and cocky expression off his face. But I knew I couldn't do that.

When I came back to take their orders, they were ready.

"I'll have the steak and potatoes," Carl said, closing the menu and setting it down.

"I'll have the double burger with fries." Andrew grinned, eyeing me with a disgusting glint in his eyes as he shoved his menu out of the way. I wrote down their orders, took their menus and headed back to the counter where Danielle was watching me with a very concerned look on her face.

"What's going on?" she whispered.

I took a steadying breath and reached inside my bag, leaning down behind the counter to quickly text Iain. I had to let him know that I would be late getting to him. There was no way I wanted to chance walking to his house after this encounter. I clicked send with shaky hands, peering up at Danielle. She was still watching me with an overly concerned look on her face, and sadness too.

"It's...nothing," I said again. I wanted to tell her, I did. "I just don't feel very well. I'll be fine."

"It's him, isn't it?" Danielle whispered, crouching down so she was level with me. I nodded, looking at her for a reaction. "I was afraid so. My friend had an...encounter with him a few months ago."

I stood up quickly, making sure I brought up more napkins from under the cash cubby. Danielle followed suit, and we began folding napkins in relative silence until the kitchen bell dinged, alerting us an order was up.

I walked over to the order window, grabbing the two plates

that waited for me, and walked back to the last table on earth I wanted to serve.

"Enjoy," I said, my forced smile now gone.

"Oh, I'm sure we will." Andrew's voice was full of unspoken innuendo. I met his leering gaze with a challenging one of my own, my chin held high. I couldn't think of a single thing to say, but I was hoping the look of ice I sent him would say all that I couldn't. I turned around and headed back to the cash counter.

Danielle was serving a few of her customers their orders, so I was alone at the counter folding napkins for a few minutes. I kept glancing in the Coopers' direction, catching Andrew staring at me with open intent. I inwardly shivered.

The diner bell chimed again, and another customer walked in. I looked over, quickly schooling the shock on my face as Iain made his way to my section, to a table in the back corner where he could easily see the cash counter and the Coopers' table. He didn't spare me a glance, and had his briefcase with him. He sat down, organizing some papers out of his briefcase. He looked at me then, well out of the Coopers' line of sight.

I grabbed a menu for him, knowing full well that Carl and Andrew were still watching. I walked over to Iain's table and handed him the menu. "What can I get for you this evening?" I asked, my voice softer. I was grateful he was there, but a fear welled up in the bottom of my stomach. I sent him a look that clearly said, *what are you doing here?*

"I'd just like some coffee today, please," Iain said, giving me a look that said, *as if I would leave you alone with these two.* It was bittersweet how easily we could read each other's secret looks.

I nodded, heading over to grab him a coffee, still chewing over Jake's warning and the fact that Andrew didn't seem to be scared or worried that I'd seen him last night and named him as one of the people who had jumped Ryan and me.

I didn't know what their intentions were by coming into the diner and staring at me the whole time while they ate, but the feeling in my gut told me it wasn't good.

The Coopers stayed entirely too long for my liking, eating their meals and their desserts painfully slow. Iain kept his eyes on them the entire time—and me as well. He noted every look Andrew gave me, every leer and unspoken innuendo, with his jaw set as he drank his coffee.

Finally, Andrew and Carl paid for their bill and left. They tipped me nearly twenty dollars, which I immediately wanted to give to Danielle.

"Keep it," she told me, shivering.

"You said something earlier," I said. "about your friend?" I was finally able to ask now that they'd gone.

"Yeah." Danielle sighed. "Rachel. She went to a party with a couple of our mutual friends—I didn't go, of course. But she went. He was there. She had just one drink and ended up alone with him."

"I can imagine the rest." I frowned, feeling sick.

She nodded sadly. "Yeah, it was vile. She—she was really hurt during it. Bleeding and..." Danielle took a deep breath.

"Would Rachel want to press charges?" I asked hopefully. Maybe if I got more of Andrew's victims to speak up, it would be an open-and-shut thing.

"Rachel can't," Danielle said sadly. "She's dead. She killed herself."

"Oh my god." My jaw dropped. "I'm so sorry, Danielle. I had no idea!"

"It's not your fault," Danielle assured me, her green eyes full of sadness as she glanced toward the door. The look behind her expression made it obvious whose fault it had been. My lips froze around telling her that Andrew had also jumped Ryan, the look on her face melting my words.

Iain waited until my shift was almost over to leave and sent me a text saying he'd be in the parking lot waiting to drive me home. I knew he didn't want me walking anywhere alone.

Danielle was in a quiet, sad, reserved mood that I'd never seen her in before. She was so distracted with her thoughts that she didn't even notice Iain's presence, nor did she comment on his good looks and the way he looked at me. I felt sick, knowing the cause of her turmoil. I knew the pain of losing a friend all too well.

Finally, after the diner was locked up and the fill-in dish boy was sent off, I went to the parking lot to where Iain was waiting in his car. I climbed into the passenger side, closing it quickly behind me. Iain reached across the seat and gently grabbed my hand.

"I think it's safe to say that I'm really looking forward to getting away next weekend," he said dryly.

I bit my lip.

"Do you think we should still go?" I asked, looking out the window. Iain hadn't started the car yet, and it was a little chilly.

"Of course," Iain said. "Unless you don't want to?"

"You know I want to." I gave him a look. "I'm just...I don't know. Worried."

"Don't be. I'll protect you." Iain squeezed my hand before letting go to start the car.

"Do you mind just taking me home?" I whispered, glancing out the window again. "I don't want to have to walk back later."

"I could drive you later, if you want," Iain offered. "But if you want to go home, I'll take you."

I thought about it for a nanosecond. Home to my cold

bedroom and my overly in my face mother, and possibly the overly friendly Larry, or back to Iain's warm and comfortable place?

"Only if you promise to make hot chocolate the real way." I gave him a half smile. "I'm still waiting to try that."

He laughed richly, then turned serious. "Of course. But we also need to talk. About tonight, and earlier."

I nodded as he gently put the car into drive and headed out of the diner. The drive to Iain's house was ridiculously short, almost pointless if it hadn't been for the whole "avoiding the public when together" thing. He pulled into his driveway and I pulled my hoodie up over my head. I always felt so exposed walking up to his house, and usually made sure my hair and face was blocked from anyone that happened to drive by. Kind of pointless, since I always wore the same leather jacket and shit kicker boots, but regardless, it made me feel a tiny bit better, like I was protecting Iain a little.

Iain shook his head, smiling at me as he unlocked his front door. He stepped aside so I could walk in first.

"You're cute," he said, watching me pull my hood down.

I rolled my eyes. "You still owe me hot chocolate. Don't weasel your way out of it again."

"I won't." He smiled, heading into the kitchen. I walked in as he was bending over to grab a pot from the lower cupboard. I admired the way his jeans fit snug to his body.

"Do you like the view?" Iain joked, wiggling a bit.

I laughed, rolling my eyes again. "Someone's egotistic," I remarked.

"Someone's staring," he pointed out, straightening up and crossing over to the refrigerator to grab some cream. He filled the pot up halfway with it, then added the hot chocolate mix and stirred it before putting it on the burner. "It takes a little longer this way," he added.

"That's okay." I sat down at the table, stretching a little to try to work the tension out of my back and shoulders. Iain watched me, quiet and thoughtful.

"So...what were you and Jake doing in the halls?" he asked, leaning against the counter to keep a close eye on the hot chocolate.

"Nothing. I was late for class and on my way, I literally ran into Jake and he told me some interesting stuff."

"What kind of stuff?" Iain frowned.

"Just the apparent town motto about the Coopers and how they aren't to be crossed. That they ran the girl who tried to press charges out of town. Tonight, when they came into the diner, all I could think about was Jake's warning. Then Danielle told me about her friend, Rachel. She was also raped by Andrew, and she ended up killing herself."

"Rachel McGuire?" Iain asked. "I heard about her suicide. I didn't know her, or even that the two incidents were related."

"Well, they are. She killed herself because of Andrew and what he did to her." I sighed.

Iain opened his mouth to speak, but I pointed at the stove. The hot chocolate was almost bubbling over. "Shit."

Iain quickly turned down the temperature and stirred it. Deeming it hot enough, he carefully poured it into two mugs and placed one in front of me. He sat down beside me and angled his chair toward me. He had a thoughtful look on his face.

"Okay, so 'Don't cross the Coopers' is an actual saying in this town?" Iain shook his head, glaring down at his mug. "And nobody does anything about it?"

"I don't know," I said. "Doesn't make any sense. I'm not from around here."

"Me either." Iain ran a hand through his hair, mussing it. "I'm originally from the Ottawa area."

"So, what does this mean?" I asked. "We haven't even brought the evidence to light, nor have any victims come forward to press charges, and I'm already getting visits at work." I tried to ignore the disgusting feeling in my stomach as I thought about Friday night's 'visit'. Attack would be more suitable.

"It's probably a scare tactic," Iain said. "From Carl, anyway," he added, remembering Friday night just as vividly as I did. "Andrew seems to be a loose cannon."

"What's the worst they can do? Try to run me out of town?" I asked, laughing without humor. "Oh no! Run me out of the town! I plan on leaving as soon as I graduate!"

Iain smiled wryly at me. "You're not planning on staying?"

"Hell no," I quickly said. "I mean, I want to stay for certain reasons," I gave him a pointed look, "but we couldn't suddenly become public when I graduate."

"That's true." Iain sighed.

"Let's not worry about all that right now," I said said, wanting to ease the mood. I was tired of feeling anxious and wound up. "In fact, let's just wait and see what Jenna says. If she doesn't want to press charges, there isn't much more we can do other than keep the evidence I compiled until another girl comes forward."

Iain nodded, sighing again. "I guess that's all we can do. But, Harlow, I really don't want you to become 'another' girl."

"I know," I said softly, my voice wavering slightly. I didn't want that either.

CHAPTER EIGHT

The next week passed by without any more weird incidents at the diner. I didn't see Andrew or Carl Cooper around town, and there also weren't any crazy parties going on. It was...quiet. Jenna continued to hang out with Tara and Callie during the day (although she often remarked about how she was tired of their antics), while I stuck to hanging out with Jake, Cory and Troy. Or I kept to myself. After school, I'd either be working or with Iain.

On November 15, Jenna and I skipped class again, this time to go to Sudbury for her ultrasound. When we parked the car, Jenna fished out huge bulky sunglasses and a hat to hide her hair. "I don't want to risk the chance of running into anyone," she explained when she caught me staring at her. I shrugged, trying to hide my smile.

"Suit yourself," I said, realizing how ridiculous I must look taking the same precautions going into Iain's house. I pushed open the car door and stepped outside. It was cold out, but I still inhaled the fresh air deeply as we walked up to the hospital. It stung my lungs, but I wasn't looking forward to the sterile environment. I hated the smell and taste of hospitals. I always had, but it got worse after the accident.

"When is your appointment?" I asked, trying to prevent my thoughts from drifting to the past as we stepped in through the revolving doors.

"Five minutes." Jenna shrugged carelessly. She was trying to appear unworried, but I could tell how nervous she really was. I didn't blame her. I couldn't imagine what it felt like.

Occasionally, I thought about having babies. Not in an obsessive *I need to get pregnant* way, but in a curious way. Would I mess up my kids? Would I even want kids? I still didn't have the answers, but I know I definitely wouldn't want to be pregnant as the result of a rape.

We followed the arrows that pointed to the X-ray and ultrasound department. It was relatively empty of people, so Jenna stepped up to the receptionist to sign in. I didn't know what else to do, so I grabbed a chair and picked up a magazine. My phone chimed in my coat pocket. I reached for it, seeing that I had one new text. It was from Iain.

I miss you. All ready for tonight?

I smiled, excited that the day had finally come. As soon as I got back from Sudbury, Iain and I would be heading out to Niagara Falls. I'd packed my overnight bag a couple days ago, and brought it over to his house after work last night. He already had it in the trunk of his car.

I'd been surprised at how little my mom questioned me about the trip. I told her I was heading down to Niagara Falls with some friends; she barely questioned me at all about which friends. I think she was excited to get an entire weekend alone with Larry. I shuddered at the thought, but to each his own. At least the weird meeting with Larry a month ago hadn't repeated itself. Probably because I was rarely home, and when I was they were already sleeping.

I texted him back "*Of course*" and a little kiss emoticon, and put my phone back in my pocket as Jenna fell into the chair beside me. She was looking at me curiously.

"Who were you texting?" she asked, shoving a flyaway hair back under her hat.

"Oh...just...someone," I replied awkwardly. Jenna continued to look at me inquisitively with one eyebrow raised in disbelief.

"Do you consider me a friend, Harlow?" she asked, almost timidly.

"Yeah, I guess I do," I answered honestly. "I'm here with you now, aren't I?"

She smiled weakly. "Thanks for that," she said. "I...I'm glad you're here."

"Do you consider *me* a friend?" I asked, curious for her answer as well.

"Yeah," she replied. "I mean, you're really nice to me and you haven't told anyone about...this. And you've been here for me the entire time, so yeah."

"Well then, besties for life?" I joked. She rolled her eyes, but laughed.

"Only if you tell me who you were texting," she pressed, looking hopeful. "Come on, distract me! I'm nervous!"

I sighed dramatically. "Okay, I'm texting my...boyfriend."

"You have a boyfriend?" Jenna looked surprised. "I thought you were single?" she asked, making reference to the first day of school. I cringed.

"Yeah, well. I have one now."

"Who? That Jake guy you're always with?"

"You don't know him, he's from back home," I lied quickly and easily.

Jenna smiled. "What's his name? Could I see a picture?" she asked. The old Jenna was popping through a little.

"His name is...Ben," I said, thinking of the first name that popped into my head. Then I cursed myself, hoping it wasn't too obvious. "And I actually don't have a picture of him..."

"How do you not have a picture of him? Everyone has Facebook these days!" Jenna scoffed.

Before I had to think of another excuse, the radiologist appeared with a clip board. She was a petite woman with a warm smile. "Jenna?"

"Please come in with me," Jenna whispered, looking panicked and ill.

"She will have to wait until we are done with the initial testing," the radiologist said kindly. "I can come get her toward the end."

Jenna looked at me, panic still enveloping her features.

"It'll be okay," I said, patting her arm awkwardly. I wasn't used to touching her, but it was all I could think to do. She nodded, biting her lip, and stood up to follow the radiologist into the ultrasound room.

When the door shut behind them, I got out my phone to check my texts. Iain had sent a few more texts in response to the lips I'd sent him, and they were leaning a bit on the steamy side. I felt my temperature rising just reading them, and some-how...that felt wrong while sitting in an ultrasound clinic. I almost laughed out loud.

*Oh, the things I want to do you...*the first one read, followed quickly by one that said, *I know you aren't really in a location that sets the mood...but...* then he went on to describe the delectable things he wanted to do to me that weekend. By the time I finished reading them, I was definitely looking forward to the weekend in many more ways than I had been before. I couldn't help but smile as I texted my seductive responses with a little too much detail. I wanted him to be just as bothered.

Try teaching class now, Iain, I thought with a mischievous look on my face.

"Harlow Jones? You can come in now," the radiologist said some twenty minutes later. Startled, I fumbled with my phone and nearly dropped it. I shoved it quickly into my pocket and stood up, following her into the ultrasound room. Jenna was lying on the table, forcing herself to stare at the wall.

"Alright," the radiologist said, turning the screen so we could both see. Jenna kept her eyes on the wall, determined not to look. A single tear ran down her cheek.

I glanced at the radiologist, ready to tell her not to bother, when my eyes went to the screen.

"This is the baby. See that? That's the baby's heartbeat. You're about 12 weeks pregnant. Your estimated due date is May 30." The radiologist said all this with a gentle smile on her face.

Jenna struggled to keep her gaze averted, but she lost the battle and looked at the image on the screen. I thought it looked like a tiny peanut. I couldn't tell what Jenna thought. "Oh," she simply said, a waterfall of tears streaming down her face. "It looks so real."

"It is real," the radiologist said gently. She printed off some pictures and handed them to Jenna.

"I don't want..." Jenna trailed off, unable to tear her gaze from the pictures. The radiologist gave her an understanding smile as she gently wiped off the ultrasound gel.

Jenna asked me to drive since she was too shaky. "You have your license, right?"

I nodded as she tossed me the keys, climbing into the passenger side. She didn't say anything the entire way home, and I felt it was the wrong time to press about the whole charges thing. I hadn't even told her that the Coopers had shown up at my work the next day.

She dropped me off at the diner after I told her I had to work. That was a little lie, but I did need to walk to Iain's and the diner was close to his place.

"Jenna, if you need me there when you tell them, I'll be there," I told her. She nodded at me, giving me a small, thankful smile.

I watched her drive away before I started walking, pulling my hoodie up over my head again. I kept an eye on my surroundings, but didn't notice anything out of the ordinary.

Iain wasn't home from school yet, so I unlocked his door using the spare key he'd given me the night before. He knew I'd likely beat him there.

I didn't have to wait very long. Iain came in some ten minutes later when I was walking from the kitchen to the living room. He tossed his briefcase on the floor and walked over to me, gently grabbing my face with his hands and kissing me with a burning passion that had obviously been growing all day. He nibbled on my lip and I moaned, leaning against him, begging him to take me.

He laughed into my mouth, trailing kisses along my neck to my ear. "That's for turning me on so much I had to sit behind my desk for a solid thirty minutes."

"Oh, I bet it was a solid thirty minutes," I retorted, pushing him away with a smile. He laughed back, pressing against me so I'd feel just how solid it had been. My humorous mood evaporated as I was filled with a burning need. He saw the change in my eyes and instantly brought his mouth down to mine again, kissing me intently while his arms roamed my body over my clothes.

"There's no way I can make that drive until I've satisfied your craving," Iain said, scooping me up in his arms and carrying me up the stairs toward his bedroom.

"My craving?" I asked, lowering my eyelashes.

"Mine too," he assured me, dropping me gently onto the bed and crawling slowly over top of me, kissing me.

"Well, we're going to be a little later getting to the hotel now," Iain joked, backing out of his driveway. It was nearly 6 p.m. "We'll miss our reservations at that fancy restaurant and have to grab something along the way, but I'd say that was more than worth it."

"I agree." I smirked, reaching across the seat to touch his inner thigh.

"Do you ever want to get there?" Iain joked, gently removing my hand while he drove toward the highway.

"Eh, I'll have you anywhere, Mr. Bentley." I winked. Then I remembered telling Jenna about him—vaguely. Frowning, I grabbed a strand of my hair to twist. "So Jenna asked who I was texting today."

"What'd you tell her?" Iain asked as he merged onto the highway with skill and ease.

"I told her I was talking to my boyfriend. Ben." I smiled weakly.

"Ben?" Iain asked, laughing. "I get it—Bentley, right?"

"I just hope she doesn't get it," I said this with concern.

"I think she's a little wrapped up in her own life right now," Iain assured me, taking my hand and holding it in my lap. "Besides, lots of guys are named Ben."

"Yeah..." I sighed, looking out the window. Iain's reassurance had brought on thoughts about Jenna's current predicament.

"Where are you?" Iain asked gently, brushing the inside of my hand with his thumb.

"I'm just thinking about all that...worrying. Wondering.

The usual," I answered, shifting in my seat a little. "It'd be so much easier if I could talk to another girl who...got run out of town. To see what I'm up against."

"That's a good idea," Iain nodded. "I could have my friend look into it."

"Who's your friend?" I asked.

"He's on the police squad, actually," Iain said, giving me a rueful smile. "Hates it there, hates how Cooper is a dirty cop and everyone covers him and his...offspring."

"What's his name?" My curiosity was growing. I thought back to the officer with curly brown hair and green eyes, the one that had given me his card.

"Mike Turner," Iain replied, confirming the name on the card.

"I met him," I said, fishing the card out of my jacket pocket where I'd left it. "At the hospital, when I was giving my statement about what happened to Ryan."

"Oh?" Iain looked almost relieved. "That's good. That's really good. He's one of the only cops in this town not on the Coopers' side, although he's very careful about revealing that."

"Why?" I asked, looking at Iain, my eyebrows knitted together with confusion.

"To protect himself," Iain answered honestly. "Trust me, Mike is very interested in exposing Carl Cooper. I'm sure he would know exactly who they ran out of town."

"Oh, well. Makes sense I guess," I said, still frowning. I looked out the window at the scenery, barely seeing how gorgeous it was. We were in the Canadian shield, and there were plenty of icicle waterfalls to look at in the rocks that lined either side of the highway. I couldn't see that though.

"Harlow?" Iain asked gently, squeezing my hand again. I looked at him, noticing how concerned he was.

"I'm okay," I said, smiling to reassure him. And I was. I was with Iain. Iain had a tremendous way of making me forget everything, and at the same time I felt like I could tell him anything. I decided to focus on us this weekend, not the drama of the Police Chief's son. It was easier to do with every mile that we drove further away from North Bay. "I'm excited. I've never actually been to Niagara Falls."

"Really?" Iain asked, his blue eyes sparkling.

"Really." I laughed.

"Well, good." Iain gave a half-smile and brought my hand up to his mouth so he could kiss it. "I can't wait to take you out to dinner," he added, smiling at me. My heart skipped a beat. It would be the first time we ever went out in public together. I had to physically restrain myself from squealing like a school-girl—which I was, more or less.

This weekend we could act like more of a couple. We'd be far away from anybody that knew us. That prospect excited me, and I knew it excited him too. His hand was still holding mine. I was excited for the five-hour car drive and the whole weekend. Although we tried to spend a lot of time together, between working and pretending to not be involved with one another, we only really got to see each other alone a few times a week and on weekends. During the week, we jumped into bed with one another as quickly as we could to fill those urges that we both worked hard to repress all day long. On weekends, we were able to take a little more time together, but my mom was becoming overly curious about my long disappearances. In fact, I'd been shocked that she hadn't put up a total stink about me wanting to leave town for the whole weekend, but the woman worked in mysterious ways. She probably knew that the likely reason I was gone so much was a guy, and a few times she had expressed an interest in meeting him. I kept telling her there was no guy, but she didn't buy my excuses. She just nodded and smiled knowingly, then told me he was welcome to come around when I was ready.

We stopped at a drive thru a few towns away for coffee, and continued driving. We held hands practically the entire time, sometimes silent, sometimes talking. Now that we had an entire weekend to spend together, things didn't have to be rushed. We didn't even turn the radio on at all.

We finally got to the hotel around 11 p.m. The moment we got up to our hotel room and dropped our bags on the floor, we fell in a massive mess of tangled limbs and clothes onto the bed. Iain peeled off my layers one by one, tortuously slow as he kissed me and pressed into me with his own longing. I moaned eagerly into his mouth, willing him to just rip off my pants and get at it. He took his time though, and afterwards, I was grateful.

The next morning, Iain presented me with an "early" Christmas present before I was even awake: a Polaroid camera.

"What's this for?" I smiled, rubbing the sleep out of my eyes.

"Taking pictures, duh." He rolled his eyes. Iain set it up and turned to me, aiming the lenses at me. I was lying tangled up in the blankets, not wearing anything. He took a picture of me seductively looking at him and waved it to dry. "Yup, keeping this one," he said after looking at it. "I just love Polaroid cameras," he added appreciatively.

"You're a dork." I laughed, rolling my eyes and watching as he set it on the end table beside the bed.

"Sure am." He grinned wickedly, a dimple appearing on his left cheek. "Now I regret to inform you that you must cover up that gorgeous body. We're going out for breakfast."

"I could go for breakfast," I said, my stomach growling in agreement. I stood up, walking over to the bathroom naked. "I want a shower first though."

"I'll join you." Iain threw back his blanket and sauntered over to the bathroom, coming up behind me and putting his arms around my waist. He nestled his head against my shoulder, kissing me.

"I really do need to shower, though." I laughed, leaning backwards into him. Having his arms around me felt amazing.

"So do I," he agreed. He released me and turned on the tap, adjusting it so that it was perfectly hot—the temperature I loved. I stepped inside it, sighing contently as the hot water instantly hit the top of my head and cascaded down my body. I opened my eyes to see Iain staring at me with a smile on his face, his eyes bright and happy. I felt vulnerable. I had never had a shower with a guy before; the concept seemed strange.

"You're gorgeous," he said, stepping in to join me. Before I could respond, he was squeezing the hotel shampoo into his hand and started to massage it into my hair.

"Are you washing my hair?" I asked, tipping my head back and enjoying it. I could get used to this.

"It would appear so. You're not very observant this morning. Didn't you get enough sleep last night?" he joked.

"Surprisingly, no. Someone kept me up all night," I replied. I moaned as his fingers massaged my head with expertise. He worked the shampoo in and rinsed it, making sure none of it remained. It took him a while, as I had a lot of hair, but he insisted on doing it by himself. He trailed kisses down the back of my neck after he was finished.

"Alright, your turn," I said, squeezing some shampoo into my hands. Iain stepped under the water, soaking his own hair, and allowed me to wash it for him. He had to bend his knees and duck his head for me to be able to reach him. He groaned with pleasure and smiled at me after he rinsed it out.

I lathered up the rest of his body, taking extra time down there. It was a good hour before we finished in the shower, and what a finish it was.

"Okay, now I'm *really* hungry." I laughed, my stomach growling. I quickly started braiding my hair, not wanting to spend time blow-drying it.

"Me too," Iain agreed, stepping into a fresh change of clothes. He was wearing snug jeans that fit him in the most complimentary way, and a gray waffle shirt that made his blue eyes appear almost gray. He styled his hair quickly, and was ready to go while I was still braiding my hair. I envied men and how little they had to put into their efforts to look good. I put a headband on, then left the bathroom to go find Iain.

He was standing by the window in his quiet perfection, staring out the window. I snuck over to the bed, grabbing the Polaroid he'd given me. I stood a little ways behind him and snapped a picture, focusing on the scene he was looking at. I waved it the same way he did and waited until the picture came into focus, and when it did, I put the camera and photo down on the end table and went to stand beside him to see the view firsthand.

"Whoa..." I said in wonderment as Iain wrapped his arm around my waist and pulled me close to him. He smiled down at the expression on my face, gently kissing the top of my head. Our hotel room window faced the Falls, and we had a perfect breathtaking view of it. "It's...beautiful."

"I know," Iain said, still looking at me. I got the feeling he wasn't talking about Niagara Falls.

A few minutes later, we were on our way down to the dining area of the hotel to have the continental breakfast. It was both thrilling and odd holding Iain's hand the entire way down. Usually, we acted as if we weren't a couple. We never went out in public together and we tried our best to ignore each other at school. Holding his hand and having him pull me close to him was great, but I felt a twinge of sadness that it couldn't always be like this.

The rest of the weekend was just as amazing. Iain took me to several wax museums, on a boat tour, and to see a movie. We went out for lunch and dinner, and before I knew it, it was time to head home. The small twinge of sadness I'd felt Saturday morning at breakfast had grown...a lot. I wished we could always be like this. I think Iain knew what I was feeling, and I think his emotions mirrored mine. As we stood in the elevator riding down to the lobby, our bags at our heels, he pulled me toward him and tipped my chin up.

"We'll do this again, very soon," he promised, touching his forehead to mine. His lips found mine and he kissed me deeply, intensely, longingly. The kiss only lasted a moment, and when he pulled away he smiled at me. He opened his mouth as if to say something, then closed it and sighed.

"What were you going to say?" I asked, curiosity over-whelming me. The elevator came to a stop at the lobby and the doors dinged open. Iain swooped down and grabbed both our bags with one arm, and took my hand with the other. We walked toward the receptionist to hand back our key and check out.

"Nothing." He smiled, secretive. I frowned. It hadn't seemed like nothing. He caught me frowning and sighed. "I just didn't want to tell you in a hotel lobby...that *I love you*," he whispered into my ear before releasing me and stepping up to the clerk to check out.

I stood there, probably with my jaw on the floor, watching Iain as he took back his credit card from the receptionist. He... loved me? Loved...me? I just couldn't wrap my head around it.

"Don't look so shell shocked," Iain said, approaching me with half a smile on his face. "You're giving me a complex. Should I not have said anything?" he added lowly, looking around the lobby. It was so weird seeing him vulnerable, but there he stood. I brushed my hair back behind my shoulders, biting my lip softly. I knew what I felt for Iain was strong—*very* strong. I'd never felt anything like it before.

"No, it's just...hard to explain," I said, smiling. "I think I'm very close, if not already there..."

"You don't need to feel obligated to say it." Iain spoke softly, tipping my chin up ever so slightly so I was looking into his eyes. "Just because I did. I mean it, more than anything, but don't feel pressured to say it if you aren't ready."

I couldn't think of anything to say, so I kissed him. I figured it'd be the last time in a while we got to have a little PDA.

CHAPTER NINE

After we got back from Niagara Falls, I went home to have a shower and do some homework I'd been procrastinating on. It was nearly 7 when we got in, and Iain dropped me off at the end of my driveway before I shooed him away, paranoid that Mom or Larry would see him.

I had a ridiculous smile on my face the entire time I showered and got dressed. I ran a comb through my hair, practically humming. When I stepped out of the bathroom into the hallway, Mom was standing there with a peculiar look on her face.

"What is it?" I asked, a terrible feeling weighing heavily in my belly.

"I need to speak to you," she urged, motioning toward my bedroom. Larry was snoring on the couch in the living room. I followed, the dread growing.

"Sit," she ordered, pointing to my bed. She had something in her hand. I sat, robotic like. Out of the corner of my eye, I noticed my bags had been disturbed.

"You went through my stuff?" I accused, angrily standing up.

"Harlow Jones, you sit down." Mom's voice was final and struck me like a whip. I sat, mouth agape. She never spoke to me that way. Mom grabbed my desk chair, spinning it around to face me and sat down, her eyes deadly serious as she tossed the photos I'd taken with the Polaroid on the bed. "Who is he? He looks way too old for you."

I breathed out a momentary sigh of relief. Momentary. I knew that bubble would burst. It was only a matter of time before she discovered just who he was. I looked at her levelly, weighing my options. I couldn't have her find out the wrong way, at a school function or even around town with other people to tell her...*that's the English teacher at the Catholic school.* If she found out from someone else, it would jeopardize everything. Mainly Iain's career. She'd find out either way, whether I told her or whether someone else did. But what if she didn't handle the truth well? I chewed on my bottom lip, conflicted. I felt dizzy and sick. I couldn't blame Iain for getting me the Polaroid; I could only blame myself for not taking more precautions, like maybe letting him hang onto the pictures, or at least hiding them somewhere the moment I got home instead of gallivanting off to the shower without a thought for my nosy mother.

"Mom...do you believe in love?" I asked so softly she had to ask me to say it again. "Do you believe in love?"

"Of course I believe in love." Mom frowned, glancing at the photos. "But he—"

"We love each other." I took a deep breath. "He's not old; he's 28."

"That's too old for you!" Mom said loudly. I hushed her, motioning to my closed door. We both got quiet, listening for Larry's snoring. When we heard it, she continued in a softer voice. "That's over ten years older than you, Harlow."

"Yes, but Larry is 15 years older than you," I whispered,

trying to level with her. I was feeling sicker by the minute. If she was disgusted by our age difference, I couldn't see this ending well at all. I wrapped my arms around my stomach, trying to hold myself together.

"We are at different stages in life, Harlow!" Mom put her hand to her temple, aggravated. "Who is he? Where on earth would you have met a 28-year-old?"

I froze again, uncertain of what to say. "He's...important."

"Harlow," Mom said sharply, sensing it was as bad as... well, as bad as it really was.

"Mom, please." I raised my hand, silencing her. "I'll explain...I just need...a minute."

Mom's eyes were wide with worry and concern, but she nodded.

"I want to tell you this, I do, but I'm scared you'll get the wrong impression or you'll freak out," I started. "I want to make it very clear to you: he is not taking advantage of me, now or ever. Do you understand?"

Mom frowned, staring intently at me, trying to gauge my tone. I tried to express to her how serious I was being with my eyes, open and pleading. I worried that I'd chosen the wrong route, that I'd set her up for a freak out by assuring her that. I inwardly cursed myself, wishing I could take back my words, but I couldn't.

"I can't tell you any more if I don't have a promise from you," I whispered, hugging myself. "It's that you won't tell anyone. And you'll try to understand."

"Alright fine, I promise!" Mom said. "Just tell me, Harlow; who is he? How did you meet him?"

"He's....a teacher." I flinched, waiting for her to yell obscenities at me and call for Larry. "My teacher."

I couldn't look at her; I stared at the pictures in her hand. She was holding one we'd gotten a stranger to take of us standing near the Falls. His arms were around me and we both looked at each other with happiness and open affection. After several moments, I grew wary of her silence. I looked at her and noticed she was staring at the same picture, her lip trembling.

"How?" Mom asked, looking as if I had betrayed her.

"It didn't happen how you think it happened," I said quickly. "It just...happened."

"Harlow, he's twenty-eight, he's your English teacher!" Mom looked horrified. "He's taking advantage of you, baby. We'll get a lawyer, we'll—"

"Stop," I cut her off harshly, glaring. "I told you, he is not taking advantage of me. He loves me."

"How can he love you?" she asked. "You're not even 18!"

"Oh, so age determines whether or not someone can fall in love with you?" I scoffed. "Or is it because I'm too horrifying to imagine anyone possibly actually loving me?"

"That's not—"

"That is pretty much what you meant. Just because I'm young, doesn't mean I'm stupid or foolish or incapable of recognizing love. Contrary to your belief, I do know when I'm being taken advantage of. And I'm not—not by Iain."

I stood up, grabbing the pictures from her hand and clenching them close to my side. "I think I'm able to recognize the difference by now, since it's happened so many times before." I said the last part with tears in my eyes. I knew that would sting her, and she flinched against the harshness of my words, but I didn't care. At least not in that moment.

"Harlow, I just want to protect you and make sure you're safe," Mom argued, pulling on my arm to get me to sit back down.

"You can't protect me from everything, as we both already

learned. And I am safe. At least with Iain," I answered. I opened my mouth, about to tell her about the Coopers, but stopped.

"There's more, isn't there?" she urged. "Are you pregnant?"

"No," I spat.

"Thank God." She closed her eyes. "Harlow, listen to me. You need to break things off with him before anyone can find out. Your entire academic year could be questioned if this ever came to light."

"It's not going to," I said, unsure. Thoughts of Carl Cooper came to mind, but I tried to repress them.

"I don't want you seeing him anymore," Mom said, fresh tears welling in the corner of her eyes. "Please, call it off."

"I can't, Mom, I love him. I want to be with him," I whispered. I was in too deep to just stop everything, and it was the last thing I wanted.

"If you really love him, you'll walk away," Mom said, shaking her head and standing up. She walked toward my door, resting her hand on the doorknob before she turned back to look at me. "Not only could this ruin any chances you stand on getting into university, but it could ruin his career too. Think about that."

She closed the door behind her with a firm click.

It took me ages to fall asleep that night. I kept tossing and turning, worrying that Mom had told Larry, worrying that he had called the cops and had Iain arrested. I woke up with extreme bags under my eyes.

I could hear Larry and Mom talking in the kitchen before he left for work. The smell of coffee assaulted my senses as I quietly got ready for the day in my bedroom. I waited until I heard the front door shut behind Larry before I went to find her. I had already slipped into my winter gear and grabbed my backpack, knowing that I didn't have long before the bus arrived to pick me up.

"Mom?" I asked timidly, seeing her standing by the sink. She was scrubbing a plate with much more muscle than required. She didn't answer me, but I knew she heard by the set her shoulders took. "Did you...did you tell Larry?"

She sighed deeply, letting the plate fall with a soapy clatter into the sink. "No, Harlow. I didn't tell Larry. I don't really think that conversation would go over well, do you? 'Oh, good morning honey, my daughter is sleeping with one of your employees.'"

"How do you know I'm sleeping with him?" I demanded. Mom gave me a sarcastic glance over her shoulder. I closed my mouth, feeling ashamed. It was just like that time she'd heard the rumours from one of the PTA moms. Remembering that sent a wave of anger pumping throughout my bloodstream, and I heatedly took a step toward her with my finger raised. "Is it because you think I'm a giant slut?" I asked. "Do you think I'm sleeping with the whole town now too? Just like old times?"

"Harlow," Mom said evenly, trying to calm me down, but she'd already set me off.

"You know what I never told you before?" I shot back, anger surging out of every pore. She stood silent, watching and waiting. "I never told you that yes, I did have sex with every single guy on the basketball team the same night. Against my fucking will. I never told you that sweet little Cole—who you loved so much and thought was so great for me—and his buddies drugged me and took turns raping me, and that I don't even know who I lost my virginity to. But yet you believed all those moms on the PTA, didn't you?" I was blind with tears and anger. I could barely see her shocked face. She looked as if I'd slapped her.

"I never told you that I'd wanted to die after that, and that Lauren had been the only person who gave a shit enough to see past the rumours and see me. I never told you that Lauren saved my life, did I? Because she did. Without Lauren, I'd probably be dead by now. And now she's gone, and I'm stuck with you, who would trust the gossip of a few PTA moms than her own daughter."

Mom was sheet white. Her mouth opened and closed, as if she wanted to say something to me but couldn't find the words.

"Iain is the first person to bring me back to the light since Lauren died—something you never even tried to do. Something you probably didn't even *care* to do. And he doesn't use sex to do it. Now you want to tell me to walk away from the one slice of happiness I've had in a long time? The one chance at feeling this? Go fuck yourself," I spat out harshly before fleeing out the front door.

It was hard to wipe the tears from my eyes as I walked to my bus stop; my hands shook so badly. The last thing I wanted to do was go to school, but I certainly didn't want to stay home with her after all I'd told her. I hadn't meant to tell her all that. It just sort of exploded out of me.

"Fuck," I practically yelled, turning the corner and seeing the bus pull away from my stop. Fresh tears poured down my cheeks, and I wiped them away furiously while I fished out my phone. I sent a text to Jake, asking if he'd mind picking me up. I didn't want to go home and risk seeing my mom again. I told him to meet me a couple blocks over. I walked as quickly as one can walk through snow and slush. November weather in North Bay certainly wasn't like November weather down south. I was nearly at the street corner I'd told Jake to meet me at when a police cruiser pulled up beside me. Fear shot through me as I instantly assumed my mom had called the police, and that they were bringing me in for questioning and arresting Iain. The window rolled down and I startled when I realized it was Carl Cooper and his partner. Seeing Carl Cooper's face did nothing to ease my anxiety.

"Beautiful morning, huh?" Carl drawled, taking in the sight of me. He took a leisurely sip of his coffee, eyes never leaving me.

"Stunning," I replied dryly. "What can I do for you, Chief?" My heart was pounding so loudly in my chest that I was almost certain he could hear it.

"Oh, nothing at all, my dear. I just wanted to remind you to be very careful. It's slippery out here," Carl said, giving me a searching look. "You could get hurt really easily."

"So I've heard." I gave him a challenging look, trying to keep my eyes fixed on his calculating brown ones.

He chuckled, deeply amused. "You have a good day; we'll see you around," he said, nodding to his partner to continue driving. I released the breath I hadn't known I'd been holding. Seriously? Could this day get any better?

"Harlow?" Jake shouted from inside his vehicle, a few houses down. He looked concerned as he watched the cruiser disappear down another road. I finished walking toward his Jeep, slipping and sliding the whole way. My eyes felt dry and crusty. I hated that after-crying feeling. I hopped into the passenger seat and pulled down his mirror to inspect the damage. My waterproof mascara and liquid eyeliner had held up surprisingly well after my morning cry fest. I applied some fresh lipstick and tried to ignore Jake while he stared at me, clearly waiting for an explanation.

"No, I have no idea what that was about," I finally said when I realized Jake wasn't about to start driving until I answered. I drew in a sharp breath. "He told me it was slippery out and to be careful."

"That's...odd." Jake pondered, concern on his face as he finally stomped on the gas. I didn't bother telling him that everything Carl Cooper had said hadn't been spoken, it would probably confuse him too much. I personally didn't understand it all that well myself.

We were nearly 15 minutes late for first period; I walked into Iain's class when he was in the middle of handing back our book reports.

"Nice of you to join us, Miss. Jones," Iain said, but his eyes betrayed his concern. I quickly averted my gaze and shrugged, making my way to my seat. "Anyway, the majority of you really need to pick more advanced novels," Iain remarked, handing a book report to Riley. "Unfortunately, *Goosebumps* doesn't really count as your grade level."

"Seriously? *Goosebumps*?" Callie scoffed.

"Didn't you do *The Baby-Sitters Club*?" Jenna said sharply, causing the entire class to laugh.

Callie shot her a death glare.

"Someone's a little testy today. Didn't get enough to eat this morning?" Callie questioned, her voice dripping with fake concern and looking pointedly at Jenna's stomach.

"What's that supposed to mean?" Jenna demanded.

"Oh nothing, just that someone's been packing on the poundage lately," Callie chuckled. "You should really try to eat better, Jenna."

"Ladies, that's quite enough," Iain's voice sharply rang out, cutting off Jenna's reply.

Jenna tossed her stuff heatedly into her bag and kicked back her chair, leaving the classroom without a second glance. The entire class "Ooo'ed" and "Ahh'd" as Callie laughed about how Jenna couldn't take a joke.

I gave Iain a look and he nodded. Standing up, I grabbed my own bag that I hadn't even unpacked yet and followed Jenna out of the classroom.

I knew I'd find her in the same bathroom on the second floor where I always found her. She was crying softly in one of the stalls.

"Jenna? Are you okay?" I asked, knocking against the door.

Jenna opened it, her cheeks wet with tears. "No, I'm not okay! I don't want this baby. I don't want to get fat. I don't want people knowing and thinking...things about me."

I glanced around, making sure we were alone. "If they knew the truth, they'd never think anything bad about you," I told her. "You're doing an admirable thing that most women aren't strong enough to do."

"What if *I'm* not strong enough?" Jenna whispered, staring at her feet. "What if I don't want to do this anymore?"

"There's still...that other option," I reminded her. "You could still get an abortion, up to 20 weeks."

"I can't do that," Jenna wailed, chewing on her lip. "I spent all fucking weekend looking at that picture. I can't...I can't do any of this!"

"Jenna, calm down," I r, drawing her close to me and putting my arms around her. "It's going to be okay. You just... you just need support. Apparently I'm not very good at it."

"No, you are." Jenna wiped at her tears, backing away from me. "I can't expect you to be at my every beck and call. I need...I need my mom. But I'm so scared to tell her."

"Do you want me to go with you?" I asked gently. Jenna nodded. "Okay, I'll go with you then. I already told you I would. Whenever you want me to, I'll be there."

"Can we go now?" Jenna asked, surprising me. It was the last thing I expected her to say, but then again, she looked like a girl who desperately needed her mother.

"Now?" I repeated, confused. She nodded, looking away and biting down on her lip.

"My mom is the only one who's home right now. I couldn't stand to tell them both at the same time...it's...it's too much."

"Then, okay," I said, picking up my bag off the floor where I'd dropped it. "Let's go."

Jenna pulled into the driveway of her house and turned off the car, taking deep and shaky breaths. She was practically hyperventilating. We got out of the car and I wrapped my arm around her protectively as we came up the walkway.

Jenna pushed open the front door, calling out for her mom. I was kicking off my boots when Jenna's mom appeared in the foyer.

"Jenna! Why aren't you at school? Is everything okay?" she asked. The woman looked very similar to Jenna—same blonde hair, same blue eyes and petite features. Her face was lined with age and experience though.

"No." Jenna started to cry and hyperventilate. Her mother and I led her to the living room, and Mrs. Burke tried hard to calm her down. Finally, she got up and grabbed a glass of water.

"You need to breathe, Jenna," I whispered, rubbing her upper back with my hand. "Breathe..."

When Mrs. Burke came back with the water, Jenna had nearly gotten it under control. Her tears were now silently falling as she took a sip of the water and hiccupped.

"Who is this young lady?" Mrs. Burke asked, eyeing me with open curiosity and wariness.

"I'm Harlow Jones," I said, extending my hand across Jenna. She shook it.

"It's nice to meet you," Mrs. Burke said, still frowning as she watched Jenna cry. "Now Jenna, what's going on? Why aren't you in school?" she asked, sitting on the ottoman across from Jenna.

"I'm...I'm pregnant," Jenna wailed.

"Okay, probably not the best way to break it to her," I sighed, speaking loudly over Jenna's cries.

"Mrs. Burke, a few months ago...Jenna was raped at a party. She's...pregnant from the rapist."

If people could actually die from shock, I honestly worried about Mrs. Burke. She went pallor white to sea green in a matter of seconds.

"Honey...is this true?" she asked, her eyes darting back and forth between the both of us.

Jenna nodded. "I wanted to tell you sooner, but I was ashamed." Jenna hiccupped again. "I know I shouldn't have gone to that party, but Callie said it'd be fun. And...and I only had one drink, Mama. Just one. Then I couldn't remember anything but bits and pieces and pain and Harlow came in and—"

Mrs. Burke had gotten on her knees and was frantically brushing the hair from Jenna's face. "Jenna, relax, baby, relax," she said, cradling her close. To me, she asked, "You were there?"

"Yeah," I answered, softly. "And yes...I saw who it was. Fought him, actually...kind of." I shrugged.

"Who was it?"

"Don't," Jenna interrupted. "Don't, Mama. It doesn't matter."

"Of course it matters, Jenna. If you know who it is, we can do something about it." Mrs. Burke spoke softly, reassuringly stroking Jenna's hair. She fell silent against her mother. "Now who was it?"

"Andrew Cooper," I answered after a moment of silence.

"Carl Cooper's son?" Mrs. Burke asked, stunned. I was stunned myself. I hadn't realized she would know who he was. But then again, the entire town seemed to know who the Coopers were.

I nodded. "I've told Jenna, I will testify in court if she chooses to press charges." I told Mrs. Burke seriously. I'd also given thought to telling her about Jake, but I couldn't speak on whether or not he'd testify too. Though he'd been there and helped prevent it from being a lot worse than it was, for me anyway, and had helped me get Jenna home...I hadn't even talked to him yet about the possibility of testifying.

"Thank you so much," Mrs. Burke said, tears running down her own face. "Jenna, baby, we'll figure this out, okay? Don't worry, you aren't in trouble," she added, speaking into Jenna's hair.

I felt awkward standing there, watching them embrace. "I'm...gonna head home. Okay, Jenna? Call me if you need anything."

She nodded, or at least I thought she did. I put my boots back on and scooped up my bag, looking toward the living room one last time. I could hear Mrs. Burke gently speaking, calming Jenna. I couldn't help but feel an ache and a tug in my heart as I thought about my own relationship with my mother.

Jenna didn't live insanely far away from where I lived, but it was quite the trek through all the snow. Had I not had a massive fight with Mom before school, I would have called and asked for a ride. Stubbornly, I pressed onward, shivering.

The walk gave me plenty of time to think. I thought about how Mom had reacted to learning about Iain. I thought about Iain, and my feelings for him, which grew stronger every day. I hadn't realized just how strong my feelings were until our relationship had been jeopardized. I thought about Jenna, and about the Coopers.

There was so much going on in my head that I didn't think there was enough space to absorb anything else.

I was nearly home, about a block away, when a big blue Ford 150 came barrelling from behind me. I heard the squealing of tires and glanced behind me in time to see it dangerously close to me. I recognized the truck instantly, although the driver was a blur. I leaped sideways at the last possible second, falling into the muddy, slushy, snowy ditch hard enough to knock the wind out of my lungs. Gasping, I sat up and stared after the truck. It kept driving as if it never nearly run me over in the first place.

"Are you fucking kidding me?" I couldn't stop myself from yelling as angry tears spilled over. "What the fuck is with today?" I tried to stand up, but I had twisted my ankle in the jump. Of course. I couldn't just nearly get hit by a truck, and not just any truck but a truck that looked exactly like Andrew Cooper's. I also had to injure my ankle enough to not be able to walk on it. I could feel it swelling already, my boot digging painfully into it.

Tears nearly blinding me, I pulled my phone out of my coat pocket and called my mom.

She was there in less than five minutes, parking horribly on the side of the road and running down into the ditch to me.

"Harlow! Are you alright?" she asked, looking positively terrified.

"I'm fine; the truck didn't hit me. I just twisted my ankle or something jumping out of the way."

"It's broad daylight! How did the driver not see you?" she fretted, trying to examine my ankle through my boot.

"Oh, I think he saw me alright," I muttered angrily.

"What are you talking about?" Mom asked, staring at me.

"It's a long story. I'll tell you if you help me out of this cold ditch. I can't feel my ass anymore."

Mom tossed my arm around her shoulder and pulled me up, helping me climb out of the ditch. She opened the passenger side and I slid in, tenderly lifting my ankle and wincing when I accidentally set it down too hard.

"We're going to the emergency room," Mom declared, slamming her door shut and starting the engine. I nodded, figuring that was probably a good idea. I watched her for a moment, taking in her tired eyes and the worry lines creasing her face. There was a sadness in her expression that only I seemed to bring out. Guilt overwhelmed me.

"I'm sorry, Mom," I whispered, looking at her.

"No, I'm sorry, Harlow." She sighed. "I always knew I'd failed you the first time. I failed to protect my baby. But I hadn't realized I'd failed you a lot more after that."

"It wasn't your fault...any of it," I told her.

"Being a mother is tough," Mom told me. "When things happen to your children, you can't help but feel the weight of guilt at failing to protect them. Maybe one day you'll understand."

"Maybe," I said distractedly, forcing myself to not even entertain that thought. I bit down on my lip again, thinking that I should tell her about Jenna and Andrew. I wasn't used to sharing things with her, though.

"As for Iain—" I started to say.

"Don't," Mom instructed, lifting her hand. "Right now, I'd like to just get you to the hospital. I can't even think about that."

I nodded, feeling a little disappointed. She still sounded ashamed. I stared out the window, willing myself to not cry. While I wasn't ashamed of what Iain and I had, I was ashamed of the circumstances and how it made us both look.

Mom pulled into the hospital parking lot and helped me inside.

I ended up spending four hours in the waiting room to find out that I had a fractured ankle. I missed my shift at the diner and was told to use crutches and take it easy for a week or so.

After I got home, Mom helped me into bed and I grabbed for my cell phone and the card that Mike Turner had given me. Iain had texted me, demanding that I call him immediately. I listened to it ring, my heart pounding in my chest loudly.

"Officer Mike Turner," he greeted, his voice full of bored authority.

"Officer Turner? It's Harlow Jones...I—" I started to say, taking a deep breath.

"I remember you." Mike's voice had changed, softened a bit. "How are you?"

"Not so good..." I answered honestly. "This afternoon, I was nearly hit by a truck that looked a lot like Andrew Cooper's truck."

"That's...interesting," Mike said heavily. "Are you alright?"

"I have a fractured ankle, but am otherwise okay. I dove out of the way before it could hit me," I told him, drawing in a shaky breath. "The thing is...I think he's stalking me. Trying to get me to leave town. And I'm not sure what I should do."

Mike took a deep breath himself. "Hang tight," he answered seriously. "Don't go anywhere alone, ever, and constantly be aware."

"That's the only advice you have?" I asked, feeling aggravated.

"I'm collecting evidence," Mike said in a hushed tone. "But all the people who could potentially help end up getting run out of town. So I need you to stay local and not let them get to you. Don't go anywhere alone. Don't put yourself in jeopardy. Any more issues arise, call me immediately, at the scene of. Program this number into your phone," he instructed.

"Okay..." I trailed off, feeling overwhelmed.

"And be careful," Mike added.

CHAPTER TEN

Although I was off work for the week, the next morning I still went to school. I didn't want to fall too behind with exams looming in the near future.

"What happened to you?" Jenna demanded, catching me walking alongside Jake in the hallway. She stared pointedly at my crutches.

"Nearly got run over by a truck walking home from your place," I answered, pausing for a moment. I was leaning the majority of my weight on my other leg.

"Wait, what?" Jenna frowned, hugging her binder to her chest.

"A truck—"

"I heard that part." She hesitated for a moment, exchanging a look with Jake.

"What color was the truck?" Jake demanded.

"Blue." I shrugged, uneasy at their stares and solemn faces.

"What make?" Jenna was now deadly serious. Even though I already had my suspicious, their reactions made me even more uneasy, as most things these days.

"Looked a lot like Andrew's truck," I said, adjusting the strap on my shoulder bag.

Jenna's face was ashen as she looked around the hallway at the students walking around us. "Harlow, he tried to run you over?"

"Yup, unless there are more blue Ford truck owners with a personal hate on for me," I replied warily.

"I didn't think he was actually that fucked up," Jake said, shaking his head.

"You don't know him as well as I know him," Jenna whispered, crushing her binder to her chest as she spoke. Jake looked at her sympathetically. I hadn't told him about the pregnancy, but he had been there that night too.

"Jenna, we should..." I motioned to Jake with a tip of my head. He was still looking at her.

"Not right now," she said. "We've got more important things to worry about. Like Andrew trying to turn you into road kill." Jenna's voice was quiet but still earned a few glances from a couple passing by students. She noticed, and instantly froze. "We'll talk about this later."

"Yeah," I agreed.

"But seriously, Harlow, get a ride from now on. From either me or Jake," Jenna added, looking at Jake to make sure he was alright with that. He nodded, looking at her intently.

"I think you guys are overreacting," I said to Jake, watching Jenna walk away.

"I don't think so," Jake told me, turning his serious eyes to mine. "He tried to run you down in broad daylight."

"How could I forget?" I looked down at my ankle pointedly. I knew they were right, but I didn't want to appear as scared as I felt.

"I guess this is what they mean when they say don't cross

the Coopers," Jake said, looking pensive and almost fearful for me.

The whole situation unsettled me to no end. I was anxious, wound up tight and ready to fall apart at the same time. All I wanted was to escape in Iain's arms. I didn't have any classes with Iain all day, and I knew he was desperate to see me.

I mulled over the entire situation all day long instead of paying attention in class. Several times, I was called on to answer a question in history class and couldn't even recall what the topic was that we were covering.

By the end of the day, I'd gone over it enough. Jenna was waiting by my locker, ready to drive me home. I'd texted her telling her that we needed to talk.

"So, what's up?" Jenna asked, eyeing me warily.

"Well, hello to you, too." I smiled. "And plenty of things are up, obviously." I raised my eyebrows slightly, silently reminding her about all the things Andrew Cooper had done to the two of us.

"And?" Jenna raised a dainty eyebrow, willing me to continue.

"Are we going to just let him continue to try and run down your friends and other random town folk?" I asked, cutting to the chase.

Jenna winced then sighed. "No, we're not." She looked around again, paranoid that someone was listening.

"We can wait until we get in your car." I bit back my irritation. I was getting extremely impatient with the paranoia— mine even more so. I was now conscious of all the listening ears and watchful eyes around us. It felt like people were staring at me more than usual.

I hobbled down the hall beside Jenna toward the doors that led to the student parking lot. We passed Iain, who was talking to Mr. Bookings near his classroom. I met his gaze and held it momentarily, willing myself to communicate without words that I missed him and wanted to see him. The likelihood of that happening was slight, at least for the next little while. I couldn't very well have Jenna drop me off at his house, and walking wasn't really an option. I dropped my gaze as I hobbled passed him.

Jenna held the door open for me and I awkwardly maneuvered my crutches through.

"That's got to be...interesting," Jenna remarked, watching me struggle to keep my book bag from knocking the crutch on my left side from under my arm.

"Hmmph," I muttered, taking care to not slip on the icy patches in the parking lot. Jenna pulled out her remote starter and unlocked the doors, then she held mine open for me and took my crutches so I could crawl into the passenger side. She opened the back door and placed them gently across the back seat, then closed both the doors and made her way to the driver's side. I watched her, curious. She had a very slight pouch. It wasn't quite recognizable as a pregnancy belly yet, but it was getting there. She saw me staring and frowned, zipping up her coat.

"It's alright, you don't have to do that." I rolled my eyes. "I kind of know."

"It makes me uncomfortable to have people...look at it," Jenna answered, her voice small and vulnerable. I could imagine her exact feelings toward it; a constant reminder of that night. "Even you."

"Sorry." I cringed. I hadn't realized how sensitive Jenna still was about it all. "Did your dad freak out?"

"Kind of, but not in the way I thought he would." Jenna's voice was shaky. She took a steadying breath and put the key in the ignition, refusing to meet my gaze.

"Well?" I looked at her, impatiently.

"He is hiring a lawyer. Taylor Thompson. The best lawyer in Ontario, pretty much," Jenna answered. "Guess I'm pressing charges after all."

"That's great!" I said, struggling to hide my smile as she backed out of the parking spot.

"No, not really." Jenna gaped at me, stopping the car. "Andrew nearly ran you over, and you've barely done anything. If I press charges...I can't even..." she shivered, still half pulled out of her spot. Some kids in an old Sunfire honked at her, irritated. She hopped back to attention and finished backing out, joining the line of students exiting the parking lot.

"I think you're safe," I answered honestly. "I can't imagine them being stupid enough to try anything to harm you when you go to press charges. That would be a little obvious, don't you think?" I hoped my words were true. Andrew had done enough to Jenna.

"Let's hope so." Jenna absently rested a hand on her stomach. I didn't even think she was aware of the action.

The remainder of the drive was relatively silent; both Jenna and I were lost in our own thoughts. I was thinking about how we'd need to talk to Jake and track down other victims of Andrew's. Building a strong case was crucial. Not that I had to worry about that anymore. Jenna's lawyer would handle all of it. Hopefully, if he got names anyway.

"Thanks for the ride," I said after she pulled into the driveway at Mom and Larry's. Jenna nodded, biting on her lip.

"Um. Harlow? Could I...hang out with you for a bit?" Jenna asked, looking awkward. "I...I don't want to go back to my house right now. I don't want to have my parents looking at me the way they've been looking at me."

"Yeah, sure," I answered. Truthfully, I was a little caught off guard. I had skipped several classes with her, hung out at her place to watch movies, accompanied her to her ultrasound appointment and had been with her when she told her mother she was pregnant, but she had yet to meet my mom and Larry. In fact, I'd told Mom and Larry very little about her. The details of my life were kept fairly silent, and I often didn't divulge information unless I absolutely had to. Like the whole Iain thing.

Jenna tried to rush around to the other side of her car to help me out and get me my crutches, but I half-beat her to it. I hopped on my one foot and opened the door by the time she'd gotten over to my side of the car. She reached around me, grabbing the crutches, and handed them gently to me.

"Thanks," I told her, feeling a little awkward. I wasn't really used to having someone help me. I made my way up the front steps and into the house. Mom and Larry were both still gone, so the house was empty. Mom's grey tabby cat, Felix greeted us at the door, nearly tripping me as he weaved around my crutches.

"Seriously?" I grumbled. "Damn cat never pays me any attention until I come home with these. Suddenly he's always under foot." Maybe it was in cahoots with the Coopers.

I cringed at my own inward joke. It really wasn't funny. At least I could be thankful that I hadn't blurted that aloud with Jenna standing close to me.

Jenna cooed at him, picking him up. It was evident by the look on her face that she loved cats. Felix purred loudly as she stroked behind his ears. I was more of a dog person.

"He's so cute!" she told me, carrying him into the living room.

"Oh yeah, he's super cute. Especially when he's puking all over my comforter." I yawned, feeling a little worn down. Walking around in crutches was hard work. "Do you want anything to drink or eat? Mom's kind of on a healthy food kick but the red pepper hummus is great with pita bread."

"That sounds amazing," Jenna said, gently putting Felix down. "I can get it—just direct me, you sit down."

"No really, I'm fine. I still have my foot—it's not cut off or anything," I argued, making my way into the kitchen. I opened the fridge and awkwardly leaned forward, grabbing the hummus. Then I used my armpit to move the one crutch as I held the tub of hummus in my hand and grabbed the bag of pita bread off the counter.

"Okay, on second thought...maybe you could grab a couple bottles of water," I added. Jenna nodded, going back to the refrigerator and grabbing two bottles of water from the door shelf.

We parked ourselves in front of the TV, changing the channel to MTV for some terrible reality shows to watch while we vegged out.

It was weird. I hadn't done anything like this since before Lauren died. She used to come over to my place, or vice versa, nearly every day after school. We would pig out on junk food and watch crappy TV, talking nonstop about whatever topics came to mind.

I felt a pang in my heart, a pang that I was almost accustomed to feeling. It was the sting of missing Lauren and remembering that she was gone. I swallowed hard, willing myself to come back, and muted the TV.

"So, what do you think of Jake?" I asked, needing to distract myself before the grief overwhelmed me. Jenna's jaw dropped open in surprise.

"What do you mean?" she asked, looking at me cautiously.

"I mean...what do you think about him?" I didn't really know what I meant. I didn't know if I was asking her if she'd ever be into him, or if I was just looking for a gateway into broaching the topic of how we needed to ask him about possibly testifying. I figured lawyer speak would be too heavy, although I wanted to talk about it. I knew the reason she didn't want to go home immediately was so that she could avoid lawyer discussion for a bit. "He's cute, right?"

"Yeah, I guess so." Jenna shrugged, biting her lip. "I'm not really looking for a guy right now...you know." She glanced down at her stomach and swallowed hard. "I've got a lot on my plate."

"I know," I said quickly, inwardly kicking myself. I really lacked tact. "It's just...I get the impression he's fond you." It was true. I did get that impression. I'd noticed the way he had started looking at her in the hallway.

"He pities me, Harlow." Jenna rolled her eyes. "It's not the same thing. Besides, I really...couldn't."

Before I could reply, I heard the front door close with a click and someone put their keys down on the little table in the foyer. Seconds later, Mom walked into the living room and leaned against the doorway. Guilt and shame welled up in the pit of my stomach. We still weren't exactly on speaking terms.

"Hey, Mom. This is Jenna," I said, trying to keep my voice even.

"Oh, hi!" Mom said in the warmest tone she had used in days. "It's nice to finally meet you! Harlow's mentioned you before, but to be honest, I kind of thought she invented you."

"No, I'm real." Jenna smiled, giggling. It was the same giggle I'd heard on the first day of school.

"Well, that's great." Mom smiled, meeting my gaze. "We'll talk later, okay, Harlow?" she said pointedly. "Have fun, you two," she added before walking off to do whatever it was that she did when she wasn't hovering around me.

"Your mom seems nice," Jenna remarked, taking another pita and dipping it in the humus.

"Hmmph." I nodded, my thoughts stuck on Mom's pointed comment about talking later. I could only guess what she wanted to talk about.

Almost unaware I was even moving, I grabbed my phone out of my pocket and checked my text messages. I'd had about six missed texts. A couple were from Jake, asking if it was cool that he pick me up in the morning, but the rest were from Iain. He'd texted that he missed me and couldn't wait to see me, and that if circumstances were different, he'd be visiting me and taking care of me. It warmed my heart and made me feel sad at the same time as I too wished for the millionth time that circumstances were different.

"Seriously, this is ridiculous. It's been two weeks—why can't you guys stop babysitting me?" I demanded as I flopped dramatically into Jenna's car after school two weeks later. My ankle was fit as a fiddle again, and I was tired of the chaperones. It made getting to see Iain incredibly difficult, especially with my mom keeping me on almost lockdown too. Every night when I worked, she'd show up to pick me up 30 minutes before my shift ended so I'd have no choice but to go straight home.

My stress level was at an all time high. I hadn't physically been with Iain for far too long for my liking, and it was looking like another night would pass without seeing him. It was getting harder and harder to not jump him in the middle of English class. I knew he was feeling the tension too, and I knew that our steamy texts didn't help either of us. I hated that I was that dependent, but I had never felt that way before.

"Better to be safe than sorry," Jenna said, shrugging.

"Besides, I thought you liked hanging out with me," she added, looking a little hurt.

"I do." I sighed, feeling a little guilty that I'd upset her. It was getting easier to do, but I attributed that to the pregnancy hormones. "I just haven't seen...my boyfriend in a while."

"You're still with him? Ben, right?" Jenna asked, surprised. "I kind of thought you weren't anymore, since you haven't mentioned him or anything..."

"Yeah, I'm with him. He just can't come see me right now, so that sucks. I guess I'm moping," I answered, thankful she reminded me what name I'd given Iain.

"Well, that's been obvious," Jenna remarked. "I thought it was just exam related."

"No," I groaned, thinking about how they were supposed to start tomorrow. We would have two exams per day, all week long. Then it would be Christmas break. I was both looking forward to Christmas break and dreading it. I had no idea if my lockdown was going to lessen. Since Mom knew about Iain, it wasn't likely, but she was starting to give me a little more freedom, at least when it came to Jenna.

"We'll study at your place if you want," Jenna offered. "I spent all last night making cue cards."

"You do that too?" I asked, surprised. I hadn't pegged Jenna as the cue card type.

"Yeah." Jenna shrugged. "I always have. Bet you thought I 'studied' like Tara and Callie, huh?"

"The thought crossed my mind," I joked. I knew Jenna didn't talk to Tara or Callie anymore. After the heated exchange on the day I fractured my ankle, those friendships had gone up in smoke. Jenna didn't seem bothered by it at all. She was hanging out with me more and more, and I didn't mind it either. although I did really miss Iain. I frowned, thinking about him again.

"What's wrong?" Jenna asked.

"Ben. My Mom doesn't really like him," I answered, partly telling the truth. "She's forbidden me to continue seeing him, and has graciously offered to keep the information from Larry."

Jenna nodded in sudden understanding. She'd met Larry a handful of times now, and he gave off the same stern, religious aura as per usual.

"So what, he's like...a bad boy or something?"

"He's just...not my type." I shrugged. "Or so they think."

"Ah, it's a race thing." Jenna nodded wisely. I bit back my laughter, deciding to let her think what she wanted to think. There was a pause in our conversation, then Jenna looked at me. "You could always tell them you're spending time at my house and go see him...if you want."

"Oh, Jenna, you've got enough to worry about, excluding my petty dramas," I quickly argued.

She shrugged. "You've done a lot to help me, and you've been a really great friend so I want to help. I don't mind covering for you."

"Well, thanks," I said, chewing on my lip. "Do you mind... covering for me Friday, maybe?"

"Sure." Jenna smiled. "Sleepover at my place?" She winked.

That evening, we spent a couple of hours studying at the table until Mom and Larry came home from whatever church potluck function they'd attended. Mom carried her half-empty casserole dish to the counter and gave us a warm smile. She seemed to really like Jenna.

"Hey, Mom, Larry, could I spend Friday night at Jenna's?" I asked.

"We're planning on having an 'end of term' girls' night," Jenna added easily. "Pedicures, manicures, facials and the latest Ryan Gosling movie."

"Oh, well...alright," Mom said, looking back and forth

between us. I knew she liked Jenna, but she still didn't trust me, although she couldn't exactly express that without giving away, well, everything.

"Great." I grinned. "The new Ryan Gosling movie, eh? Is every girl obsessed with him?"

"You would have to be dead not to be," Jenna rolled her eyes. "Not only is he incredibly hot, but he's a great actor!"

"What's this movie about?" I asked, trying to appear serious.

"Um..."

"All you're able to think about right now is Ryan Gosling's abs, am I right?" I laughed. Mom smiled, put at ease by our bantering, and followed Larry into the living room to watch TV.

We continued to study for another hour before Jenna finally called it quits.

"My brain feels like mush," she said, yawning and shoving her books and notes back into her book bag. "I'm done. I'm going to go home and sleep for a thousand hours."

"You'll miss the exam," I pointed out.

"I know," she said, yawning again. "Obviously that's just wishful thinking. But I'm headed home anyway."

"Alright. And don't worry about me in the morning—Jake's got it covered," I told her, rolling my eyes dramatically. She nodded, yawning again as she stood up.

It was nearly 10 p.m., and I heard Mom and Larry turning off the TV in the living room. She came into the kitchen, where I was still sitting with my notes spread all over the table.

"Get some rest," she told me, kissing my forehead and pausing for a moment. "You need sleep almost as much as you need to study."

"I know. I'll be going to bed in a bit," I told her, suppressing a yawn. She opened her mouth, about to say something, when Larry appeared in the doorway.

"Good night, Harlow," he said.

"Night." I barely looked up from my notes, highlighting another not-so-important part. Mom and Larry left the kitchen and I heard them getting ready for bed. I sat at the table, listening until I couldn't hear anything anymore. Then I pulled out my cell phone to text Iain.

I miss you. 'Rents are in bed...maybe I'll pop over, I clicked send and double checked that my volume was on mute. Iain took less than a minute to reply.

I wish. Not a good idea. See you tomorrow after exam?

I bristled, angry. Iain had been shutting down every attempt I tried to make to see him. A tiny wave of insecurity swelled in the pit of my stomach. A small voice whispered, *Maybe he just doesn't want to see you anymore.*

I frowned, not bothering to reply. I was a little bit frustrated. Since the accident, I had barely seen him. I felt his desire roll off in waves every time I walked near him, but I couldn't understand why he was keeping me at arm's length.

My phone vibrated again, and I opened the latest text message. *Mike is over, we're having beers.*

Sighing at how ridiculous I'd been, I texted him back with *Okay, see ya later then.* I put my notes back in my bag and went to my room. Tomorrow was going to come quickly, and Mom was right. I did need my sleep.

Thankfully, exams went by quickly, and before I knew it, Friday had arrived and I was preparing for a "sleepover" at Jenna's house.

"We might make it into a weekend thing," I told Mom,

swinging my bag over my shoulder as I stood in the front hall. I'd packed a change of clothes, something to sleep in, and my work things—I had to work tomorrow morning. "Jenna's having a bit of a rough time right now."

"I meant to ask," Mom said, hesitating by the doorway, a dish towel in hand. "Is...she..."

I held my breath, waiting for her to continue, but she wouldn't, she just stared at me, waiting for my answer. I sighed, tightening my grip on my bag. "Yes, Mom. She is."

"That's—"

"Not what you think," I corrected her, giving her a stern look. "Jenna was...she didn't consent to it, and she doesn't want—"

"Oh." Mom's voice was tiny. She looked genuinely shocked. I glanced at the clock on the microwave and sighed.

"I went to a party at the beginning of the year with Jake. I walked in on some guy with Jenna. She was crying, hysterical, begging him to stop. He didn't..." I still had difficulty saying the word 'rape,' and avoided it entirely with my mom.

"That's terrible!" Mom said, putting a hand over her mouth. "Does she know...?"

"Yes," I said quickly. "Her dad's hired a lawyer. But please don't tell anybody; nobody knows but me and now her family."

"I...I won't, I promise." Mom looked overwhelmed. I knew she felt the burden of carrying secrets more than most, especially all the ones I had dumped on her recently.

"Thanks, Mom..." I trailed off. I knew I could always tell her more, and that I probably should, but I couldn't bear to add to the overwhelmed look on her face. "So, I'll be home Sunday afternoon at some point?"

Mom nodded. I knew she wanted to ask me about Iain. but at the same time, she wanted to avoid the subject. I followed suit with the second motion, and turned around to leave. I told Mom I would walk to Jenna's.

Iain knew I was coming ahead of time, so he left the door unlocked. I let myself inside, and I could hear him in the kitchen.

"Hey," he called out, coming into the foyer and drying his hands on the back of his jeans. I smiled at him, instantly put at ease at the look on his face as he walked over to where I was standing. He gently tipped my chin up and lowered his lips to mine in a slow and tender kiss. It had been a while since he'd been able to kiss me. Instantly, his kiss turned from tender to urgent. My hands tangled in his hair, he slid my jacket off my shoulders and it fell to the floor.

He pressed me against the wall, his hands roaming my body. He gripped my right thigh and pulled it up over his hip, pressing me back against the wall and never breaking the kiss. I wrapped my legs around his waist and he carried me out to the living room. Candles lined the coffee table and end tables, and there were even rose peddles strewen about. I pulled away, taking it in with surprise. Iain continued to kiss my neck.

"You did all this?" I asked, motioning to the roses and candles. He smiled against my skin, not breaking away to look me.

"Yes," he murmured, his voice vibrating against my neck. I shivered with pleasure and brought my mouth back to his.

His blue eyes were aglow with desire, and I knew what he wanted instantly. I pulled him hard against me, urging him on. I needed it as much as he did. When he finally found his release (just after I found mine for the fourth time), he traced slow kisses up my collarbone and went to speak.

He was interrupted by the shrill screeching of the fire alarm.

"Shit," he said, diving off me and rushing toward the

kitchen. I couldn't help but laugh as his naked body disappeared around the corner. I pulled my jeans and shirt back on before I went to find out what disastrous thing awaited me in the kitchen.

Iain was prodding at a very black lump of meat on a cooking tray with a solemn frown on his face.

"Um...did you cook dinner too?" I asked, putting my hand to my mouth to silence my laughter.

"I tried to," Iain confessed, sighing. He wiped his moist brow with his left hand and tossed the fork down with the other. Then he turned to look at me with a sheepish smile on his face. "Mind if we order in?"

I took another look at the black lump and nodded eagerly. As much as I loved Iain, I knew I couldn't stomach whatever that was. I wasn't even sure if I could chew it.

"Chinese it is," Iain sighed, reaching into the top drawer and pulling out a menu. He quickly placed our order while I continued to inspect him. He was still naked, standing in the kitchen without a bother. He saw me watching him and gave me a knowing smile.

"Yes, that's delivery. 48 Orion Street," Iain said, staring at me. "Twenty minutes? Perfect." He hung up the phone and I walked over to his open arms.

"It means a lot to me that you tried to cook," I told him, smiling against his chest. He chuckled.

"Yeah, cooking's never been my strong suit. I'm much better with a take-out menu," Iain replied, rubbing the small of my back.

"Yeah, you're great at eating out," I joked.

He laughed, pushing me away gently but grabbing my hand. "So I've been told," he replied, cockily. "Do you mind if I get dressed?"

"Yes, I do. Remain naked," I ordered, following him back

into the living room. He released my hand and picked up his t-shirt.

"Unfortunately, I have to answer the door and I don't really want to do that naked," he said, pulling his shirt over his head and slipping into his jeans. I frowned, disappointed. "Don't worry, I'll be naked again very soon," he predicted, kissing me again.

Then he sat down, pulling me on top of him. I straddled him, peering down at him through the dark curtain of my hair. "So, it's been a while. What have you been up to, Mr. Bentley?"

"Oh, you know. Work, sleep, that kind of thing." Iain shrugged. "It's been boring here without you," he added, taking a strand of my hair and gently toying with it between his fingers.

"Well, I would have been over in a heartbeat if you hadn't kept rejecting me," I answered, trying not to pout. It had really gotten under my skin. Iain looked at me, seeing that, and sighed.

"Harlow, you know I wanted to see you. But it wasn't practical. Mike was over, and you nearly got run over—"

"Yeah, I know, I'm aware," I huffed, irritated. I looked away, not voicing that my desire had been to see him there for me. He knew it though; I could tell by the torn look in his eyes.

"You know I would have been there, if circumstances were different," Iain said softly.

"I—" I trailed off, hit with the sudden realization that I hadn't even told him that my mother knew. It had honestly gotten pushed to the very back of my mind between Jenna, the accident, and not being able to see Iain. It hadn't felt like a topic that I could broach over text messaging, or in class for that matter.

"What is it?" Iain froze, seeing the look on my face.

"I have something to tell you..." I sighed.

Iain waited, patiently looking at me with those deep blue eyes.

"My mom found out about us," I replied, cringing at the shocked look on Iain's face. "When we got home from Niagara Falls. I had a shower, and when I was in the shower she snooped through my bags and found the photos we took..."

"Whoa," Iain breathed, still stunned. "And you didn't feel that this was something I needed to know? Where does she think you are right now?"

"Of course I felt like you needed to know," I snapped. "I was kind of recovering from nearly getting run over, and I didn't feel it was a conversation to have over texting, since you didn't come around."

"I couldn't," Iain protested.

I clenched my jaw and sighed. "I know. I'm sorry. I'm just...overwhelmed."

"What did she do when she found out?" Iain asked.

"She got pissed and told me to not see you again."

"Where does she think you are?" Iain's jaw was tense.

"At Jenna's. But that doesn't matter, does it? Nobody would want us together and it's not like I'd disclose where I was if she didn't know."

Iain paused, considering. "That's true."

"Mom doesn't want to...rat me out to Larry. I know she won't. If I know her like I know her, she's going to pretend that I called it off like she asked me to, even though I told her I wasn't going to. She won't ask about it, but she'll probably try to keep grounding me—just in case."

"What do you want to do, Harlow?" Iain asked, his voice heavy and loaded with uncertainty.

"What we're already doing," I whispered, kissing his jaw line gently. "I want to be with you, however I can be with you."

"I knew this would be difficult." Iain sighed, turning his

lips to mine. He smiled warily. "I just didn't realize how hard it'd be to keep my distance from you."

I looked at him curiously. I wasn't sure if he meant the last few weeks, or if he was talking about putting distance between us now. He kissed me, and my questions evaporated on the tip of my tongue. His hands tangled in my hair as he deepened his kiss. We pulled away slowly when the doorbell rang. Iain gently lifted me off his lap and headed toward the door, pulling his wallet out of his back pocket.

He returned moments later with our food, and we ate in the living room, bathed in candle light. When we finally finished some time later, Iain discarded his carton on the table and turned to face me.

"Mike's been doing some sleuthing," he said, getting straight to it. "He's managed to track down a few names of other victims. He has a list of three girls."

"Has he contacted them?" I asked, my light, joyful mood suddenly serious.

"No, not yet, but he's biding his time. He needs a victim to come forward before he can contact the others."

"Well, that will be sooner than he thinks. Jenna finally told her parents," I told him, proud of my friend. "Her dad has hired a really good lawyer."

"That's awesome!" Iain said, looking relieved.

"I'm going to be testifying about the night of the party, you know, since I was there." My throat was dry, so I took a sip of the can of Pepsi he'd set out for me.

"Will Jake?" Iain inquired, gently squeezing my thigh.

"Not sure. I haven't reminded Jenna about him yet," I confessed. "I'll do that next time I see her. But right now, no more talking." I set my can of pop back on the coffee table.

"What else would you like to do?" Iain asked, wriggling his eyebrows suggestively.

"Cuddle?" I asked, sounding just as vulnerable as I felt. Iain smiled warmly at me, reaching for my hand. He gently pulled me on top of him and fixed an afghan around the both of us. He grabbed the remote and switched it to some Discovery Channel show, and I fell asleep with my head resting on his chest, listening to the sound of his heart beating.

CHAPTER ELEVEN

The next morning, I woke up feeling as if a slight weight was lifted off my shoulders. Mike had a list of Andrew's victims; Jenna had the best lawyer and was going to press charges. Hopefully one day soon, the town would know about the Coopers. Both of them.

It was a relief for more than that, really. Originally, I'd wanted to track down every single girl myself and talk to them each, help them realize how important it was to take a stand against Andrew Cooper, but now that Jenna's dad had hired the best lawyer to handle the case, I wasn't sure what to do. On the one hand, I didn't want to tamper with anything. On the other hand, how did I know this new lawyer wasn't on the Coopers' payroll? When I expressed my concerns to Iain, he nodded in agreement.

"I spoke to Mike about that too," he told me. "And no, Taylor Thompson is not on the Coopers' payroll. He's a big lawyer in Ottawa, probably never even heard of the Coopers before."

"Okay." I nodded, feeling slightly more reassured.

"Relax, Harlow." Iain smiled, gently squeezing my shoulders. "Mike will handle it. You've got to trust the professionals here."

"Forgive me, trusting the law enforcement in this town is a little hard to do," I said sarcastically.

After my weekend with Iain came to a close, I stopped in at Jenna's place. Her parents were out grocery shopping, so Jenna and I sat in the living room comfortably.

"So, how was your weekend?" she asked, her voice light and happy.

"Good." I smiled. "We just...hung out—something we haven't been able to do for a while."

"Ah, forbidden love. Like Romeo and Juliet." Jenna smiled wistfully. "I wish I had that."

"You wish you had a forbidden love?" I asked, raising my eyebrow.

"Well, you know what I mean." Jenna frowned. "A love of any kind, really."

I could tell we were both thought about how hard it was to go through what she was going through alone, with nobody—aside from her parents—to hold her hand. I felt another wave of guilt. If only I'd arrived even five minutes earlier.

"It's not your fault," Jenna added, as if sensing my thought process.

"It's his," I agreed, anger rising again as I thought about Andrew's smug face. "And speaking of which...you told your lawyer that I would testify, right?"

"Yes." Jenna picked at a tiny thread on the cushion in her lap. "He actually wants to call you to set up a meeting."

"That's okay. You know, Jake might be able to testify too, if you asked him," I said, drawing in a breath between my sentences, unsure of how she'd react.

"I know." Jenna smiled sadly. "He's already told me that."

"Really? When?" I asked, shocked. I hadn't even realized they'd been talking without me.

"A couple days ago." Jenna shrugged. "He added me on Facebook a few weeks ago and we've been messaging each other."

"Oh." I tried to hide my smile, but Jenna caught it.

"Don't go there," she warned. "I'm still...in no position...for that."

"I didn't say a thing." I grinned.

Taylor Thompson ended up calling me that night to book an appointment the same day that he'd be meeting with the Burkes. His office was in Ottawa, and Iain jumped at the opportunity to make a three-day trip out of it. I got Danielle to cover my shifts, and told my parents I had to go to Ottawa to meet with Jenna's lawyer with her family. I did get a ride with them there, to ease Mom's worry lines and the anger I could see simmering, and Jenna covered for me when they offered to get me a hotel room. She'd told her parents that I would be visiting with my cousin at the University of Ottawa, and that I didn't need a room or a ride home. They didn't even question this; they were far too concerned about Jenna. The next few days was going to be busy for them too. I knew Jenna had a meeting at an adoption agency in Ottawa. She was still leaning toward putting the baby up for adoption, and her parents were supporting her decision. I knew that would swallow them up for the next couple of days.

Thompson first met with Jenna and her parents. I waited in the office waiting room, tapping my feet impatiently and texting with Iain. He was waiting in a nearby hotel—not the one where Jenna and her family were staying. He'd made sure of that. He'd also left town a little before Jenna's family and I left.

I got in touch with Mike once more before leaving with Jenna's family and told him that my friend would be pressing charges against Andrew for sexual assault—that I was on my way to meet with her lawyer, as I was testifying. I'd given him the name and number of Thompson, just in case he had any evidence of his own that he wanted to share with him. Mike had been surprised and wary of my call, but thanked me. I didn't know if he would call Thompson, but at least he knew that something was brewing.

I had never been in a lawyer's office before. Lauren's death had been open and shut. Rhys was charged once he tested positive for being completely out of his mind on coke, and he confessed. As far as I knew, he was still in jail for manslaughter and driving while intoxicated.

Finally, after nearly an hour, Jenna and her parents came out looking serious.

"He's ready to see you now," Thompson's secretary said, motioning for me to go inside. I went, clenching the folder to my chest a little as the door closed behind me.

"Good evening, Ms. Jones." Taylor Thompson smiled, shaking my hand. He was surprisingly young for a lawyer. I had pictured a portly elderly dude, like in the Stevenson & Stevenson Law commercials, but Taylor Thompson looked to be in his late thirties. His dark hair was just dusting with grey around the roots, and his eyes were bright and intelligent behind square framed glasses. "I've heard a lot about you."

"I'm sure you have," I said, instantly uncomfortable. The whole situation was extremely overwhelming. I wished for the thousandth time that morning that Iain could have come in with me. I knew I would have drawn strength off his mere presence.

"So, I understand you were there on the night of the incident?" Taylor Thompson asked, sitting down in his plush chair and getting right into it. He stared at me with an unwavering gaze.

"Yes..." I said, still uncomfortable but fighting not to show it. "I was. I walked in on it just as the slime ball crawled off her. I saw his face. I know who he is."

"Were you drinking that night?" Taylor Thompson asked.

"No," I shot back, a little angrily. "Even if I was, what does that matter?"

"Because the defence will ask you that," Thompson said evenly, writing something down in his notebook.

"Okay, well no. I wasn't drinking. I don't drink," I replied honestly. "I saw, I got into a fight with Andrew and he came at me. My friend, Jake, came in and scared him off. Then Jake helped me get Jenna home."

"Why didn't you take her to a hospital?" Thompson inquired.

"Because she wanted to go home." I stared right back at him. "I wasn't going to force her to do something she wasn't ready to do."

Thompson nodded, jotted something else down and looked at me again.

"I have a friend that I work with, Danielle. Her best friend was also...raped by Andrew, a few months ago," I told him. I'd forgotten to tell Jenna that, but I'd get around to it.

"Is she willing to testify?" Thompson asked, continuing to write on his legal pad.

"No, she's dead," I answered stiffly. Thompson's eyes shot up at me. "She committed suicide shortly after the rape."

"That's terrible," Thompson said, his voice nearly void of emotion.

I nodded; it was all I could think to do. "Andrew has also almost run me over and has tried attacked me twice while I've left my place of work," I added after a moment of silence that stretched too long for my comfort.

"Did you report it or press charges?" Thompson looked up quickly again, keen interest in every feature on his face.

"No." I shook my head. "Well, the second time, when he jumped a friend of mine, I gave a statement, but I'm not sure what the police did about it. Probably nothing. Andrew Cooper's father is the Chief of Police."

"So we've heard." Thompson sighed. "Look, next time Andrew comes near you, you call the police. Even if his dad is the Chief of Police. Keep reporting it; they can't keep covering it up."

"Okay." I felt like I was getting reprimanded by a fatherly figure for not doing my chores or getting good grades. It was a little unsettling.

Thompson sighed. "Would your friend...Jake, was it?" I nodded, and he continued, "Would he go to trial and say that he'd been there?"

"I think so," I answered.

"Will you?"

"Of course, why else would I be here?" I resisted the urge to roll my eyes.

"That's great. Anything you can get me is extremely helpful."

"You could probably talk to Danielle about Rachel, the girl who committed suicide."

"Would she cooperate in the trial?" Thompson looked back up at me, waiting for my reply.

"I could ask," I answered. I was sure that she would, but I

didn't want to commit her to something without even talking to her.

"Okay, good."

"When is it going to trial?" I asked, watching Thompson as he continued to write on the note pad.

"As soon as I get my case together. It's my top priority right now, but I don't want to rush things. It could take anywhere from a month to three," Thompson said, looking back at the paper.

I nodded, standing up. Thompson reached into a cardholder and selected one, handing it to me. "That's my card. Please call if you have anything else."

I left his office, seeing Jenna and her family still waiting for me.

"We're going to head back to the hotel; did you need a ride?" Mrs. Burke asked, standing up and sliding into her coat.

"No, thank you, my cousin's waiting for me here," I answered, smiling.

"Okay," Mrs. Burke nodded, looking at Jenna and her husband.

They both stood up and Mr. Burke reached out and took my hand. "I want to thank you again for doing this, Harlow," he said, his voice serious.

"Don't mention it," I replied, a little uncomfortable. Mrs. Burke smiled at me, and gently put her hand on her husband's arm.

"Text me, okay?" Jenna ordered. "When you get to the campus."

"I will," I assured her. She surprised me by wrapping her arms around me in a hug.

"Thanks again," she whispered. I felt a tear on my ear from her eye. She pulled away and smiled, her eyes still moist.

I walked with them out into the office lobby, then watched

them head to the underground parking lot. I called Iain, telling him I was ready. Ten minutes later, his car pulled to a stop in front of the office building. I walked toward it quickly. A car that looked like Mr. Burke's Impala drove by as I opened Iain's car door. I thought I saw Jenna's blonde locks, but couldn't tell if they'd seen me, or worse, Iain. I ducked inside, my heart racing. I hadn't even thought to double check my surroundings, as my mind had been so clouded with thoughts of the meeting with the lawyer.

"Everything okay?" Iain asked, looking at me.

"Yeah," I muttered, pulling my hair out from under my jacket and twisting it up into a bun to give my hands something to do.

Iain reached over and took my hand gently in his. "Okay," he said simply, pulling away from the office building. I watched in the rear view mirror until I couldn't see it anymore. Iain squeezed my hand gently, bringing my attention back to him.

"Sorry, what did you say?"

Iain smiled. "I asked if you wanted to go out for dinner."

"Oh." I thought about my earlier scare. "Could we order in?"

"We always order in." Iain frowned slightly. "But alright...if that's what you want." He pulled into a parking spot at the hotel and we got out of the car. I grabbed my bag and followed him inside. He took my hand and led me toward the elevator. He was working his jaw, a sign that he was aggravated. The moment the elevator doors closed, I shoved him roughly against the wall and started to kiss him intensely, determined to melt his aggravation away. He moaned, his hands pulling my jacket closer to him roughly. All too soon, the elevator dinged at our level. I gave him a mischievous smile and pulled him out of the elevator, laughing at the surprised expression on his face.

"What room are you, Mr. Bentley?" I purred.

His eyes heated, and he quickly led me down the hall to the room. He pulled out a key card from his jacket pocket and held the door open for me. I walked inside, turning to face him and backing up slowly as I started to take off my jacket and shoes. He shut and locked the door behind us, staring at my little show. I pulled my jeans off and slipped my shirt over my head. I was wearing a new matching set of a red lace thong and bra; I could practically see Iain salivating. I motioned for him to come over, and he did, slipping out of his own clothes.

Quickly, I forgot about my paranoia. In fact, I forgot almost everything but the feeling of Iain's lips on my body. Afterwards, as we lay entangled in the bed, Iain tracing kisses on my collarbone, I thought about it again. I winced.

"I think Jenna maybe saw us. Maybe. I don't know. I don't know if it was Jenna, or if she just saw me, or what..." My eyes were closed when I said this. I was scared of his reaction. He did pause and lift his lips slightly, but then I felt him shrug and go back to kissing me. "You're...not worried?"

"Can't do anything about that right now." Iain shrugged again, shifting so that he was supporting his weight on his left arm and running his right hand along my outer thigh. "Besides, maybe I want people to know," he added, pulling me forcefully onto him.

I laughed, straddling him. "You can't mean that," I whispered, leaning so that my face was inches from his. My hair fell like a curtain, obscuring the view from either side.

"I do," Iain answered, looking at me with sincerity. "I want more than anything to let everyone know how much I love you." My breath caught, and I stalled. He ran his hand up the small of my back, gently stroking. "Obviously, I know there are many implications and I can't...but I still want to."

I relaxed a bit, satisfied that he wasn't going to announce to our English class that he was in love with me. "But I have been thinking..."

"About?"

"About after you graduate," Iain answered, smiling. "Would you like to come with me?"

"Come with you where? Where are you going?" I stammered, confused.

"I'm not going anywhere, per se," Iain replied, still tracing his hands along my body. "In June, my post is finished. I'll be looking for a new job. I want to look wherever you're going to go to college."

"I...I don't know where I'm going," I said, taken aback. I couldn't help but picture it: him and I, living together. A couple in every way, not just in the ways we already were a couple. An involuntary smile touched the corners of my mouth, but I tried to repress it.

"That's alright." Iain smiled. "I'm not saying you need to make a decision now. Just let me know a few months ahead of time when you do." He paused. "Unless you'd rather—"

"No, I want...that," I cut him off, kissing him and leaning onto him. He hungrily kissed me back, his hands still tracing gentle patterns up my spine. I pulled away gently and laughed against his lips.

"What?" he asked, smiling.

"I'm hungry," I answered. "Let's go get something to eat."

"Really?" Iain's eyes lit up and I smiled.

"Yeah, really," I said, grabbing my clothes.

I dressed quickly, pulling my messy, tangled hair up in an equally messy high sock bun. I fixed my makeup while Iain waited patiently on the bed, fully dressed. It still amazed me how patient Iain constantly was. He never made any quips about me taking forever, like most waiting boyfriends would... even if I'd only taken 10 minutes. Rhys used to complain whenever I wasn't immediately ready to go with whatever plan he had, which usually was just attending some party with Lauren and Alex. Rhys had never taken me out on dates.

I forced that thought down. I didn't want to think about him while I was with Iain. I wouldn't let those memories sour our weekend. Instead, I looked at Iain's face and felt that happy glow returning to me.

"I'm ready," I told him, standing in the bathroom doorway. I had freshened up and hoped that I looked a little older than my actual age. Iain appraised me with a devious grin on his face.

"You look gorgeous, as always." Iain stood up. I smiled at him, slipping my leather jacket on, my sour mood replaced. "I'm curious about that jacket," Iain confessed, smiling ruefully. "You always wear this...it must be important to you?"

"It is," I said simply, turning my back to him so I could grab my purse off the floor. "It belonged to my dad. It's the last thing I have of his."

"Well, you wear it beautifully," Iain remarked, his breath warm on my neck.

I smiled again, taking his hand. "Let's go, I actually am seriously hungry," I said, dragging him out of the hallway.

We walked to the elevator, hand in hand, and out to his car. Darkness had fallen, and I took comfort in that. I don't know why I was still paranoid. I was miles away from home, but Jenna and her family were still in town...somewhere. I chewed on the inside of my cheek, worrying about this. I highly doubted they'd be spending a romantic evening out, as Iain and I were about to, but I still felt a prickly sensation on the back of my neck. Iain soon had me forgetting my worries though, as he kissed me passionately while opening the passenger door to his car. Hungrily, I ran my hands through his constantly mused hair, kissing him deeply back and moaning softly.

"Keep that up, and we won't make it anywhere," Iain said, chuckling and gently pulling away. He kissed me once more, then released me. I fell back into the seat with a genuine smile on my face. I watched as he walked around the front of the car, sweeping off the snow that had accumulated when we'd been in the hotel. Ottawa seemed to get hit just as badly as North Bay did. I was toasty warm in the car, thanks to Iain's remote starter.

When he finished clearing off the car, he jumped inside quickly, rubbing his hands together to warm them. "It's chilly out," he laughed.

"Well, it is winter," I pointed out.

"Where do you want to go?" Iain asked, putting his car in drive.

"I don't know. Aren't you from Ottawa? Don't you know all the great places?"

Iain looked at me as if he wanted to say something but thought the better of it. "Yeah, I do," he said instead, pulling out of the parking spot and driving.

I wasn't familiar with my surroundings, and have a horrible sense of direction regardless, so I had no idea what direction we were driving in. We arrived at a fancy looking restaurant ten minutes later. Iain easily found a parking spot while I tried to casually search for an Impala. I came up blank in my search; no Impalas in sight, so I relaxed a little. I glanced at Iain, and he was staring at me with a smile on his lips. I leaned over, kissing him gently.

"Seriously...I'm hungry. Let's go." I smirked, opening my door.

Iain laughed. "Let it be known that I should never forget to feed you," he joked, catching up with me and taking my hand. We walked into the warmth of the restaurant.

"What is this place, anyway?" I asked, impressed with the modern décor.

"It's my favorite Thai food place." Iain smiled. "It's gotten a few updates since the last time I've been here." He glanced around, taking in the modern lightening.

"Can we get a secluded table?" I whispered to him when we came up to the hostess. He nodded, repeating my request to her. She led us to the back of the restaurant, to a small table almost tucked away in the corner. Iain smiled at me, squeezing my hand encouragingly. It wasn't like we'd never gone out to dinner in public before. We had in Niagara Falls. But I still felt uneasy.

"What if we run into someone you know?" I whispered after the hostess left to get our drink orders. I kept my eyes on his, gauging his reaction.

"It's not like I'm going to introduce you as my almost 18-year-old student." He shrugged, a slight smile playing on his lips as if he found the whole thing humorous, and maybe he did.

I rolled my eyes. "Well, obviously." I looked at the menu, searching for something that looked appealing. I'd actually never had Thai food before. The only Thai place near our apartment in Toronto had been sketchy, and North Bay definitely didn't have anything Thai.

"I recommend the Thai Pad Siew," Iain suggested, winking. "You'd like it."

"I bet you're right," I told him, closing my menu and smiling coyly at him. "You seem to know exactly what I like, Mr. Bentley."

Iain's eyes smouldered, as they usually did when I called

him Mr. Bentley. He cleared his throat, about to reply when the hostess appeared with our drinks. He'd ordered Tiger beer, and I had asked for some strawberry fruity non-alcoholic drink. I took a sip while Iain ordered for us. I found myself staring at Iain's beer curiously. I knew it was imported from Thailand.

"Have a sip," he told me after he'd poured it expertly into his tall beer glass and let it settle.

"No, thank you." I looked away, smiling. He cocked his head, his eyes full of curiosity, but he didn't ask the questions I knew he had. Besides, I had a feeling he already knew the answers.

"Tell me more about your life here in Ottawa." I wanted to break the silence, but I also wanted to hear about it.

"Okay, well. We moved here when I was twelve, and I grew up here...went to university here...there's not much to tell, really," Iain answered, taking another sip of his beer.

"Is your family still here?" I asked, hesitating briefly.

"Yeah. But don't worry, they very rarely venture away from home-cooked meals and Hockey Night in Canada." Iain winked. "Besides, none of my family likes Thai food."

I opened my mouth, longing to say I'd love to meet them some day—the standard girlfriend response—before I realized how...ridiculous that would be. The questions that would arise. The spot he'd be put on. I swallowed the lump that suddenly welled in my throat and looked down at my glass.

"Hey," Iain whispered, reaching across the table and tipping my chin up so I'd look at him. "I want you to meet them too. And you will...one day."

I smiled sadly at him, touched that he'd known my train of thought even though I hadn't said a word, but I still felt solemn. I didn't believe that. I mean, I did...but I didn't. I knew he wanted me to meet his family, but I knew it wasn't that simple. I'd been a dirty little secret for so long, and there was so much at stake.

The waitress interrupted us with our plates, and we ate in almost silence. Iain watched me carefully, worry tracing the corners of his eyes.

CHAPTER TWELVE

After dinner, we returned to the hotel room. I wanted to forget my worries and get lost in him entirely, and I did that. I allowed myself to just...be. We fell asleep entangled in each other's arms, my head comfortably resting on his shoulder.

I woke up early the next morning to the sound of Iain walking about the hotel room, talking on the phone in a hushed tone.

"I know. I wish I could pop in too. But I'm swamped with work," he was saying. I watched him as he leaned against the window, the light of the full moon illuminating his perfect athletic body. He was only wearing a pair of boxers. "Okay. I love you too. I'll talk to you later," he said, ending the call. He remained in front of the window, staring out.

"Who was that?" I asked. I knew it was intrusive, but I figured I had a right to know. Iain startled a little, turning to look at me.

He smiled, no trace of uneasiness in his features. "Just my mom." He shrugged, crossing over to the bed and crawling into it.

"Oh," I whispered, thinking about the turn our conversation had taken the night before.

"What is it?" Iain asked, frowning at the look on my face.

"Nothing," I said, trying to brush off the conversation. It was definitely not one I wanted to have at 5 in the morning.

"Harlow, please," Iain begged, angling his face so that our eyes met. "I need to know what's on your mind. I need to know if you're....regretting us."

"I'm not regretting us!" I was shocked that he'd jump to that conclusion.

"Then tell me what it is, because I'm not getting good vibes from you lately. You're on edge, and you're closed off. You don't seem happy." Iain sounded vulnerable and hurt. It was my turn to startle. I hadn't realized I'd been so easy to read.

"It's just..." I hesitated, wanting to find the correct words. Iain watched me patiently. I got the impression that I could take a lifetime and he'd still be quietly waiting for me. Patiently. I sighed. "I'm never going to be the girl that you can just bring home."

"And why not?" Iain asked, surprise crossing his features.

"Because Iain, I'm barely 18. You were my teacher when we met, when we...got together, even if you aren't teaching any of my classes next semester. How do we tell that story to your family over dinner? How do we explain ourselves to anyone?"

Iain opened and closed his mouth as he thought about what I'd said and how best he could argue it.

"You love me," I said, gently placing my index finger over his lips to silence him. "I know that. And I love you, more than anything. But every time I think about the future, I get scared." My confession hit a sore spot within Iain. I saw pain reflect in his eyes. It was fleeting, but it was there.

"Don't be scared," he whispered, stroking my cheek to

soothe me. "All that matters is if you want the future. Do you want the future, Harlow? With me?"

I nodded, about to tell him how stupid he was for asking me such a thing, but he continued talking. "Then that's the important bit. The rest of it is just technicalities. I know that my family is very embracing and understanding. My younger brother? He's gay. It doesn't matter to any of us. You love who you love."

"You love who you love," I repeated, a real smile lifting the corners of my lips for the first time in a while. I'd been mulling over the bleakness of our situation for too long, moping about it, when really, so many people out there faced similar issues. So many people were "not supposed" to love who they loved.

"You love who you love," Iain said again, firmly this time. He took my face in his hands and passionately kissed me. "And I love you, Harlow Jones. We'll figure the rest out when the time comes."

I smiled against his lips, pulling him back on the bed against me.

"Mom? Is there anything I can help you with?" I asked, hesitating by the doorway. She was in the kitchen, preparing dinner. Larry was in the living room, watching some sports show on his new flat screen TV with glee. His hooted excitement over goals and the "clarity" of the TV was amusing to listen to.

"Yeah, sure honey...if you'd like to peel those carrots?" Mom gestured to the sink where a pile of carrots was waiting, freshly washed. I walked over, picking one up and grabbing a peeler. I set to work, stealing glances at her from out of the corner of my eye.

Since getting home the week before, I'd thought a lot about the conversation Iain and I had in the hotel room in Ottawa. *You love who you love.* That sentence kept ringing out in my head, over and over again. Since returning home, I had wanted desperately to talk to Mom about Iain again. She was still pretending that he didn't exist. Pursing her lips whenever I said I would be home late, but unable to keep me on lock down. She knew that every time I said I was headed over to Jenna's, I wasn't always headed over there, although I did visit with her quite a bit. At first, I'd wanted to gauge out if she'd seen anything in Ottawa. She hadn't seemed like it though, and after we hung out a few times, I was able to relax a little. But we definitely didn't have sleepovers, like I told Mom and Larry. I think Mom knew that, though, but she couldn't call it into question with Larry around, and with her sheer determination to deny it was happening.

I kind of expected her to rat me out, but she hadn't yet. My curiosity as to why was overwhelming. I figured it was probably because she didn't want to deal with the fallout, and she also didn't want to betray me. We were on shaky ground.

I wanted to blurt it all out then and there, but knew that tactic likely wouldn't work with her. So I decided to go for the full-disclosure route.

"So Jenna heard back from that agency," I said, rolling my neck to work out the kinks as I picked up another carrot.

"Oh?" Mom asked, her voice piquing with interest.

"Yeah, I think she's picked a family," I answered. "Or at least narrowed it down to a few."

"How does she feel about it?" Mom inquired, sounding generally concerned with Jenna's feelings, and I'm sure she was. She checked the temperature of the turkey and had her back to me.

"Sad," I said. "Overwhelmed, but relieved. She still thinks it's the best route for her and the baby."

"What do you think?" Mom's question caught me off guard.

"Well, I don't know." I shrugged. "It makes sense to me." Mom nodded in agreement, and put the turkey back in the oven. "Jenna also told me they picked a trial date...February 24."

"So soon?" Mom asked, surprise on her face as she turned around to look at me. "I thought it'd be another couple of months."

"I guess things are coming together quickly." I shrugged again. "I know that Jake is willing to testify, and Thompson's gotten in touch with a few of Andrew's...other victims. There's a lot of evidence, and I think they are even going to bring Carl Cooper's role to light, exposing him for obstruction of justice."

"It'll be here, though?" Mom asked, leaning backwards against the counter.

"Yeah, Thompson will travel here," I answered, wiping the back of my hand across my eyes to push some stray hairs that had fallen from my sloppy bun. I was nearly done peeling the carrots. Mom started on the salad, humming quietly to herself.

"Mom...I was wondering something?" I asked, timidly peeling another carrot while watching her. I saw her back stiffen.

"Oh? What's that?" She was forcefully working to keep her tone joyful and even as she tossed the salad, mixing in the dressing.

"Do you support gay marriage?" I asked. My random question threw me off guard, and she turned to look at me.

"Yes..." She gave me a peculiar look, wary of where I was going with it.

"So...if I were a lesbian...that wouldn't bother you?" I raised an eyebrow, waiting for her response.

She stole a look to the living room, then looked back at me. "What are you getting at, Harlow? Are you a lesbian now?" she asked, scoffing at the notion.

I stared at her, keeping my expression serious. "If I were a lesbian, and I loved another girl, would that bother you?"

"I would still love you," Mom replied, exasperated. Impatience showed in her eyes.

"So why is my relationship with Iain so hard to handle?" I asked lowly, keeping my eyes on hers. She wavered a bit, but tensed her jaw.

"Because, Harlow," she whispered, glancing back to the living room again. Then she walked toward me, stopping when she was less than a foot away. "It jeopardizes your credibility as a student. It pulls into question your grades, and both of your morals."

"Mom." I rolled my eyes. "I've always gotten good grades. Do you mean to tell me I've slept with every teacher I've ever had?"

"No, of course not," Mom said, her voice desperate. "But what I think doesn't matter. It's what the school board would think if this ever went public. You're still technically a minor. It's sick of a teacher to pursue a student."

"But I consent, regardless of my age."

"Age matters, for you, right now. The age you are...that matters," Mom hissed, gently but firmly grasping my upper arms with her hands. She didn't look angry, just desperate.

"I want to protect you," she added, her voice gentler but still pleading. "I know how this will play out. Haven't you followed any news coverage of student-teacher relationships? They always end badly. The teacher usually gets charged and thrown in jail, and if the student isn't victimized, their academic records are called into question."

It was my turn to waver, ever so slightly. "We love each other..."

"That may be." Mom's voice was as stiff as her posture. "But there are laws against this kind of thing, Harlow! I could press charges against him. You are a minor and you are my daughter."

"You wouldn't," I said confidently, although I really wasn't sure. "You wouldn't because you know I'm in love with him, and that he makes me happier than I've ever been. You haven't told Larry because of it."

Mom opened her mouth, but was silenced by Larry walking into the kitchen. "Tell Larry what?" he asked, looking curiously at the two of us. Mom's hands dropped to her sides and she quickly smiled at Larry.

"Oh, nothing, dear," she said. "Just girl talk."

Larry shrugged, unconcerned, and attempted to sneak some food from the dishes on the counter. Mom swatted him away and shoved him back toward the living room with a genuine smile on her face as she told him that dinner would be ready soon.

"This conversation is over for now, Harlow. I mean that," Mom whispered.

Shortly after Christmas dinner, when the dishes were cleaned and Larry was passed out in his recliner in front of his new TV, I slipped out into the front hall to get my jacket and boots on. What I really wanted was to continue the conversation with Mom, but I didn't know what else I could say about it. She had her points (valid ones at that) and I had mine as well. I didn't want to face the fact that maybe, there was a grain of truth to her words.

"When will you be home?" Mom whispered, coming into the foyer as I finished lacing up my boots. I thought about Lauren, briefly. She was the one who used to call them my shit-kicker boots. A wave of sadness rose in my chest, but I shoved it down. Now was not the time to think about Lauren. It was surreal, how she'd well up in the most random of times.

"Dunno," I replied honestly, scooping up my overnight bag. I'd packed a few gifts for Iain and some overnight clothes. "I'm doing a Christmas...thing...with...I'll be home tomorrow."

"Harlow." Mom glanced to the floor, avoiding my gaze. "I do want you to be happy."

"I know, Mom." I sighed, also avoiding her eyes. "He... makes me happy."

"I can see that," Mom remarked, her voice sounding defeated. I stole a glance at her, and she did look defeated. Bone weary and tired.

"You love who you love," I said, borrowing the line that was now permanently etched in my mind. I opened the door, giving her one more look over my shoulder before I closed it. I couldn't make out her expression, but that didn't matter. I knew she wouldn't tell on us.

It was snowing heavily, the big snowflakes that fall from the sky and bring magic to Christmas. Iain was parked on the next street over, waiting for me. I climbed into the passenger seat, leaning over to kiss him hello.

"Merry Christmas," I whispered, smiling.

"Merry Christmas to you too." Iain grinned. He started driving toward his place, asking me about my day. I filled him in on bits and pieces of it, but left out the conversation with my mom. I was trying to ignore how certain things she'd said hit home for me, since it felt like Iain and I were constantly hashing out those "technicalities," as he called them. I wanted our first Christmas together to be special.

And it was, Iain made sure of it. We exchanged gifts in front of a burning fireplace. Iain had bought me a dainty necklace with a heart and key, a leather bound journal and ink pens. I bought him the entire boxed set of *Dexter*, a show he was obsessed with, although I felt insecure in my choice. His gifts were so personal, so me. Nevertheless, Iain was so excited about it that I couldn't help but allow him to talk me into watching nearly the entire first season in 24 hours while we cuddled on his couch.

I returned home for a few days, awkwardly spending it with Mom and Larry when I wasn't working, and spent the New Year at Iain's house. We sipped champagne in his bed, and welcomed the new year with intimacy and tangled limbs.

My birthday fell on January 4, the last weekend before the new semester started, and I spent the entire weekend with Iain.

"Where are we going?" I asked yet again, watching as he tossed some clothes into his overnight bag. Mine was already packed. Iain shrugged, a quiet smile on his handsome face.

"That's a secret," he said alluringly.

The secret ended up being a cozy cabin even more north than we already were. He took me skiing for the first time ever, and laughed with delight every time I fell on my ass. By the end of the weekend, I was sorer than I'd ever imagined possible, but also incredibly happy. I was still riding on those feelings of euphoria when we returned for the new school year. Jenna was waiting for me by the cafeteria doors. She was wearing a baggy cardigan and had angled her bag to cover her stomach. She wasn't noticeable as she was still quite tiny, but it was almost getting to the point that you'd be able to tell. I knew she was extremely insecure about it.

"What's got you all happy? Did Ben spoil you this weekend?" Jenna asked, a hint of a mischievous grin on her face. She glanced around, trying to see if anyone was staring at her.

"That he did." I smiled. We started walking upstairs toward our first period class: art.

"Where'd he take you?" Jenna asked, brushing back a strand of her blond hair and sliding in behind me to avoid a cluster of giggling girls.

"A cabin up North. We went skiing," I replied. We entered room 302 and found seats near the back. "It was my first time. He taught me how to stay on my feet...kind of."

"That's so romantic." Jenna sighed, leaning back in her chair beside me and looking away dreamily. "I wish I had that."

"Looks like you did already," scoffed a familiar voice. Jenna and I both looked with surprise at the speaker. It was Callie, and she was leering at Jenna's belly pointedly. Tara giggled beside her, and they dramatically tossed their hair over their shoulders and found seats further away from us, but still in view. They immediately started whispering and giggling, glancing over toward us with malice.

"Ignore them. They're bitches," I told Jenna gently, leaning in toward her. She was breathing heavily, panicking almost. She'd moved her bag over her stomach, and was ghostly pale.

"Oh hey, didn't know you guys had this class," Jake said, sliding into the seat beside Jenna. He paused for a moment. "Is...everything okay?"

"Everything is fine," I told him, glancing over at Callie and Tara and sending them a glare. "She's just not feeling good."

"Yeah, the first day back makes me feel ill too," Jake joked, looking at Jenna with concern. He started talking to her, distracting her away from her panic. Slowly, she calmed down, and was even starting to laugh when the final bell rang. I observed them with a quiet smile on my face, impressed with Jake's skill at easing Jenna's panic. It was effortless for him.

Our art teacher was a kooky lady named Ms. Higgins. She had wild red hair and big square purple glasses. She handed out sketchbooks and kits and told us to draw whatever we wanted for our first day back. She disappeared in the supply room for a bit, leaving the class to their own devices. Conversations erupted around us, people chatting about their holidays while they doodled. Apparently, Riley had had another party over the holidays. I overheard a lot of people talking about how hilarious that had been. But two sets of voices rang out over all the others.

"I couldn't believe it either; obviously someone just wants attention," Callie was saying haughtily, tossing a glance over to our direction.

"Still, that's a really dick move," Tara was saying. "So she just up and charged Andrew?"

"Yeah," Callie tittered, turning to look at her friend. "Andrew said they hooked up at a party, but that he didn't really want to. She wouldn't stop coming on to him after he told her that he wanted to get back with me. Now she's saying he sexually assaulted her because he doesn't want to be with her. Such a whore."

"I heard that—"

"Oh yeah, but it's not his," Callie cut Tara off quickly, shushing her with a glare. "Andrew always uses protection."

"Of course you'd know," Tara giggled. "So what, you guys are back together now?"

"Well...kind of." Callie smirked. "I'm making him work for it."

"You go girl!" Tara cheered.

Their conversation was making me feel ill. I stole a glance

at Jenna, and it looked like she heard everything too. I closed my sketchbook, shoving it into my book bag.

"Come on," I told her. "Let's go." Jenna numbly shoved hers into her bag and stood up with me.

"Skipping class? I'm in too," Jake decided, grabbing his things and following us.

"I hear morning sickness is a drag," Callie drawled, pouting as we walked by their table.

Jake gently steered both Jenna and I out into the hall before I could walk over and punch Callie's smug expression off her face. I had been tempted, and had he not taken action I probably would have.

Jenna was ghostly white and shaking. "I can't be here anymore."

"Do you want me to take you home?" Jake offered.

"I drove..."

"I don't think you're in any condition to drive," Jake pointed out.

"What's that supposed to mean?" Jenna snapped, glaring at him.

"I just mean...you're upset, and you shouldn't drive." Jake raised his hands in surrender. "I mean no harm."

"Sorry," Jenna said. I stood nearby, watching the exchange with a peculiar look on my face. The gentle kindness and sincerity on Jake's face was very sweet.

"Let Jake take you home," I told her. "I'll drive your car back, then he can take me back to school."

Jenna looked back between Jake and I, then toward the classroom and sighed. "Fine. I just want to get out of here."

She offered her keys up to me and I took them. The three of us started walking toward the parking lot doors. I saw Iain exiting a classroom and I froze temporarily, caught off guard by the sight of him in the school, dressed his pressed pants and blazer.

"Shouldn't you three be in class?" he asked, his voice full of authority. Memories of the weekend we'd just had flooded my mind and I flushed, almost feeling his lips on my neck. Jenna was looking back from Iain to me, curiosity on her face.

"Yeah...sorry, Mr. Bentley. We're taking Jenna home... she's...sick," I answered awkwardly. Iain studied Jenna for a moment. She avoided his gaze, frowning at the floor.

"Very well. Make sure you get passes from the principal's office," Iain instructed, continuing on his way.

"We'll get them later." Jake shrugged, unfazed. Jenna was still looking at me curiously. I avoided her gaze and kept walking toward the parking lot doors, knowing they were behind me.

I found Jenna's car easily enough. Jake parked on the other side of the lot, so we met up at Jenna's house as planned. I drove slower, allowing them time to talk and maybe get to know each other. I wasn't intending on playing matchmaker, but I did think it was good for Jenna to be around Jake. He was sweet, funny, and caring. Sure, he sold pot to high school students and smoked it, but that wasn't really a bad thing. I mean, there were definitely worse character traits in a person.

By the time Jake and I returned to school, we were greeted by crazy amount of gossip. Rumours were spreading. I hadn't realized that the local paper had released a story about the sexual assault charges that were pressed against Andrew, but they had. They didn't release Jenna's name, but the school would figure it out soon. Especially with Callie fuelling the rumours. She knew exactly who had pressed charges; Andrew had likely told her.

As the weeks passed by, the town's interest in the upcoming trial grew. I heard the gossip when I served coffee to the towns folk at the diner. I heard the gossip in the hallways. The trial was all everyone could talk about. I felt like if I heard one more person talking about the trial, my brain would explode.

Danielle was the only one who remained uncharacteristically silent and solemn as we waited tables. I knew she was listening, hearing it all.

"That sweet Andrew couldn't have done that," an elderly lady was tittering to her friend, sipping a tea I'd brought her. "He shovels my driveway, that one, every winter all winter long!"

"Well, he does...quite regularly!" I interrupted rudely, unable to stop myself. Both elderly ladies stared at me, mouths agape, and the entire diner seemed to pause, ears tuned to the three of us. "I mean, do you want some more hot water for your tea?" I asked, my voice dripping with false sweetness. The ladies looked back and forth from me to each other and nodded, unsure of what to do. I filled their tea pots up with more boiling water and carefully put it down on their table before stalking off to the cash. I could feel their eyes on me as I stood with my back to them and the rest of the diner.

The trial was still several weeks away. I rubbed my temples, trying to ease the tension headache I seemed to have constantly since the news broke. Thompson had warned us all of the implications, but I hadn't expected...well, this. Neither had Jenna. I knew she was panicked about it, spending more and more time at home. She had all but stopped going to school. I would drop in after school with Jake to drop her homework off to her. I knew it wasn't just the fear of being discovered that kept her home. Her belly had grown in the past weeks, and now there was no denying that she was pregnant.

"Hey, are you okay?" Danielle asked from behind the

counter. She was leaning forward, putting a gentle hand on my forearm to get my attention.

"Yeah, sorry," I muttered, sighing. "I just can't take this 'Andrew's such a saint' bullshit."

"I know." Danielle frowned, looking back at the masses of people that had finally gone back to their meals. Only the two elderly ladies sipping tea were staring openly at me, conversing with each other out of the corner of their lips.

"Did you think about...what we talked about?" I asked, looking out the door.

"Yeah." Danielle took a deep breath. "I will. I'll call that lawyer guy tomorrow."

I nodded, unable to think of anything else to say. I felt terrible asking Danielle to relive the trauma her friend had gone through, and her friend's death, but I really felt what she had to say would make a difference.

The diner bell chimed and two figures walked in, letting brisk late January wind nip at my exposed skin. Goosebumps arose as a hush fell over the diner. Before I even turned to look, I knew who was there. I stiffened, watching Carl Cooper and his partner, Officer Reid, walk to the back of my section.

"Fuck," I muttered, grabbing a menu. The last thing I wanted to do was serve Carl Cooper, or any of the Coopers for that matter. Begrudgingly, I walked toward the back and dropped the menus on their table. They were still dressed in their uniforms, their navy blue winter patrol coats thick with snow. Some of it fell onto my shoes as Carl shrugged out of his coat.

"Can I get you anything to drink?" I asked stiffly. I was having a lot of difficulty keeping my tone pleasant.

"Yes, you can," Carl Cooper answered, exchanging an amused look with Officer Reid. "We'll both have coffees."

I nodded, heading to grab them coffee. I hadn't realized

that almost every eye in the diner was on the two policemen that had come in, but then, why *wouldn't* they be staring? They'd spent the majority of the morning talking about the breaking news of the charges pressed against Andrew.

Carl Cooper also ordered a plate of bacon and eggs. He ate slowly, probably extremely aware of the fact that all eyes were still on his turned back. When he and his partner got up to leave, Carl finally turned around to face the diner at large. Everyone fell silent as his gaze penetrated through every single conversation.

"Many of you have probably heard about the ridiculous charges pressed against my son." His voice was quiet, yet full of authority. He had every single person's attention, even those in the back kitchen. "I just wanted to say that those charges are false, brought on by a sad little girl seeking attention and validation for her mistakes. I have no doubt that these charges will be dropped." He said this last part while looking directly at me. I glared hotly back. Doubtful.

Unfortunately, I still had to ring in the egotistic Chief of Police's order. He smiled at me, a smile that coiled the nerves in my stomach, and handed me a wad of bills.

"Take care, Ms. Jones," he said, giving me a look that chilled me to the bone. My hand trembled against my will as I accepted his money and handed him his change.

"You too, Chief," I said, my voice as strong as I could make it. He chuckled, giving me a firm look that said, *watch your tone.*

As soon as the diner door closed behind Officer Reid, everyone started talking. I couldn't hear a single thing; their voices faded into a buzz. I brushed back a strand of my hair that had fallen from my ponytail, trying to steady my breathing. It didn't matter what anybody said; the truth would come out.

"Are you okay?" Danielle asked, her voice full of concern.

"Yeah, I'm...fine. I just..."

"It's okay. Head out," Danielle said, motioning to the door. "Trixie will be here in less than twenty minutes. I'll tell her you weren't feeling well."

"Okay." I nodded. Quickly, I went into the staff room and grabbed my jacket and bag, barely uttering a good bye to the kitchen guys.

I knew exactly where I was headed. I pulled my hood up, looking cautiously around me. There were plenty of people around, heading into the diner and leaving it, but nobody was paying me any attention and there were no police cars nearby. I walked as quickly as my legs would carry me, not even pausing to knock on Iain's door. I just walked straight in and kicked off my boots.

Iain was in the living room, a bunch of papers spread out in front of him. He looked like he was in the middle of marking assignments.

"Whoa, hey," he said, leaning back into the couch and watching me walk into the living room. "I wasn't expecting you until after dinner."

"I know, I bailed on my shift," I said, leaning against the doorway. "We had visitors at the diner. Carl Cooper and his partner."

"Not surprising. I saw the paper." Iain sighed, nodding toward the local paper on the coffee table in front of him. The front page headline read Chief of Police's Son Charged with Alleged Sexual Assault.

"Nobody knows that it's Jenna who's charging him, right?" I asked, grabbing the paper. I'd seen it on several customers' tables, but I hadn't been able to get my hands on it to read it yet.

"No, her name is protected...right now," Iain answered, running a hand through his hair in a distracting manner.

"For now?" I pressed, my eyes widening.

"The details will leak eventually. They always do during big profile cases."

"This is a big profile case?"

"Yeah, it involves a possible cover up by the Chief of Police. Of course it will be high profile," Iain said patiently. Of course, I knew that...sort of. I'd seen enough CSI shows to kind of put that together, but I hadn't been thinking about that the past few weeks. I'd just been thinking about my statement and what I was going to say.

"Relax, Harlow," Iain finally said, seeing me stressing and worrying about it. "She's safe."

CHAPTER THIRTEEN

The town gossip increased in the weeks that led up to the trial. Iain was right; the case had everybody's attention. Anywhere I went, I heard about the scandal. Most of the townspeople were torn: many of them stood by the Coopers with unwavering support, but more and more were questioning Carl Cooper's morals and ethics. The department had begun an internal investigation on Carl Cooper. I wasn't sure what they would find; I didn't know how good Carl was at covering up his tracks. The whole thing had me on edge.

It was late one Sunday night, three days before the trial was set to begin, and I was working a shift at the diner. Danielle was working alongside me, although the place was nearly dead.

"Go home," I told her, motioning to the door with my head. "I've got it from here."

"But..." Danielle hesitated, looking at me with concern.

"I'll be fine," I said firmly. "Go home to that little boy of yours."

Danielle chewed on her lip, clearly conflicted. I knew she

was hesitant to leave me alone in light of the chaos of the trial. It wasn't like I was being harassed. In fact, I hadn't heard or seen the Coopers since Carl's grand speech in the diner a few weeks before.

"Seriously, I'm fine." I rolled my eyes. "Besides, Ryan's here."

Danielle gave me a look. After the accident, Danielle and Ryan started seeing each other. Their relationship was still new, still sweet and innocent. Danielle was taking her time, and Ryan was just happy to be with her after months of pinning for her.

"I'm sure we'll be fine," I said. "Ryan's good now." It'd been months since we'd gotten jumped outside of the diner, and Ryan was better. He'd actually gotten a gym membership and started working out, taking self-defense courses. He'd beefed out a little in the muscle department, and was determined to never let anyone get him on the ground again.

Danielle pursed her lips, considering. Ryan came out of the kitchen with a tray of clean utensils.

"Ryan, tell Danielle to go home, that we'll be alright," I demanded, rolling my eyes toward her. Bemused, Ryan set the tray down and leaned over the counter. He smiled at her.

"Babe, we'll be fine," he said reassuringly. He looked ecstatic that she was worried about him, that she cared. He showed off a muscle, flexing it for her. "See? All good here."

"Alright, alright! Put the gun show away." Danielle laughed. I could tell she wasn't quite sure still, but I shoved her coat and bag at her anyway.

"Just go," I said. "No sense in both of us being here."

"Alright, I'm going..." Danielle said, sliding into her coat. She waved at Ryan, mouthing for

him to call her later. He nodded, heading back into the kitchen with bins full of dirty dishes.

I watched as Danielle left. I locked the door behind her quickly, after all...it was after hours and the diner was deader than dead—it had been for the past hour or so. I began my closing prep. I vacuumed the floors, cashed out the till while Ryan waited, laying down in an empty booth across from me.

"How's Danielle doing, really?" I asked him, looking up briefly.

"She's...good, I guess," Ryan said, still lying in the booth. "She's distracted with this whole trial thing. I think it's dredging up bad memories."

"No kidding." I sighed, leaning back in the chair I was sitting in. "Did you know Rachel?"

"Kind of." Ryan shrugged. "It's a small town. Everyone kind of knows everyone else. Plus she'd come in with some of their mutual friends when Danielle was working the breakfast shift. She also attempted working here. Didn't last long, she was the worst hostess ever."

I was silent, thoughtful. Unable to think of a reply, I headed to the office to drop off the cash out. I slid into my coat as I walked back out to the dining area. Ryan was standing, waiting by the back door. I quickly punched in the lock code while Ryan waited outside. I made sure the door was locked, then adjusted my jacket collar. The February air was sharp and chilly, slicing at my exposed skin like tiny razors.

I noticed that Ryan was staring toward the parking lot with a look of mounting concern and anxiety on his face. "What's your deal?" I asked. He was tense, his fists clenched at his sides as if he was awaiting a fight. I followed his gaze, noticing the heavy-set man walking toward us with a folder. His heavy coat and hat obscured his facial features, and I didn't recognize him at all.

"What do you want, man?" he called out, trying to keep his voice from shaking. I knew he was having flash backs to the last time someone approached the two of us after work. I was too.

"Ms. Jones?" the man asked, approaching us and ignoring Ryan.

"Yes..."

"This is for you," he shoved the folder at me and started walking in the other direction. I clenched it in my hands, unsure of what to do.

"What was that about?" Ryan demanded, staring at the folder with open curiosity.

"I don't know," I answered honestly. I didn't know what was in the folder, but I knew that it couldn't be good. What good news was delivered by an unfamiliar, heavy-set man in an abandoned parking lot late at night? None.

I knew that Ryan wanted me to open the folder, but I couldn't bring myself to do it. The sticky, horrible feeling I had in the pit of my stomach was mounting.

"I'll be alright," I told him, motioning for him to go on without me.

"Don't be ridiculous." Ryan frowned. "That? Was creepy. I'm walking you home. Who knows where that guy went."

"I just want to be alone, okay?" I said somewhat harshly. The surprised and hurt look on Ryan's face made me feel guilty, but it couldn't be helped.

"If you're sure..."

"I'm sure," I snapped. "I'm a big girl; I can take care of myself."

"I don't doubt that," Ryan remarked, frowning again, taking offence to my words although I hadn't meant it that way. "Whatever...your choice," he added before walking in the opposite direction of where I wanted to go. I watched him walk for a bit, feeling guilty, then I quickly headed to Iain's.

Iain's porch light was still on when I came up to his house.

I walked inside blindly, my fingers numb from the cold and from clenching the brown envelope so tightly.

"Harlow?" Iain called out from upstairs when I kicked the door shut behind me. I didn't answer; I could scarcely hear him as my shaky hands opened the envelope. I gasped, seeing the contents inside, and dropped the whole thing. Pictures floated to the ground absurdly slow. Distantly, I heard Iain saying something to me as he ran down the stairs. I couldn't truly hear him though, and I couldn't form a single worded reply. My words were frozen in my throat, just as the stunned expression was frozen on my face as I stared down at the photos of Iain and I together. Photos neither of us had taken. I fell back against the door, sliding down to the ground just as Iain reached my side. He picked up one of the photos, stared at it for a moment, and swore.

He pulled me toward him, hard against his chest, and held me close. "It's going to be okay, Harlow."

"No, it's not," I whispered. I felt like crying, but no tears would come. My heart was pounding. I knew what this meant. I'd seen enough law dramas to know when I was being blackmailed. I knew who it was from too, although the folder hadn't come with any words or names at all.

He didn't argue; he just held me for what seemed like hours. I couldn't move. I was rigid, trying to think my way out of this messy situation. My mind was whirling, and all I could think about was quietly backing out of the trial and getting the hell away from this town, and Iain, before I screwed everything up for him...and before he ended up in jail.

"Should I—"

"Don't go there." Iain sighed, cutting me off before I even had a chance to finish my sentence. "You need to go to the trial. You need to speak about what you saw, and what happened that night. It's imperative that you do."

"But what about you?" I asked, my brows knitting together in frustration and concern.

"Don't worry about me." Iain tipped my chin up, looking straight into my eyes. "This is a tactic to try and get you to hush up. What non-guilty party spies on people to get dirt on them to have them back out?"

"I don't think that matters..." I hesitated, still frowning. "You could still get arrested."

Iain bit his lip, looking at the wall just behind my head. He knew he couldn't argue with that. He knew the possibility was there, and it was real.

I looked away too, feeling the burn of tears in my eyes. I should have listened to Mom. I should have walked away. I shouldn't have remained involved with Iain, especially when all this court shit loomed. A part of me wanted to shove away from Iain's embrace and flee from his house, but a bigger part kept me rooted. I didn't want to lose what we had. I rested my forehead on his and allowed the tears fall, shaking as silent sobs escaped.

Eventually, Iain scooped me up in his arms and carried me to the couch. I was still wearing my jacket and boots. He left them on, not caring that the snow was melting from my shoes onto his living room floor. He made me tea—his go-to calming method—and held it out to me. I shook my head; the mere thought of swallowing anything made me want to vomit. My nerves were so frazzled.

"Iain...we need to do something," I said, my voice shaking.

"I plan on it," Iain assured me, looking angrily out the window.

"What's your plan then?" I asked, curiosity getting the better of me.

Iain sighed, looking back at me with a sad expression on his face. "To be honest? I have no idea."

I thought back to what my mom said about how "she could press charges if she wanted to." Momentarily, I wondered if this had been her. I just as quickly dismissed the thought. "You know...my mom knows about us."

"I know," Iain hedged, frowning slightly.

"Well...she said that she could press charges if she wanted, but I know she would never do that. Maybe she'd stand up for you." I shrugged. "I could talk to her about it."

"I don't know...".

"Well, I don't know what else to do, okay!" I snapped.

Iain sighed again, running a hand through his hair in thought. "It's okay," he said easily. "We'll figure it out."

"You could call Thompson," I suggested, gently lifting my tea off the coffee table. I'd calmed down enough to drink it. My mouth was dryer than cotton balls.

"No, that's a conflict of interest," Iain said, picking up the folder again. "My lawyer will handle this...if anything comes of it." He looked at the photos for a second time, working his jaw thoughtfully.

"What is it?" I held the mug of tea tighter in my hands. I took another sip, my hands still trembling ever so slightly.

"Well, there's nothing here that suggests a sexual relationship between us," Iain said, calmly laying the photos out for me too look at again.

"So? It shows us together..." I trailed off, confused. He was right though. There was a photo of me outside his house, two of us in his car. The two car photos were blurry, and the one of me walking up to his house didn't show my face. Luckily, our mutual agreement on no public displays of affection had prevented the photographer from getting a photo of us in any incriminating positions.

"They'd need to prove beyond a reasonable doubt that our relationship was sexual," Iain explained. "These photos don't do that. They don't prove beyond a reasonable doubt. They barely even subtly hint. You can't tell for certain if you're in the car photos, or if that's you..."

"You can tell that's me," I said, pointing to the one of me walking. "You can see the same leather jacket I always wear."

He nodded, agreeing. "But, again, this photo proves nothing."

"How do you know all this?" I demanded, perplexed. My eyes dropped to the photos in Iain's hand. He gave me a foolish half smile.

"I looked into it," he said, shrugging. "Just in case."

"Well, our relationship *is* sexual," I whispered.

"I know..." Iain said, hesitating for a moment.

"What is it?" I demanded, an icy cold fear gripping my heart as Iain's sad eyes met mine.

"If I were to get charged...it'd be with sexual exploitation." Iain looked as if he was having difficulty speaking.

"It's not though, we're in love. The age difference doesn't matter," I argued, the fear growing so large that it almost choked me.

"It doesn't matter to *us*," Iain corrected, "but it would matter in the courtroom. There is no Romeo and Juliet clause to save us. I'm a teacher and you're my student. The outcome isn't good."

"What are we going to do?" I asked, both dreading and knowing the answer.

"We need to cool it." His voice broke a little, as if this was the last thing in the world he wanted to do. Fresh tears pooled in my eyes, and I tried to blink them back as I nodded in understanding. He kneeled on the floor, gently taking the tea from my hands and setting it on the coffee table. He took my hands in his and looked at me intently. "Please know, Harlow," he said, "that I love you more than anything. The only reason why I'm suggesting this is because I don't want to give them anything else. I don't want them hinting toward anything to paint you in a negative light. That will be their intent if they can't scare you away from giving your testimony. Plus...I really don't want to go to jail," he confessed.

I nodded, the tears escaping down my cheeks. I understood; I truly did. The last thing I wanted to do was to have Iain go to jail. We'd been lucky so far. And incredibly foolish. I couldn't risk having that luck run out.

"When this is all over, we will be together," Iain promised softly. "Just be patient." He kissed me gently on the lips, tasting the salt of my tears. I kissed him back, heartbreakingly slow. When we pulled away, I noticed that his eyes were wet too.

I hated to leave him, but I had no choice. He was right.

I walked home, tears freezing on my cheeks in the arctic weather. It took the same amount of time to walk home that it usually did, but I barely registered the time. It could have been hours or minutes; I was indifferent to the passage of time.

I took my jacket off in a trance, hanging it up in the front hall closet. The house was silent and dark. I didn't think anyone was up. I was grateful for that. I couldn't face Mom or Larry right at the moment. I knew I was undoubtedly wearing the shock from the photos and the hurt from the departure on my face.

I quietly treaded down the hallway and went straight to my bedroom. I didn't bother with my nightly routine of washing the makeup off. I fell onto my bed, allowing the

exhaustion I'd been feeling for days overcome me. Sleep merci-
fully came quickly.

A couple days passed without any further incident. Then it was
the morning I was to give testimony at the trial. The trial had
already been going for a couple of days, and the jury was
supposed to reach a decision by the end of the following week.
My testimony was right in the middle of it.

I awoke to Mom pulling the blinds open in my room. She
rushed about, trying to get me up and ready for the trial start
time at ten. I showered and dressed, worrying about the
upcoming day. When I stood up and said my piece...what
would happen? Would we be exposed?

I'd seriously considered not speaking up in the trial, but
only for half a minute. My silence would just help Andrew get
away with another rape. This had to stop, and it was bigger
than my relationship with Iain.

In the end, I had to tell myself to do what was right.
Speaking up against the Coopers, helping Jenna's case in the
trial—that was what was right. Iain and I weren't seeing each
other anymore. We were "cooling it," as he put it. I knew it was
for the better, but it still stung.

I washed the soap out of my hair, shaking my head slightly
to clear it. I need to get back in the now, in the present.
Thompson had warned me that Andrew's lawyers would likely
try to pick apart every single thing that I said. I had to be at my
most aware.

Choosing to go a more natural look than my usual liquid
eyeliner cat eye, I applied my makeup carefully. I dried my long
hair with my blow dryer and brushed it out, leaving it down.
I'd chosen simple yet snug black dress jeans and borrowed a

dress top off my mom. It was a simple cream cashmere sweater, but far more appropriate than anything I'd had in my closet. I evaluated myself in the mirror critically. Would I pass the judgmental scrutiny of the jury? I chewed on my lip, absently fingering the necklace Iain had given me at Christmas.

"Come on, Harlow; we're going to be late!" Mom hollered. I sighed, giving up, and left the bathroom. Mom was already in the front hall. She was dressed in her best coat and shoes. She was clenching her purse in her left hand, the keys in her right and looking at me with a look that clearly said Hurry up. I went to put on my boots, feeling sheepish that I hadn't considered court shoes. "No," Mom said quickly, she reached to the top shelf of the front hall closet and grabbed a shoe box. "Wear these."

I opened the box, looking at the plain black pumps she'd purchased for me. I smiled gratefully as I slid into them. She offered me the simple black dress trench jacket that she'd bought me a year ago in hopes that I'd take to it and stop wearing Dad's old leather jacket. I put it on, grateful that she hadn't thrown it out.

"Let's go," she said, nodding in satisfaction. I followed her out to the car, which was already warming thanks to the remote starter Larry had gotten her for Christmas.

We drove in silence to the court house, found a parking spot with some difficulty, and raced up the front steps. I had ten minutes to get back into the judge's chambers. Thompson was pacing the floor, and let out an aggravated sigh of relief when he saw me approaching.

"Good. You're here. You need to wait in that room until we're ready for you, and you'll have to sit in the audience," Thompson said quickly. He pointed to a room on his left and motioned for Mom to follow him.

"Good luck!" she whispered, kissing my cheek before she headed off after him. I took a deep breath and pushed open the door. The room was empty. Thompson had told me that we would all have our own waiting areas. I fell onto the leather couch and sighed.

I hadn't bothered bringing my phone, since I knew I wouldn't be allowed to use it today anyway. My fingers tapped impatiently against the leather as I stared at the clock. Ten minutes passed, and I sighed. I stood up, deciding to explore the room to keep myself occupied. There was a bar fridge and a small table. I went to the bar fridge, opening it and peering inside. There were a couple cans of pop, some water bottles, some juice boxes, and some yogurt. I grabbed a bottle of water, closing the door and twisting off the lid. I was about to take a sip when the door opened.

"Ms. Jones? They're ready to see you now," the bailiff said. He stood aside so I could exit the room. He led me to the court room, where all the proceedings were taking place.

I walked into the court room. I'd been expecting a full house, with all the talking that our town had been doing...but the room was surprisingly nearly empty. A few people sat in the rows of benches behind the plaintiff and a handful sat behind the defendant's side. The bailiff led me straight to the stand, where I had to swear on a Bible before sitting down.

I stared directly at Andrew, my solemn eyes unwavering as he shifted uncomfortably in his chair. He was looking fearful now.

His lawyer, a small rat of a man, stared at me with watery eyes the entire time Thompson asked me to recount the night of the party. I told them about going into the room and seeing Andrew climbing off Jenna. I told them about the altercation we had, about how Jake came in just in time and how Andrew had taken off. I told them about Jake helping me get Jenna home. I didn't leave out a single thing about that night.

Thompson asked me about the following day, when Andrew chased me down the street, and when he and his friends jumped a co-worker and I after work.

When Thompson was done asking me questions, he went to sit down at the plaintiff table beside Jenna. She was trembling slightly, tugging the large sweater she was wearing tighter to her body. As far as I'd seen, Andrew had not so much as tossed a glance in her direction. I wasn't even sure if he knew that she was pregnant.

Andrew's lawyer stood up and walked toward me. He cleared his throat to gain the attention of the jury. I felt dizzy, like I couldn't focus. I tried not to appear that way, though. I raised my head proudly and stared at the approaching lawyer. Thompson had told me his name was O'Neil.

"Ms. Jones?" he started. "You are aware that you took an oath swearing to tell the whole truth and nothing but the truth, correct?" I nodded, waiting for him to proceed. "When is your birthday, Ms. Jones?"

"January 4, 1988," I replied.

"Who are your parents?" O'Neil questioned.

"Lisa Stevenson and Randy Jones," I answered, not pausing.

"Randy Jones?" O'Neil asked, looking deeply interested. "Wasn't he in that band in the 80s? The 'Screaming Dragons'?"

"Yes," I answered stiffly.

"He overdosed when you were three. Cocaine?"

"How is this relevant?" Thompson demanded.

"Overruled, that doesn't concern this case O'Neil," the judge said, his voice thick with authority as he frowned down at O'Neil. He nodded, waving his hand in understanding before fixating his eyes on me again.

"So, tell us about the night of September 15...this party that you all went to. Was there drinking?" O'Neil asked, his voice slick like oil.

"Yes, but I wasn't," I answered honestly. "I don't drink."

"You don't drink?" O'Neil said, disbelief clear on his expression and his voice as he tossed a bemused look at the jury as if they were in on the joke. He looked down at some papers in his hand. "On the night of October 28, 2008, you were in a car accident with a couple of your friends. Your alcohol content level was 0.09."

"I don't drink *anymore*," I amended angrily. "My friend died that night, in case your notes don't say that."

"So you haven't had any alcohol since the night of this accident," O'Neil continued, ignoring the bit where I mentioned my friend's death. "Yet my client says he saw you with a red cup."

"I had the cup, yes. Riley gave me it and I dumped it all over the floor when Andrew came at me," I answered.

"Oh, sure," O'Neil said, smirking.

The rest of the trial session carried on in the same matter. O'Neil kept asking me ridiculous questions, hinting that I'd been drinking that night, trying to make me look bad. I was prepared for this, though, and I breezed through his questions and attempts at debunking my testimony. I left the stand an hour later feeling extremely exhausted and frustrated. I'd wanted to kick O'Neil in the balls when I walked by, but I didn't.

The bailiff escorted me back to the same room I had been waiting in before I gave my testimony. I had to wait there another two hours until court ended for the day.

Finally, Thompson came to alert me that it was time to leave. "You did great," he told me, smiling as he held the door open so I could walk out. "Your mother is waiting out front."

"Okay. Am I done?" I asked, gesturing back to the court house. "Because if I have to go in there again, I may not have as much restraint in kicking O'Neil in the nether regions."

Thompson chuckled. "Unless they come up with more questions, you should be okay. I don't foresee that. You were very descriptive and cooperative."

I nodded, thankful.

I found Mom near the doors, looking for me. I accompanied her down the stone steps, ignoring the few reporters that had gathered at the bottom of the steps. They fired question after question at me, but I ignored them and followed Mom straight to the car. She turned on the engine, driving us home wordlessly.

She didn't speak until we got inside the house and I flopped down on the couch in exhaustion. She sat down beside me, angling her body so that she was facing me.

"Harlow, if there's anything you need to tell me..." she said, hesitating as she looked at me with her big, caring green eyes. "You know you can, right?" I looked at her—*really* looked at her —for the first time in a while. I got the sense that she meant that, that she wanted me to open up to her and that this time she'd listen. "You haven't been yourself the last few days. I can't tell if it's related to this trial...or what. But please know that I'm here."

I stared back at her, longing to tell her about the man with the folder and about Iain. I opened my mouth, drawing in a breath.

"It's...fine," I said finally, unable to get the proper words out.

Mom looked at me skeptically. "I can't help you if you don't talk to me." She sighed, brushing back a strand of her short hair. She'd recently cut it into a bob. It suited her.

"You can't help me even if I talk to you," I muttered, looking out the living room window at the large snowflakes that had started to fall.

"What does that mean?"

"It means that I'm past helping," I clarified, sighing deeply.

"Is it...Iain?" Mom said his name with complete distain. I stole a glance at her, noticing her wrinkled forehead. It was as if we were discussing dissecting a frog, not the love of my life.

"There is no more..." I trailed off, searching for the right words. I knew that's not what Iain meant, but it was the easiest way to get her off my case. Maybe it was easiest if I started thinking that way, too. Mom looked surprised.

"I thought you were still together?" she asked, not bothering to hide her pleasure.

"No, not anymore," I answered, looking back out the window and glaring as I thought about the pictures, and the cooling it. Iain was right; it was necessary. As much as it pained me to be separated from him, it was in both our best interest. She was silent for a moment, still as she watched me. She sighed, reaching her hand out to brush my hair out of my face.

"It'll be okay, Harlow," she told me. "He wasn't right for you anyway."

"How do you know that?" I demanded, unable to stop myself. I looked at her with anger. "You don't know what he's like—who he is."

"All I'm saying, Harlow, is that there is something wrong with a guy that goes after his student. You're eleven years younger than he is!" Mom said defensively. She had recoiled at the harshness of my outburst.

"It wasn't like that." I shook my head, bewildered. "He didn't go after me. We just...fell for each other. I already told you that."

"Did you sleep with him?" Mom demanded, outright. I

shook my head, unable to answer. I knew it was a lie, but I couldn't help but think about what Iain had said...beyond a reasonable doubt. "Well, that's good then." Mom decided. "We'll put this behind us."

I stared at her, flabbergasted. Put what behind us, exactly? Years of her back and forth parenting? Trusting, understanding, caring mother one minute, judgmental PTA mom the next? I shook my head, watching her walk off to the kitchen.

CHAPTER FOURTEEN

I awoke to a brisk knocking at my door. I startled, my heart racing. My eyes felt crusty and gross. I wiped at them, trying to clear them out.

"Who...?" My voice was still full of exhaustion. Although sleep had come quickly the night before, I restlessly tossed and turned. My dreams had been full of images I didn't want to see. Iain being forced into a police car, handcuffed. The Coopers getting away with everything. I didn't feel rested at all.

My door was pushed open, and Mom stood in the hallway with her hands on her hips. "Harlow Jones. It's nearly nine thirty. What are you doing still in bed? You're late for school!" she scolded.

"Sorry...I...I'll get ready now," I muttered, pushing my blankets off and standing up. She nodded, satisfied with my answer, and headed back toward the kitchen, leaving me to get ready. I swung my legs over the side of my bed, rubbing at my eyes again. They were itchy and swollen.

I stretched a little before grabbing my cell phone off my night stand. For the past week, every time I woke up I felt a sinking disappointment in my chest upon checking my phone and seeing that I had no new text messages. Prior to us "cooling it," I received a good morning text every single morning, and several throughout the day and one right before bed. I swallowed hard as I looked at the screen. No new messages. I scowled, my heart rate increasing as I remembered my dreams from the night before.

Knock it off, Harlow, I chided myself. *Everything is fine.* I stood up, making my way quickly to the bathroom for a much needed shower. I brushed my wet hair and applied makeup with a quick, unwavering hand. The restless night of sleep had shown too much on my face to avoid makeup, although I seriously wanted to. I felt as if my limbs weighed a thousand pounds each. I was moving slowly, almost sloth like. I couldn't believe that I was feeling like this after just one day in court, a couple hours on the stand.

"I'll drive you to school," Mom said, tossing a muffin at me. I caught it, but set it on the counter.

"I'm not hungry," I said, looking away. Mom's lips pursed, she was concerned. "It's okay, I'll get something at the school for lunch," I added. That seemed to appease her, and she shrugged, grabbing her keys from the table.

"Are you ready to go?" she asked.

I nodded, slipping into my boots and coat. I picked up my bag slowly, following her out to her car. She turned it on prior too, so it was nice and toasty warm when we got in. Still, my wet hair had frozen in places. I shook my head, breaking the frozen bits apart with gentle fingers. Mom looked at me again, concern clearly radiating off her as she backed out of our driveway. She was silent the entire drive to the school, and didn't say anything until she pulled up front.

I glanced at her, muttering a quick thanks under my breath, and jumped out of the car. I swung my bag on my back as I made my way down the main foyer of the school. I walked into the principal's office, ignoring the plump secretary as she disapprovingly signed me in and gave me a hall pass. I took it off her, meeting her eyes with a firm gaze.

"Have a good day now, buh-bye," she said pointedly. I walked away, stealing another glance at her as I left. She was shaking her head in disdain.

I really couldn't figure out why the school's secretary hated me so much. It couldn't just be that she saw my tattoos on my first day of school and hated them. That seemed to be the turning point in her behavior to me. But regardless, I didn't care enough to really read into it. Shrugging, I pulled open the door and made my way to my second period class. I already knew Jenna wouldn't be there, she was officially doing corre-spondence at home, so I kept to myself for pretty much the whole day. At the end of third period, I was at my locker grab-bing my math textbook. Jake found me there. He leaned against the locker beside mine and grinned.

"Hey," he said. "You weren't in homeroom!"

"Yeah, I know. Slept in. So how did your...thing go?" I asked, shoving a book into my bag. I went to close the door; it was slightly warped, so I had to shut it with force. It slammed, drawing the attention of a couple students passing by.

"Fine." Jake shrugged. "How's Jenna doing? I was hoping I'd get to talk to her after...but..."

"She's fine. I thought you had her number?"

"No." Jake's smile was almost wistful. "We talked on Face-book a few times...but then she deleted it."

"Oh?" I hadn't realized Jenna had deleted her Facebook. Granted, I hadn't been on it in a couple weeks. "Do you want her number?"

"I don't know if she wants me to have it." Jake shrugged again. "But if you talk to her...give her mine."

"Okay," I said, almost bewildered by his behavior. He was acting shy.

"Cool, well. I've gotta run." He started to walk away, but paused and looked at me. "Did you want a ride to work tonight?"

"Thanks, but I don't work," I answered, smiling. "I'm going to Jenna's."

"Really?" Jake looked thoughtful.

I rolled my eyes. "Yes, you can give me a ride."

"Alright alright, I'll give you a ride," Jake joked, grinning at me. "See ya after school!"

I watched him walk off, smiling and shaking my head. I could read people fairly well, and Jake had a thing for Jenna. It was sweet to see. I was wondering how Jenna felt about Jake when I caught Iain's eye from across the crowded hallway. He was walking down toward the parking lot exit, holding his briefcase. He had a peculiar look on his face, an odd set to his mouth like he was displeased by something. My breath hitched. Was he displeased by the mere sight of me, or had it been Jake and I talking? I couldn't ask him, not with all the people around, and he'd turned his head the moment he saw me looking at him. He walked down the hall with determination, not stopping to smile at the students like usual. Something was up.

The bell rang, and students started walking with more purpose toward their last period classes. I hesitated, filled with the drive to follow Iain's retreating figure down the hall and into his abandoned classroom. I needed a moment with him. Just a moment. Fourth period was a spare for him as well, and he used that time to catch up on his lesson plans and marking. He paused with his hand on the door. I knew it'd look suspicious if I just followed him inside, so I spoke up, my voice calm.

"Mr. Bentley...Do you have a moment? I wanted to talk to you about a university referral letter?"

He looked at me, the surprise and tension quickly fading to amusement, then he schooled his features to indifference and nodded. "I have a few to spare." He held open the door for me, allowing me to walk in. We both tried to remain natural, but it was hard to resist the pull we had toward each other. I was relieved that it was still there. The dark, taunting voice in my head had nearly convinced me none of it had ever happened.

I waited until Iain set his briefcase down on his desk and sat, motioning to one of the empty desks in front of him.

"It's very wise of you to get referral letters from all your teachers," Iain said, his voice full of authority and approval. I could tell by the glint in his eyes that he meant it. "Have you figured out where you want to go yet?"

"I'm leaning toward the University of Ottawa," I replied breezily, leaning back in the desk chair while I remembered our weekend in Ottawa.

Iain smiled, remembering it too. "It's a good university. I believe you'd be a great fit. What are you hoping to take?"

"I hope to get an MA in English, maybe with an emphasis on women's studies." I shrugged. I still wasn't entirely sure what I wanted to do. I knew it was going to involve my love of the written language—and the further away from this town I got, the better.

"Well, I'd be happy to write a referral," Iain said, looking at me steadily. I grinned. Seeing his expression in the hallway had me worried. It was nice sitting there talking to him, even if it was about school. "You should also book an appointment with the guidance counselor, about getting started on your university application. It's a tedious process."

"Okay." I nodded, figuring that'd be a good idea.

"It's time you got back to class though, Harlow," Iain told

me, giving me one last longing look. He didn't promise to call me or text, and I somehow knew that he wouldn't.

I hurried to my final class—math—and apologized to the teacher before finding my seat. I forced myself to pay attention to his monotone voice to almost no avail. My mind kept drifting to Iain, the trial, the photos, university, and Iain again. I accepted our latest assignment before the bell rang. I didn't even know what he'd been lecturing us on. Irritated with myself for having zoned out, I shoved the assignment paper in my bag and stood up. I darted past the students taking their time leaving the classroom and hurried to my locker to grab my jacket. Jake was waiting, leaning casually against the lockers, texting on his phone.

"Hey," I said.

"Hey," Jake said, nodding. He waited for me to grab my coat then we headed out to the parking lot to his Jeep.

I reached into my coat pocket, pulling my phone out. Just as I thought. There were no messages from Iain. Wrinkling my nose in minor disappointment, I quickly typed out a text to Jenna: *On my way over. Jake is driving me. Want anything?*

I waited less than a minute for Jenna's reply: *DQ Blizzard?*

"Seriously? It's freezing out!" I said out loud, shaking my head. Jake sent me a curious look. "She wants a DQ Blizzard," I answered his unspoken question.

"Ahhh." Jake nodded, looking amused. "Okay, that's doable. But I want a coffee."

"Me too." I yawned. My energy was spent. My body felt numb, although my mind kept whirling about everything. It was a lot of drama for one to handle. I suddenly missed Lauren with a furious pang in my heart, but I tried to shake it off without success. As if you could shake something like that off. It always welled up in me, catching me off guard. With Iain distancing himself from me, I felt vulnerable and alone. This was a time where I'd normally lean on Lauren.

Jake fired up his Jeep and drove us to the nearest Tim Horton's while I sat in silence, looking out the window, brooding. Jake tried to make conversation a few times, then gave up and put on his stereo. Lorde pumped through the aftermarket speakers.

"Lorde?" I raised an eyebrow, impressed with his music choice.

"Yeah." He shrugged, grinning. "She's got a great voice." I nodded in agreement as he pulled up to the Tim Horton's drive-thru window. Jake looked to me expectantly, and I told him my order. He repeated it and his own, and handed the teller a five-dollar bill. I insisted on thrusting some coins at him for mine and he insisted on trying to refuse.

"Don't be ridiculous," I snapped, tossing the coins into his cup holder. He rolled his eyes at my outburst.

"What's up with you?" he demanded. "Trouble in paradise?"

I gritted my teeth. "No, I just don't have any patience today, so don't test me."

"Whatever. Next stop, DQ." Jake shrugged. He ordered Jenna's Blizzard, refusing to accept my money. "I've got this one. I want to."

I rolled my eyes dramatically, trying to hide my smile. I knew exactly why Jake wanted to buy the Blizzard. His blossoming crush on Jenna was completely obvious. Jake put Jenna's Blizzard in his cup holder and started driving toward Jenna's house. Within ten minutes we were there. That was one of the perks to North Bay— you could get anywhere within ten or fifteen minutes, providing there wasn't any construction or accidents. People in North Bay seemed to know how to drive in the snow a lot better than people down south. Probably because the people in North Bay had to adjust to almost eight solid months of snow, while people down south barely got a dusting around Christmas time.

We pulled up into Jenna's driveway and Jake hesitated. I could tell he wanted to come in, but wasn't sure if he would be welcome.

"You have her Blizzard. Trust me, you'll be more welcome than me," I told him, jumping out of his Jeep and slamming the door. I nearly slipped on the ice patch under my feet, and grabbed the Jeep's handle to steady myself. My coffee sloshed over my hand, the hot liquid burning my skin slightly. "Fuck," I muttered, switching the coffee over to my other hand and wiping my right hand on the bottom of my jeans angrily.

"You okay?" Jake asked, raising an eyebrow.

"I'm fine," I said, feeling anything but.

We walked up the front steps and I knocked on the door before opening it. I'd been to visit Jenna so many times before, that I felt totally comfortable just walking in, especially knowing that her parents would be at work for another two hours at least. I kicked off my boots and called out Jenna's name. Jake followed me inside, keeping quiet as he held onto his coffee and Jenna's Blizzard.

"In here!" Jenna called back. I found her in the living room, watching MTV's Jersey Shore.

"Again?" I rolled my eyes. "This show is so stupid it's actually painful."

"What else am I supposed to do?" Jenna pouted. "There's not much on during the day."

"Read a book?" I suggested, repressing the urge to laugh at her death glare.

"I have. I've read six this week so far. My eyes hurt," Jenna retorted hotly. "Oh, hi Jake." Jenna straightened up a little as Jake walked in behind me. She self-consciously adjusted the blanket over her belly to hide it and ran a hand through her already perfect hair. She shot me a look that said *some warning would have been nice.* I figured the text would have been warning enough, but apparently not.

"Hey." He grinned, looking as if he felt a little awkward. He held up her Blizzard. "We got you this."

"Oh, thank you!" Jenna blushed, accepting it as he handed it to her. She timidly looked up at him and smiled. He smiled back.

"Oh good Lord," I grumbled, falling onto the couch opposite Jenna. Both of them turned to stare at me, Jake with an amused smile and Jenna with embarrassment. "Cut the crap, you two. It's okay to be into each other."

"I—" Jenna blushed deeper, glaring at me.

"Well, that wasn't awkward." Jake rolled his eyes, shifting his weight from foot to foot.

"Just get her number and make plans or something," I told him, trying to keep the note of bitterness out of my tone. It'd be easy for them to be together. They didn't have to worry about being discovered; they wouldn't have a forbidden relationship. Okay, so it wouldn't be as easy for them as it would for most considering Jenna's condition, but they stood a better chance than me and Iain. At least nobody would end up in jail.

"She's on to something," Jake said, looking at Jenna expectantly. "So...can I have your number?"

"Yeah...sure." Jenna's blue eyes were bright with excitement. She gave him her number as he programmed it into his phone.

"I'll text you so you know mine," Jake said, quickly typing a text into his phone. We heard Jenna's go off on the arm of the couch beside her, and she smiled.

"See? That wasn't so terrible," I remarked dryly, leaning

back. I took another sip of my still hot coffee, staring ahead of me. Jenna and Jake exchanged a look and he shrugged at her.

"I'll catch you guys later," he said, making to leave. Jenna waited until we heard him pull away from her driveway to start in on me.

"What's gotten into you?" she demanded, adjusting her body so that she was facing me. Her belly was getting rounder every day, part of the reason why she had decided to do correspondence.

I tried to think of an answer that would satisfy Jenna that wouldn't give away too much of my situation. My mouth opened and closed several times before I finally settled on my answer. "Guy troubles."

Jenna stared at me, waiting for more. She raised one eyebrow delicately. "What kind of 'guy troubles'?" she asked, even going as far as to give finger quotations.

"The kind that I can't really talk about." I shrugged. "It's complicated."

"Oh, I bet it is," Jenna said, smiling like the Cheshire Cat.

"What's that supposed to mean?" I asked. I didn't have the patience for games right now. I was in quite the foul mood, thanks to my direction of thought that afternoon. I just wanted to go home and sleep, but I had promised Jenna I would come by.

"I think I know," Jenna said softly, muting the TV to shut out Snooki's irritating drivel about guidos.

"Know what?" My frown deepened as my heartbeat increased, but I kept my hand steady as I brought my coffee up to my lips to take another sip.

"Ben," Jenna said after a moment. "He's...not really Ben, is he? It's...Mr. Bentley. I've seen the way you guys look at each other..."

I didn't say anything. I didn't know what to say. I hadn't

realized Jenna had been paying that much attention. I took another sip of my coffee, trying to buy myself some time.

"That's ridiculous," I said, giving her a look that said *you are clearly off your rocker.*

Jenna gave me a silencing glare. "Oh please. I'm not an idiot," she said, rolling her eyes. "There's an...energy, about you two." She gazed off into the distance with a small smile on her lips.

I winced, unsure of this entire conversation.

"Don't worry, I'm not going to rat you guys out," Jenna said, shaking her head to clear whatever thoughts she'd been having. "Frankly, I'm kind of impressed. Mr. Bentley is hot."

I put my coffee down on the end table with shaky hands and leaned forward, covering my face with my hands. I didn't know what to say or do. I couldn't deny it, not without really looking like I was lying. Jenna would know, and then she'd be hurt that I hadn't told her the truth.

"So..." Jenna pressed gently, her voice edging into my panicked thoughts. "What kind of trouble with 'Ben'?"

"Just...trouble. Outside influences rocking the boat, so we're 'cooling it.'" I shrugged. It was easier to talk to her when she called Iain 'Ben,' I could still pretend that Jenna had no idea who Ben really was.

"I'd show up on his doorstep, personally." Jenna shrugged. "Demand an explanation. Not leave until I got it."

"No, you wouldn't." I laughed. "You could barely give Jake your number without turning a very adorable shade of pink."

"Well, circumstances are a bit different, aren't they?" Jenna smiled sadly, absently putting her hand on her swollen stomach. "It's hard to be confident with..."

"I know," I said quickly, feeling guilty. "But it's actually tough for us too, believe it or not. Ia—Ben could go to jail for sexual exploitation. He's our teacher. Besides, I seriously don't even think Jake sees that. I mean, he sees it, but not the way you think. He sees you as a remarkably strong and admirable person."

"Why?" Jenna asked, wisely ignoring to comment on Iain and instead focusing on Jake. "How do you know that?"

"Jake's an open book, he's super easy to read," I said, shrugging. "It's the subtle asking about you every day, the way he smiles at you...that kind of thing. He's into you."

"Now is kind of a bad time." Jenna looked down at her stomach.

"Hey, if you find a guy that's willing to stick around for this? He's a keeper. If Jake's interested in you, it's because he's interested in *you*," I said.

"If you're so full of sage advice, why don't you go talk to 'Ben'? Read him." Jenna smirked.

I sighed. "Because..."

I thought about the photos, and the subtle threat behind them. I thought about our conversation the other night, about why Iain wanted to cool it. It wasn't because he didn't love me or didn't want to be with me; it's because he wanted the possibility of that happening long term. He didn't want to end up in jail. He was looking toward the future while I was rooted in the present. If we continued to see each other, that would just allow the photographer another chance at snapping a photo, and it might be one that would get Iain into serious trouble. It was better to lay low for a while.

I didn't tell Jenna about any of it. I didn't want to stress her out about the trial. "Maybe I will," I said finally, hoping to appease her.

"And maybe I'll give Jake a chance." She smiled demurely.

The next few days went by quickly. I went to school, took notes like a good little student, and booked an appointment with the guidance counselor to discuss my post-secondary education. She was a middle-aged friendly woman who was absolutely confident that I'd get accepted into the University of Ottawa, but still encouraged me to apply to a few different universities. I chose Carleton University and Laurentian University as well, not overly concerned with where I went. Carleton would be just as nice, as it was in Ottawa too.

For some reason, I was hung up on Ottawa. I felt a force, pulling me toward that direction.

I kept busy, hanging out with Jake on break and focusing as much as I could on schooling. Despite my forced smile and attempts at staying social, I was becoming numb. Each day I grew more and more anxious. The jury had requested an extra week to decide, and it felt as if the entire town stood in limbo.

I was beginning to shut down again, just like I had after the accident. Too many things were happening, and my brain felt muddled and overwhelmed. I willed myself to snap out of it. I knew not to let one person affect my happiness so much, but Iain wasn't just a guy. He was the love of my life. Besides, it was more than that. It was the fear that our secret would be discovered, the fear that he'd face serious legal repercussions and grow to resent me. What love could flourish under those circumstances?

The jury reached their decision that Friday morning. Andrew got 600 hours of community service, a year of therapy, and a smear on his permanent record. A slap on the wrist, really, but if he ever dared to sexually assault a girl again, he would face more the more serious repercussions of jail time and registering as a sex offender.

The Police Department was making a lot of discoveries in the investigation of Carl Cooper's play in it all. The Police Department had even chosen another police officer to act as Chief of Police. The word on the street was that Carl Cooper was livid.

I heard all the townsfolk chatter at work that Saturday morning—a day after the jury's decision—while I brought pancakes and plates of eggs to tables and refilled coffee mugs. It was the kind of gossip that I didn't mind hearing, despite the prickly, fearful sensation in the pit of my stomach that seemed to be constantly there.

"I bet they're ashamed," one of the elderly ladies that regularly came in to gossip was saying to another one. I was pretty sure it was the same two that were gossiping about how sweet Andrew had been. "After that scandal, I wouldn't want to show my face in public again."

"And that poor girl," the other one tittered, shaking her head remorsefully. I held back my comments, continuing past their table to the register.

I massaged my forehead, feeling stifled. Danielle gave me a sympathetic, understanding look.

"How are you?" I asked her, forgetting about my feelings. I knew how hard it must have been to relive Rachel's trauma inside a court room and in front of Andrew Cooper.

"I'm fine," she assured me, giving me a brave smile. "How's your friend? Jenna?"

"Good," I replied, doing up some rolls of utensils while we talked.

Danielle nodded. "At least the town can't ignore it now," she whispered, glancing at the patrons.

"That's true." I nodded, agreeing with her statement. There was definitely no hushing it.

The rest of my shift was the same, the entire diner full of gossip about the Coopers. By the time I headed for home, my head was nearly splitting in two.

Although I desperately wanted to, I resisted the urge to walk to Iain's house. Instead, I trekked home, keeping one hand on my cell phone and both eyes obsessively scanning my surroundings. I kept imagining Carl Cooper and Andrew trying to run me down again, only this time...succeeding. I saw no sign of a blue truck on my walk though.

I really need to get a damn car, I thought, angry at myself, tired of the fear of walking home.

Half an hour later, I was home. I slid out of my jacket and boots, and snagged a quick shower to wash the greasy diner smell from my hair and skin. As I was drying my hair, I heard my cell phone's shrill ring tone from my bedroom. I wrapped my towel around my body, allowing my wet hair to fall back down, and raced to my room.

"Hello?" I said breathlessly.

"Did you hear?" Jenna's voice was animated. "Carl Cooper is under arrest for obstruction of justice!"

"Yes!" I said, unable to stop the wide grin from spreading across my face. I sat down on my bed, wet hair still dripping down my arms.

"Yup," Jenna reported smugly. "Serves him right. I'm just surprised that he didn't try to come after me."

Frankly, I wasn't all that surprised. Carl Cooper saw me as a threat because I stood up to both him and his son. I was verbal and defiant, my attitude made me stand out while soft spoken Jenna had flown under their radar. I was pretty sure Carl hadn't even known the name of Andrew's latest victim, the one that was pressing charges, until the Burkes had already pressed them. I suppose a lot of it had to do with how influential Mr. Burke was too.

"Well, that's good, right?" I said, believing that it was. Still, I couldn't help the dreadful well of anxiety in the pit of my belly. I tried to calm my nerves, focusing on the good that this news brought.

"Yeah." Jenna paused, lower her voice slightly. "Do you think...it's safe now?" I knew what she was talking about—Iain and I.

"I don't think it will ever be safe," I said, my own voice just as low. "At least not here." I played with a loose thread on my towel.

"If I were you, I'd run away with him," Jenna said.

After hanging up the phone, I couldn't stop replaying Jenna's words in my mind. *Run away with him*, the sickly sweet voice urged. I could almost picture us...together, happy, no restrictions on our relationship. No fear looming over us at every single moment. I chewed on my lip, debating whether I should call Iain, but I knew it was best to lay low. At least for a while longer, until I was certain everything wasn't going to blow up in my face.

CHAPTER FIFTEEN

I wasn't naïve enough to think that Iain and I could immediately be together after Carl Cooper's arrest. I knew that so long as I was a student and Iain taught at my high school, it was incredibly dangerous to entertain even the thought of a future together. Someone somewhere had photos of us. It was a bomb set to detonate at any minute. I tried my best to keep myself from thinking about it. I spent too many of the weeks after Carl Cooper's arrest scarcely breathing, terrified that Iain would get arrested. Each day it didn't happen, the hope grew... as did the fear.

I focused my best efforts on my schoolwork, keeping my grades high so that the universities I applied to would have no reason to turn me away. I also finally dove into my savings and bought a secondhand car. It was nothing fancy, just a black 2001 Honda Civic. The best part about it was that it was mine. I knew I didn't necessarily need it to get around North Bay, but it helped my anxiety. No more walking alone at night, no more waiting fully exposed to unseen enemies. Besides, it'd be convenient when I left for university in the fall. I'd have my own set of wheels and wouldn't have to depend on public transportation.

"I don't know why the photos haven't surfaced," I said to Jenna one night in the middle of April. We were hanging out at her place, watching yet another Ryan Reynolds movie.

Since Carl Cooper's arrest (and the relocation of his wife and son), I'd opened up to Jenna more about what "outside influence" had interrupted our blissful state of ignorance.

"I don't know." Jenna frowned, absently rubbing her swollen belly. She was so huge, but she wasn't due for another three or four weeks. "Maybe it was an empty threat?" she offered, looking at me hopefully.

"I don't think the Coopers do empty threats." I sighed.

Jenna opened her mouth to say something, but instead she let out a choked gasp, doubling forward and clenching her stomach. Her face filled with agonizing pain.

"Jenna!" I jumped up, racing to her side.

"Arg!" Jenna groaned, her face pale. "I think it's time!"

"Really? What do I do?" I panicked, running my hands through my hair and looking around for guidance. I had no experience with babies.

"Just...call my mom," Jenna said, spacing out each word with gasps. She looked vulnerable and scared.

I grabbed her phone, searching through her contacts for her mom's phone number.

"Mrs. Burke? It's Harlow. I think Jenna is in labor," I said when Mrs. Burke answered on the third ring. I watched as Jenna doubled over in pain again.

"How far apart are the contractions?" Mrs. Burke's voice was brisk and controlled.

"Um...contractions?" I repeated, completely lost. I helplessly looked at Jenna, wondering if she knew. Jenna shrugged back in answer, panting slightly. Moisture dotted her temple.

"Take Jenna to the labor and delivery ward," Mrs. Burke instructed, realizing that I had no idea what I was doing. "We are an hour and a half away. We will meet you guys there."

"Okay," I said. I could do that. I handed Jenna the phone, searching for her purse. I found it on the dresser. I returned to the living room with it clenched in my hands. "Okay, let's go, Jenna."

"No," Jenna panted. "My hospital bag," she huffed. "By my bed. It has my docu-ments!" she yelped as yet another contraction hit her, or at least...I thought it was another contraction.

I returned to her room, snatching up the hospital bag from beside her bed. Jenna was already slipping into her boots, taking breaks as each wave of pain hit her.

"Oh my God, Jenna," I gasped, panicking again. Things were moving way too quickly for my liking. In a rush, I hurried her out the door. As soon as we got to the porch, Jenna stopped moving with me, a look of utter shock on her face as she looked down.

"I think my water just broke," she said.

I tugged on her. "Seriously, let's get you to the hospital because I cannot deliver a baby."

I drove like a speed demon, arriving at the hospital in under seven minutes. Finding parking and getting Jenna up to the labor and delivery ward took much longer, and she was nearly crying by the time we stumbled up to the nurses' station and made it into a room. She huffed through getting into a hospital gown, gripping my arm painfully tight when a contraction hit her.

"Oh my, your contractions are close together," the nurse, who'd introduced herself as Tina, said, helping lower Jenna into the bed. "I'm going to check your cervix. Is this your first?" Jenna nodded, keeping her eyes on the ceiling as the nurse went about her job. "You're about six centimeters dilated. When did the contractions hit?"

"Less than half an hour ago," I answered.

Tina raised her eyebrows. "Luckily girl, things are moving quickly then! And you arrived just in time to have an epidural, should you choose to get one."

"Yes, now, please!" Jenna begged.

Once the epidural was in, Jenna relaxed enough to demand her phone. I fetched it for her, and she scrolled through her list of contacts. I assumed she was calling her mother, so I sat down in a chair by her bed to wait.

"Hi...Sarah? It's Jenna...I'm in the hospital...in labor," Jenna said. "You guys can come if you can make it...but I'm six centimetres dilated. Things have progressed really quickly."

I couldn't hear the person, Sarah, answer, but I saw Jenna's smile. "Okay great!" she said, hanging up the phone. I looked at her questionably. "That was the...adoptive mother." Jenna made a face, and the machine strapped to her body made beeping sounds as she had yet another contraction. They were less than a minute apart, now. Jenna still wasn't feeling pain, but had mentioned several times that she felt like she should start pushing. We were waiting for the nurse to come in and check her cervix.

In the chaos of Jenna going into labor, I'd forgotten all about the very huge detail of adoption. Jenna bit her lip, looking uncertain. "Are you okay?" I asked.

"Yeah," Jenna answered, trying to put on a brave face. "I'm just really nervous."

I tried to think of something encouraging to say, but was saved by Jenna's mom and dad rushing into the room. Mr. Burke stayed long enough to kiss Jenna and tell her loved her, but left just after the nurse arrived to check Jenna's cervix. She was eight centimeters dilated, so painfully close but not quite there yet.

"I'll be back to check on you in twenty minutes," the friendly nurse assured her, pulling her surgical gloves off and tossing them into the garbage can. Jenna nodded, taking a deep, steadying breath.

"I can't do this," Jenna wailed, bursting into huge tears the moment the door clicked shut behind the nurse. "I can't...I can't."

"Shh, it's okay, honey," Mrs. Burke said, putting her arms around Jenna and hugging her close.

"You've got this, Jenna," I added, leaning forward and gently squeezing her hand. "You haven't really got a choice, have you? I mean, it can't stay in there. Think of how hard it'd be to find a prom dress to fit an 11-month-pregnant belly."

Jenna laughed weakly, her shoulders still shaking. Someone timidly knocked on the door, and Jenna furiously wiped her tears away before calling for them to come in.

"Hello," a sweet unfamiliar voice, just as timid as the knock, said. We all looked up to see a pretty, petite blonde woman with soft blue eyes, she looked vaguely familiar. She was smiling shyly at Jenna.

"Hello, Sarah," Mrs. Burke greeted her, smiling warmly and gently at the woman; the adoptive mother.

"Harlow, this is the baby's adoptive mom, Sarah," Jenna said, smiling through her tears. Jenna had been crying an awful lot. "Harlow is my best friend," Jenna explained to Sarah. The declaration surprised and warmed me, although I suppose it was true. We had gotten incredibly close over the last several months. "I'm glad you made it in time. I thought you guys would take longer..."

"I was staying with family, so I could get to the hospital quickly," Sarah replied, coming to stand at the end of Jenna's hospital bed. She tentatively rested her hands on the railing at the foot of the bed, giving me a warm smile in greeting. "Rob is on his way right now; he left the moment I called him. We live in Hamilton," Sarah said, mostly to me.

"Well, that's good," Jenna said shyly, probably feeling awkward. Another contraction hit her hard and she moaned, squeezing my hand. Either the epidural was starting to fade, or she was getting closer to giving birth. She looked at her mother frantically. "I feel like I need to push, Mom," she said desperately.

"Should I call the nurse?" I asked. Mrs. Burke nodded, so I grabbed the call button on the side of Jenna's bed.

"Should I go?" Sarah asked, her voice nervous and longing.

"I'll go," I said quickly, trying to pull away from Jenna. She clasped tighter onto my hand.

"No, I want you all to stay," Jenna said. "You two at my sides, and you right there...so you can take...the baby." Jenna groaned against the urge to push. The nurse rushed in, and the next half an hour was a flurry of activity. The doctor walked in the moment Jenna started to crown, and shortly thereafter, the baby was born. The doctor held it up and grinned.

"It's a girl!" he said, offering the messy, gooey newborn to Jenna. She shook her head, sobbing hard. Jenna didn't seem to be able to look at the baby. Mrs. Burke looked at her daughter, her heartbreak evident on her face.

"To her..." she nodded toward Sarah, who had stayed by the door the whole time. Sarah was also crying, only her tears were joyful and happy as she took the baby from the doctor.

"You did great, Jenna," I told her, but Jenna didn't hear me. She was sobbing heavily, her chest heaving with every breath. I didn't know whether I should stay or not. Mrs. Burke seemed to have a hold on the situation, but I didn't want Jenna to feel like I'd abandoned her.

I sat down, watching the two scenes unfold around me. Mrs. Burke stroking Jenna's hair in an attempt to comfort her, and the nurses across the room, checking the baby's vitals and wrapping her up in a warm blanket and hat, with Sarah standing right there smiling through her tears. Heartbreak and joy in one room. My heart felt heavy for my friend, and yet excited for this stranger's chance at being a mother. I could tell she would be an amazing one, simply from how she held the baby and looked down at the small bundle with all the love in the world.

I left Jenna's hospital room to give her, her family, Sarah, and the baby some privacy. It seemed overwhelmingly crowded in the room. Before I left, Jenna thanked me for everything.

"You've been so supportive. I don't know what I would have done without you," she said, fresh tears spilling from her tired eyes.

"You're a rock star," I told her. "I'll come by after school to hang with you. Maybe I'll bring that Ryan Reynold's movie; we'll finish it," I promised. She smiled and nodded, and I gave her a hug before leaving. I couldn't help but glance once more over at the baby, cradled in Sarah's arm. Soft blonde curls peaked out from under the pink newborn hat. Sarah was cooing at her, and didn't notice my departure. Not that I minded.

When I returned home, I crashed.

The next day, I surprised myself by getting up on time for school. I was eager for the chance to catch a glimpse of Iain in the hallways, just to see him. It'd been so long.

Only Iain wasn't there. Concern welled up in my belly. It was unlike him to miss school. I still couldn't bring myself to text him though. Instead, I stopped off to grab panzerottis, then I went to the hospital.

Jenna was in the same room she'd been in the day before, only the baby was gone.

"They moved her to a different room with Sarah," Jenna explained, catching me looking around. "I couldn't..."

"I understand, no need to explain," I quickly said, sweeping in to sit down in the chair beside her hospital bed. I pulled out the panzerottis from my purse. "I had to sneak these in, you know. Hospitals don't like it when their patients eat delicious, greasy foods."

Jenna laughed, gleefully accepting the panzerotti. "I'm so tired of the cardboard food, and I haven't even been here for a full 24 hours yet."

"That's also understandable," I assured her, grinning before I took a bite of mine. It was still hot and fresh. I wiped the greasy sauce away from the corner of my mouth.

"How was school?"

"Boring, stupid, lame, and did I mention boring?" I answered, taking another bite.

"Did anyone..." Jenna trailed off, sighing.

"No, nobody knows you had her," I said, feeling a little uneasy. Jenna bit her lip, tears welling in her eyes.

"I didn't know it would be this hard," she whispered, wiping a tear furiously away. "I can't even look...and I feel bad, because it's not her fault..."

"You chose what looks like a fantastic mother for her," I assured Jenna, leaning forward and gently holding her hand.

"She will have all the love in the world; that's all she'll know."

Jenna nodded, taking a huge shaky breath. She looked exhausted.

I stayed for another twenty minutes before Jenna started to fall asleep while sitting up. I left her room with the promise to visit again. I walked down the hallway to the elevator.

The doors were just about to close when a hand reached out to stop them. "Sorry," a familiar voice that instantly sent an electrical shock through my body said. Iain slid in, looking just as shocked as I did. "Harlow," he whispered, surprised to see me.

I stood there, staring at him with my mouth agape. "What are you doing here?"

"Visiting," Iain answered, cocking his head slightly and smiling wistfully as the elevator lurched downward.

"Who?"

"My sister." Iain laughed. "Sarah. She...well, I guess she just had a baby...adopted..."

"Wait," I interrupted. "Sarah, the birth mother that Jenna picked is Sarah your sister?"

"Yeah." Iain smiled.

"But...Jenna would have told me." I frowned. This wasn't exactly something that a good friend would keep from another good friend. Oh, by the way, my baby's adopted parents are related to the love of your life who just happens to be your teacher. Hope that's cool!

"She didn't know—doesn't know," Iain replied, stepping toward me so that his breath washed over me in a warm wave. "My brother-in-law's last name is Fetcher. Sarah has his last name now."

"Oh," I whispered. "I guess you're the family she's staying with right now."

Iain nodded, stepping closer to me. It was as if he couldn't help himself. The elevator came to a stop with his face inches away from mine. The doors opened and we jumped apart, our trance interrupted once we reached the main floor.

With heavy legs, I left the elevator, walking toward the parking lot. I could both sense and hear Iain several paces behind me. We hadn't been this close in months, but I still kept my distance, remembering his words about cooling it.

I walked quickly toward my car, Iain almost keeping pace but not quite.

"I miss you, Harlow," he said, his voice low.

"Iain." I glanced around helplessly. I couldn't tell if anyone was paying attention nearby, but it was still light out. I feared getting caught.

"I know," he assured me, reaching out to touch my cheek briefly. "I'm heading back to Ottawa next week."

"Why next week?" I demanded.

"I found a new job at a public school there. I need to get out of this town...besides, Mrs. Rush wanted to come back early. Guess her husband lost his job." Iain smiled.

"Guess I'll see you in Ottawa...maybe," I said, smiling as I opened the door and slid into my car.

"I've got no doubt about that," Iain commented, giving me a hungry look.

CHAPTER SIXTEEN

The next morning, I awoke later than I had intended. I had been unable to fall asleep; my mind just wouldn't shut off. I kept thinking about what Iain said about leaving next week. While the thought of being farther away from him pained me, I couldn't help but feel a thrill when I thought about the fact that he'd no longer be a teacher at my school.

I rushed about, trying to make it to school before the bell rang. I made it to my first period art class with five minutes to spare. As usual, Ms. Higgins was nowhere in sight. I headed to sit beside Jake at our table, ignoring the sniggering and smirking from Callie and Tara.

"Hey," Jake said, an odd expression on his face.

"What's up?" I demanded, sensing something was amiss. Everyone was staring at me, talking behind hands.

"You..." Jake started, clearing his throat and looking around uncomfortably. "You didn't see what was plastered all over the school Facebook group?"

"We have a school Facebook group?" I asked, dumbfounded. My first thought was that someone had heard about Jenna's birth.

In answer, Jake pulled his phone out of his pocket and pulled up the school Facebook group. Wordlessly, he handed me his phone. I grabbed it, my breath freezing in my chest as I scrolled down, staring at picture after picture of myself with Iain. Two were even taken last night in the parking lot of the hospital. Whoever had taken the photos from last night managed to capture both the hungry look Iain gave me and the touch of his hand on my cheek.

"People are saying..." Jake trailed off, searching for words.

"So that's how you got all those A's in Mr. Bentley's class," Callie tittered from across the room, giving me a scandalous once over before she turned back to Tara. "I knew she wasn't smart. She just screwed the teachers to pass."

"You stupid bitch," I hissed, jumping up out of my chair. It flung back behind me, tipping upside down with a clatter. My classmates fell silent, staring at me with wide eyes.

"Harlow Jones," a stern voice said from the classroom doorway. I looked up, my fists trembling. Ms. Higgins had reappeared, this time with the principal, Mr. Osborne. It was Mr. Osborne who spoke, demanding authority and attention. He was a stern-looking man in his early 60s. In the last several months, I hadn't had any run-ins with him personally but I heard a lot about what a dick he was from Jake. Naturally, the school pot dealer and the principal didn't get along. "I need you to come with me now. Grab your things."

I picked up my bag, my heart pounding and my face red with embarrassment, and followed Mr. Osborne to his office. Two policemen stood waiting.

"Harlow Jones?" the first one said. I didn't recognize him, but his partner was familiar. I'd run into Mike Turner again.

Hope fluttered in my chest. Surely it was a good sign that one of Iain's friends was on the case?

"Yes," I said, trying to keep my voice even and neutral.

"I'm Officer Hudson and this is Officer Turner. We are here to talk to you about some serious allegations that are being made about a teacher at this school having an inappropriate relationship with a student," he said. He had red hair shaved tight to his head and freckles dotting his nose. He didn't look like the policeman type.

I said nothing. I didn't know what was safe to say and what wasn't. I just stared at Officer Turner, willing him to give me some sort of sign that he'd take care of everything. He didn't. He avoided my gaze, staring instead at the desk beside me, his jaw tense.

"We'd like for you to come down to the station and answer some questions," Officer Hudson said after a moment of awkward silence.

"I want to call someone."

"You're not in trouble, Harlow," Mr. Osborne told me. "We want to help you."

"I don't need help," I blurted out. "Everything is fine." Even as I said it, the tears threatened to spill from my eyes. I was terrified for Iain, terrified about what we had done. I loved him, and I didn't want him to get into trouble. Everything certainly was not fine.

"Let's just go to the station," Officer Turner said stiffly. "You can call whoever you need on the way."

I opened and closed my mouth. It seemed like I had no choice but to accompany them to the police station. I followed them out of the school, thankful that class was in session. As it was, the few students that were roaming the halls stopped to stare openly as I walked by, being led by two police officers. Officer Hudson had his hand on my arm, gently yet firmly leading me, while Officer Turner stayed silent and stony faced. I was losing hope in the situation with every passing minute.

In the back of the police cruiser, I had time to reflect upon the situation I now found myself in. It was undeniable that Iain was arrested, or would be shortly. I wasn't clear on the details yet, but I knew that if I was being called in to the station to give a statement, that things weren't good.

"This way, please," Officer Hudson said gently, leading me down the pale yellow hallway to an interrogation room. He held the door open and I walked in, noting the room was void of everything but a table, four chairs, and a two-way mirror. Fear clenched its fist around my heart.

"I want a lawyer," I demanded, crossing my arms and refusing to walk forward at all. "I refuse to give a statement until I have a lawyer present."

Officer Hudson and Officer Turner exchanged a look with one another. Officer Turner sighed, nodding his head once. "Okay, we'll call one. Have a seat for now."

Walking into the room, my legs shaking, I sat heavily in one of the plastic chairs. The officers closed the door behind me, leaving me in the interrogation room.

I knew I wasn't in trouble, that my request for a lawyer seemed odd. I didn't want my statement to get Iain into any more trouble. I didn't want to confirm anything that would incriminate him.

I sat in the chilly interrogation room for nearly fifteen minutes. A quick knock came at the door before it swung open. Officer Turner walked in alone, holding a file in one hand and a can of Coca Cola in another. He tossed the file down, sitting across from me, and set the coke down in front of my hand. I stared at it, not making a move to touch it. He stared at me for a solid five minutes before I grew uncomfortable.

"Where is Mr. Bentley?" I asked, my voice trembling.

Officer Turner tipped his head slightly. "He's in another interrogation room," he answered.

"Why?"

"I'll cut to the chase, Harlow," Officer Turner sighed, leaning forward. "Iain is facing charges of sexual exploitation."

"But it wasn't..." I trailed off, clamping my mouth shut when I realized I'd nearly confirmed the allegations. "I want to see a lawyer," I insisted again. I was beginning to feel like a broken record. My voice was scratchy, dry and itchy.

"The lawyer is on the way," Officer Turner said. "Did you want us to call your parents?"

"I figured you would have already," I retorted, surprise flashing across my face.

"You're 18," Officer Turner reminded me. I snorted.

"Then no, I don't want to call my parents." I rolled my eyes. The last thing I needed was Mom and Larry blowing in here. Mom with her tears of guilt and Larry...I froze, realizing that Larry was a Catholic School Board member.

"He already knows," Officer Turner said, nodding once, as if he knew where my thoughts had taken me. "The school board has been notified of the charges, naturally."

"He's your friend," I shot back.

Officer Turner looked taken aback, surprised that I knew that information, and even more angry about it. "I'll be back when the lawyer gets here," was all he said in response. He stood up, leaving the room with quick steps. I stared down at the can of Coke. Condensation had formed. I was desperately thirsty, but I didn't want to drink anything that the police provided me. I couldn't help but feel as if they were the bad guys.

Nearly two hours later, I left the police station. My mom opened the passenger door to her car, and I slid in wordlessly. She'd picked me up when I called her, my voice oddly calm and my eyes dry. The lawyer they had called sat with me while Officer Hudson and Officer Turner asked me questions. She was a tall, willowy brunette with her hair pulled back into a tight bun. She looked every bit a lawyer.

She'd told me my best bet was to explain that Iain and I had been friends. After all, there was no proof of a physical relationship.

I didn't know if my statement would help or hinder Iain, and I couldn't draw my thoughts away from anything else.

"Larry is at home," Mom warned, pulling into our driveway. I'd been silent the whole ride. I didn't say anything in response. I just unbuckled my seat belt and went inside meekly.

Larry was waiting in the sitting room, tapping his foot furiously on the floor. He stood up when the door opened, making his way to the foyer. The look of anger on his face shocked me, and I took an involuntary step back, bumping into my mom.

"When I found out this morning that one of the teachers in my high school was having an inappropriate relationship with a student, I was livid," Larry started, his voice full of controlled anger. He paced into the kitchen, unable to remain still. "When I found out that the student was my daughter, I was enraged."

"Step-daughter," I corrected automatically. Larry sent a look that silenced me.

"Then when your mother told me that you were willingly having a relationship with this teacher, I came very close to snapping," Larry continued, putting the counter between us. He placed his wide palms on the top of the marble slab counter, his face red with anger. I kept my mouth shut, unable to speak. "How could you have been so stupid and naïve, Harlow?" he bellowed, spit flying from his mouth.

"Larry," Mom warned, stepping forward and reaching her arm out to me.

"And you," Larry turned to look at my mom, his face full of hurt. "I can't believe you knew about it and didn't tell me when it was happening so we could stop it."

"It ended," Mom argued, her brows creasing in anger. She put her hand on my shoulder, as a show of support.

"Regardless." Larry waved his hand, as if that detail was miniature and unimportant, and I suppose it was.

I opened and closed my mouth a few times, willing the words that sat on the tip of my tongue to spill out—*we love each other, we're in love*—but they didn't. They remained frozen in my mouth. I realized how naïve that sounded; how foolish.

Larry looked at us one last time then he sighed heavily. "Now I have a huge mess to clean up. I'll be home late," he added. He came back around the island, grabbing his coat and keys. Neither Mom nor I turned around to watch him go.

CHAPTER SEVENTEEN

In the week after Iain's arrest, the newspapers blew up with reports of the charges laid against a local Catholic High School teacher. They all painted Iain in a sick light, as if he was a predator who needed to be locked up.

Worse were the allegations being made by other students. The newspapers didn't release the names of the supposed victims, but said that several female students had come forward, saying that Mr. Bentley had "made sexual advances on them." The moment I read that, I ran for the bathroom to vomit. I couldn't believe it. I felt a tiny seed of insecurity, but in my heart of hearts, I knew it wasn't true. Our relationship hadn't been the sick, *Lifetime* drama that the newspapers and the town painted it. I spent the week after the arrest hiding out at home. I refused to go out, especially after my ten-second attempt at school the day after. I couldn't handle the gossip from my classmates or the looks of pity I attracted from every single person over the age of 30.

Despite the fact that the newspapers hadn't released my name, my photo was still all over the Internet. Larry was desperately working to get it removed, so it wouldn't taint my future academic career. I would have a week of testing to prove that my grades were earned by my intelligence and not by Iain's bias. It was both insulting and ridiculous, but I had no choice but to go through with it so that my acceptance at all the universities I applied at would still stand.

"It's not true," I spat out to Larry over a very strained dinner one evening. Mom had attempted at bringing us back to a normalized state, but I couldn't handle the stony silence from Larry. The trial had already started; the school board had gotten a very good lawyer and were proceeding in pressing charges against Iain for sexual exploitation and inappropriate behavior toward minors, and the story about more alleged victims had appeared in that morning's paper. "There are no victims. Iain and I are in love."

Larry looked as if he was having a hard time swallowing the forkful he'd put in his month. His eyes narrowed, staring at me while he took a sip of his water to clear his throat.

"I don't want to hear about it," he warned me, waving the fork at me. His face started to flush with anger. "Not another word about this, Harlow, and I mean it."

Mom gave me a pleading look, willing me to hush. I knew she was desperate for a night of normal, but I couldn't stomach it. I stood up, pushing my chair back angrily. I glared at them before I walked toward the front hall. I pulled my boots on, grabbing my car keys and jacket and fleeing out of the house before either of them could stop me. I didn't know where I was going, but I had to get out of the house.

I drove to the lake. At the beginning of May, nobody was really there. It wasn't warm enough to hang out at the beach at night. Not yet anyway. I put the car in park and started to cry, my head buried in my arms on the steering wheel.

At first, I had thought that Iain would somehow contact

me, maybe through his lawyer or something. I thought he would have me speak at the trial about how we were in love, but I hadn't heard a thing from him or his lawyer. I wasn't involved in the trial; I couldn't even watch the proceedings. The court room was closed to the public.

I knew from reading the newspapers that there were only a couple more days left in the trial. The jury was supposed to reach a decision by the following Thursday. I also knew that the Catholic school board wanted to have this "ugly scandal" dealt with as quickly as possible, so the town could forget about it.

My phone rang, breaking me from my sob fest. I grabbed it, looking at the screen before clicking answer.

"What?" I demanded harshly, hiccuping.

"Where are you, Harlow?" Jenna sighed.

"At the lake," I replied, too exhausted to deflect her. Besides, I felt like I needed company.

"I'll be there in ten," Jenna promised, hanging up. I dropped the phone back on the passenger seat, wiping the tears from my eyes as I looked at the landscape. The sun was just setting over the lake. I stared at it without really taking it in, my eyes blurred with fresh tears. I didn't bother wiping them away.

Ten minutes later, Jenna tapped against the passenger window of my car. I hit the unlock button and she slid inside, closing the door behind her. She stared at me with her wide blue eyes. She looked a lot better than the last time I'd seen her, then and again...that had been in the hospital, the day I'd run into Iain, the day before his arrest. She wore her hair in a casual braid down her back with a headband pushing back her fringe. She looked healthy and happy.

"I'm sorry," I said.

"For what?" Jenna asked, her face clouding with confusion.

"For not being there," I explained, rolling my eyes. "I kind of ditched you."

"I understand." Jenna waved her hand impatiently. "That's not important. Are you okay?"

"No, not really. No," I answered honestly, laughing bitterly. "I thought he'd call...or find a way to reach out to me...something."

"Maybe he's not allowed," Jenna offered, shrugging.

"This is all my fault," I moaned, burying my face in my hands as fresh tears poured out of me. It was the first time I really allowed myself to cry.

Jenna rubbed my back, keeping silent for a few moments as she thought about what to say. Finally, she sighed. "It's not just your fault. He knew better. He should have never...encouraged it."

"We both couldn't ignore the pull." I sniffed. "He made me feel so alive, and honestly, I haven't felt that since Lauren died. I needed that."

"Lauren?" Jenna asked, looking confused again. I froze, realizing that I hadn't once told her about Lauren. I knew, as painful as it was, that I'd have to tell Jenna about Lauren. I couldn't keep burying it.

"She was my best friend," I finally said. "She died over a year ago."

"I'm sorry," Jenna said, continuing to rub my back as I spoke about Lauren, about who she'd been and about the accident that killed her.

"I had been walking around like a zombie, after that. Iain made me feel alive. He made me feel whole."

Jenna bit her lip, considering her words. "You did that yourself, Harlow," she told me gently.

"What do you mean?" I asked, looking at her incredulously.

"I mean, *you* did that...not Iain," Jenna explained. "He just gave you an outlet. You let someone in."

The day before the jury reached their decision, more photos came to light. The photographer had captured me and Iain in a heated embrace, in the hotel that we had stayed in during our trip to Ottawa. Iain was charged with "sexual exploitation of a minor." They couldn't prove that Iain had had a sexual relationship with the other students that had come forward, but the photos were enough to condemn him. He lost his teaching license and had to serve a year in jail. He didn't reach out to me after the trial, and I sent one letter that went unanswered.

Attending school was difficult to do, but I had to. Jenna refused to let me sink into a hole of despair over it. She came over every single day to get me up and force me to get ready.

"No offense, Harlow, but you've dealt with worse things than high school," she reminded me. "Besides, we only have a few months left. Don't make me go back there alone."

In the end, I went back. I passed all of the exams that the school board gave me to test my intelligence. Jenna and I endured a lot of stares from our peers. The two of us were the most talked about girls at school.

The first few weeks were the hardest. Although I'd kept silent about what happened and although Larry had succeeded in having the photos of me and Iain removed from the Internet, the rumours still swirled about the lunch room and by lockers. Students would stare openly at me, their words hissing out in quick spurts as they gossiped. But after a while, it tapered off. People started to forget, and to move on to the next big thing: prom.

I didn't want to go, but Jenna refused to take no for an

answer. "I worked so hard to get back in shape for this," she told me as she dragged me from store to store at the mall, searching for the best prom dress. "You can't bail on me."

"Just go with Jake," I begged, rolling my eyes. "I really do not want to go." Aside from Jenna and Jake, I didn't have any friends. Nor did I want to spend the night dancing with someone who wasn't Iain.

"Seriously?" Jenna stopped looking at the dress she'd been inspecting and turned to stare at me, raising her eyebrows.

"It's just prom." I rolled my eyes again, exasperated. But Jenna was relentless, and she wouldn't give up until I finally gave in and bought a simple black dress. Finally satisfied, she allowed me to leave the mall after she found her dress—a royal blue gown with a sweetheart neckline.

Jenna, Jake and I went "together." Although Jenna and Jake were nearly a couple, they still did their best to make me not feel like the third wheel. I didn't mind going with them, especially since nobody held my interest. Nobody but Iain, that was. I still hadn't heard from him, but I had given up on trying. I knew if he wanted to reach out to me, he would. Every day that passed with him not reaching out stung, but I did my best to push through it with help from Jenna.

Jenna even applied to several of the same universities I applied to so that we could attend together. The two of us had formed an unlikely, unbreakable bond. Had someone told me at the beginning of the year that I would end up being best friends with one of the popular girls that had tossed me dirty looks during my first day of school, I would have laughed manically. Now, I was thankful to have her as a friend. Knowing that she'd be near me in university calmed my nerves.

After May, June came. I graduated as one of the tops of my class, although I was picked over to give the valedictorian speech. I knew the reason why, although they didn't officially give me one.

"You look gorgeous, honey," Mom said, seeing me in my blue gown and graduation cap as I stood in front of my bedroom mirror.

"Thanks," I said, giving her a small smile. She came into my room and sat down on my unmade bed, still looking at me with a smile on her face.

"I am so proud of you, honey," she told me. "You've come a long way this year."

"Really?" I asked, disbelief apparent in my voice and on my face.

"Yes, really," Mom answered, serious. "You've been through a lot. You've made some mistakes, but you're in a better place because of it."

I said nothing, shocked by her honesty.

"Well, it's time to go," Mom said, standing up and heading out of my room. I followed her into the kitchen, where Larry was waiting. He was dressed in a suit, rolling on his heels as if he was nervous. We hadn't really had a whole lot of contact since Iain's sentencing. He probably thought I blamed him, but I didn't. I had at first, of course, but then I realized that Iain and I were really to blame. We'd both known it was illegal, even if I had naively thought that a Romeo and Juliet cause would save him.

"You look great, Harlow," Larry said, clearing his throat uncomfortably.

"Thanks, Larry," I answered, trying to smile.

"Well, let's go." Mom picked up her purse, motioning for us to get moving. I had to be there in less than fifteen minutes.

The next hour was chaotic as the teachers organized us by last name. We waited in line then made the progression outside to where the bleachers had been set up. Family of the graduating students filled the bleachers, and in front of the bleachers was enough chairs for all of us to sit. One by one, the teachers directed us down to our seats. It was surreal, hearing all of my classmates' names called. Jake did the rock-and-roll devil sign with his hand as he accepted his diploma from Mr. Osborne, earning several laughs and an eye roll from Mr. Osborne himself. Jenna sobbed while she took hers, and I barely made eye contact when my name was called. A chorus of hushed whispers accompanied the announcement of my name. I couldn't help but feel paranoid and think that everyone was remembering the scandal.

Finally, after the valedictorian drawled on and on for a solid forty-five minutes about the next chapter of our lives, the ceremony came to a close.

That summer, Jenna's parents rented a two-bedroom apartment near the University of Ottawa, subleasing a room out to me for next to nothing. They would have allowed me to live there rent free if I hadn't insisted on paying them something each month.

We moved into the apartment in July, so that we could find part-time jobs and adjust to life before university started. I landed a job at a local coffee shop close to our new apartment. Everything was within walking or busing distance, so I sold my car, unable to really afford the insurance on it anyway, and treated myself to yet another tattoo: a colourful phoenix on my right calf, meant to pay tribute to me rising from the ashes, yet again.

EPILOGUE

I still thought about Iain often, but I never heard from him. Due to the nature of his charges, I'm sure his lawyer advised him not to contact me. I had almost expected him to do so after his sentence was up, but he never did. I didn't hear a whisper.

At first, it hurt like hell. I realized he had a lot of time to think about us, and probably had grown to resent me. I missed him, but over time the ache in my chest faded. He would always be my first true love, the love that pulled me out of the darkness and brought me back to life in a way. Jenna still insisted that it had been all me...and maybe it had been.

Two years into university, one snowy day in December, I was with Jenna at the St. Laurent Centre on a rare day off, doing some obligatory Christmas shopping. She was laughing about a pair of crocodile print leather jeans at H&M, holding them out to me and trying to urge me to try them on, when she fell silent. An odd look passed over her face as she squinted toward the front of the store.

I glanced behind me, seeing the familiar dirty blond hair and piercing Caribbean blue eyes of my twelfth grade English teacher. He was standing at the front of the store, near the mall exit, holding up a pair of jeans. Our eyes met, and I drew in my breath. He'd lost some weight, and his hair was a little more unruly and longer, but he still sent shivers of desire coursing through my body.

ABOUT THE AUTHOR

J.C. Hannigan lives in Ontario, Canada with her husband, their two sons, and their dog. She writes contemporary romance stories with compelling characters and vibrant plots that focus on relationships, mental health, social issues, and other life challenges.

http://jchannigan.com

CHAPTER 1
A NOTE FROM THE AUTHOR

If you enjoyed this story (or if you didn't), please take a moment to post a review on Amazon, Goodreads, your blog, or whichever platform you use. Reviews help other readers find books, and I appreciate any and all reviews!

Sign up for my newsletter to receive exclusive stories, sneak peeks, and updates: https://www.subscribepage.com/jchannigannewsletter

Also, I do have a reader's group on Facebook where I share exclusive sneak peeks and other fun stuff: J.C. Hannigan's FANnigans.

CHAPTER 2
OTHER BOOKS BY J.C. HANNIGAN

The Collide Series
Collide
Consumed
Collateral

The Damaged Series
Damaged Goods
Reckless Abandon

The Rebel Series
Rebel Soul
Rebel Heart
Rebel Song

The Forgotten Flounders Series
Off Beat
Off Limit

COLLIDE

Standalones